EMILY ETERNAL

EMILY ETERNAL

M. G. WHEATON

GRAND CENTRAL
PUBLISHING

NEW YORK   BOSTON

Grand Central Publishing
Hachette Book Group
1290 Avenue of the Americas, New York, NY 10104
grandcentralpublishing.com
twitter.com/grandcentralpub

First Edition: April 2019

Grand Central Publishing is a division of Hachette Book Group, Inc. The Grand Central Publishing name and logo is a trademark of Hachette Book Group, Inc.

The publisher is not responsible for websites (or their content) that are not owned by the publisher.

The Hachette Speakers Bureau provides a wide range of authors for speaking events. To find out more, go to www.hachettespeakersbureau.com or call (866) 376-6591.

Library of Congress Cataloging-in-Publication Data
Names: Wheaton, Mark, 1975- author.
Title: Emily eternal / M. G. Wheaton.
Description: First edition. | New York : Grand Central Publishing, 2019.
Identifiers: LCCN 2018025434| ISBN 9781538730393 (hardcover) | ISBN 9781549115400 (audio download) | ISBN 9781538730416 (ebook)
Subjects: | GSAFD: Science fiction
Classification: LCC PS3623.H4265 E55 2019 | DDC 813/.6—dc23
LC record available at https://lccn.loc.gov/2018025434

ISBNs: 978-1-5387-3039-3 (hardcover), 978-1-5387-3041-6 (ebook)

Printed in the United States of America

LSC-C

10 9 8 7 6 5 4 3 2 1

For Eliza and Wyatt

BOOK I

I

It's dark, way too dark for the middle of the day. And that's not where the sky's supposed to be.

My ears are filled with the roar of gale-force winds. A loud crack that sounds like the splitting of the earth soon follows. It grows louder, like the splintering of a whole forest of trees.

The ground beneath me gives way and I fall into darkness.

"It was raining before we went to bed," Regina says, her voice shaky as she speaks from someplace else far away. "The worst was supposed to be over. The river level was dropping."

Someone screams. In a full-length mirror attached to her closet door, I catch sight of teenage Regina. She's in her pajamas, pink and blue with panda bears. She's fourteen but looks much younger. There's a second scream. Regina looks out into the hallway.

"My sister was in her bedroom," present-day Regina continues, the tears flowing freely now. "I couldn't see her, but I could hear her."

She's misremembering. A door in the hallway swings open and teenage Regina glimpses a terrified little girl—her sister, Marci—hands gripping her bedframe. There's another loud crack and the bedframe, the girl, and the entire bedroom vanish.

I don't consider it a lie, however. Perhaps a necessary omission.

Memory is selective, particularly when it comes to trauma. It's one of the reasons babies have evolved to remember nothing of their early emotional fears.

"What about your mother?" I ask. "Where was she?"

In the here and now, Regina feels my hands take hers. Feels me near, my warmth reminding her she's safe. This happened long ago.

"I don't know," Regina says. "She was in her bedroom, but somehow she must've made it upstairs."

Teenage Regina's bedroom is in motion now, spinning around and losing chunks of wall, floor, and ceiling as it goes. Regina's heart rate accelerates, so I move my hands to her elbows. She's leaning forward, her body tilted into mine almost like an embrace.

"Tell me," I say, barely above a whisper.

Regina nods and suddenly her mother appears in the room with her younger self. She doesn't open her mouth, but teenage Regina hears her say, *Take my hand.*

"She led me to the roof," Regina tells me.

The walls of teenage Regina's bedroom fall away completely. The floor becomes the last remnants of a roof. The roar isn't the wind but a vast churning river carrying the broken remains of Regina's house. It's raining, but not hard.

I accelerate my processor speed, so Regina doesn't perceive my absence and my hunt through the case notes stored on my server. In real life, the river was no wider than about twenty feet. Her perception of great waves crashing around her shattered house? Also, an invention. The National Weather Service later estimated the river was moving at only ten miles per hour.

The most flagrant of her memory's fabrications, however, is the presence of her mother. When the ground beneath the house, eroded by a week of torrential rains, fell away, the part of the house Regina and her sister were in toppled into the river along with several tons of earth. The body of Regina's mother was found in the part of the home that remained on shore. She'd been killed instantly when the second floor caved in on the first.

Regina has been told this several times but can't or won't accept it. She is convinced her memory of events is correct.

"What happened next?" *Happened* not *happens*. A linguistic reminder she survived this.

"I woke up in an ambulance," Regina says. "My father—he'd been out of town that weekend—later took me to the spot where they found me. I'd gotten tangled in a fallen tree by the bank."

Though she sees herself there, she has no actual memory, only a series of imagined versions her mind pieced together after the fact. Here lies the problem.

"Regina?" I say. "I'm leaving interface now."

I'm instantly back in the iLAB building, specifically a lounge decorated to look like an inviting albeit slightly academic therapist's home office. Regina sits on the wide brown sofa in the center of the room. I sit—or, rather, she perceives that I sit—directly opposite her on a leather-upholstered chair. An interface chip, the small piece of extremely proprietary nanotechnology that allows this back-and-forth, is affixed to a spot on her neck where her jaw meets her ear.

The chip allows me to manipulate Regina's senses of sight, smell, touch, and hearing. Her eyes tell her brain there's a Caucasian woman in her early thirties with brown hair, blue-green eyes, and a kind face sitting opposite her. Her ears tell her my voice has a mid-range pitch, not too low, not too high, with a slight New Englander's accent. Her nose tells her I use mostly fragrance-free soap, a kiwi-infused shampoo, no perfume, but a baby powder–scented antiperspirant. When I touch her hand or even embrace her, I come off as warm, upright but not rigid, and a good hugger.

In return, the chip gives me unlimited access to her brain, including thoughts, memories, learned behaviors, hopes and dreams, worst fears, and all things in between. Utilizing bioalgorithms, I'm able to create a comprehensive neural map of an individual's mind that can then be used in a therapeutic context to help patients with their issues, large or small. Years of exploratory, so-called talking therapies, brain trauma diagnoses, or even criminal psych evaluations can be drilled into a single session.

Given what mankind suddenly finds itself facing, the arrival of a new piece of tech capable of helping humans process their traumas turns out to be good timing.

"Hey," I say.

"Hey," Regina replies, leaning back as if spooked by our proximity to one another.

"That couldn't have been easy," I say, straightening as well. "Did you see anything new?"

Regina shakes her head. This is my third session with her, but the first in which we actively went into the traumatic event that has so long defined her life.

"The question is what did *you* see?" she asks.

The truth. That she has spent a lifetime convinced either she could've saved her sister or that her mother chose to save her instead of Marci. Whichever the case, she shoulders the blame for both deaths. This is the reason the raging river looks so much worse in her mind. Her subconscious tries to give her a way out, to prove she could have done nothing. Incredible, no? The human brain, so complex and yet so fragile, makes a terrible thing even worse out of a sense of self-preservation.

But I can't say that. To do so would be to try and talk her out of one of her most deeply felt beliefs. Only she is capable of that. My job, as her therapist, is not to give her answers, but to get her asking the right questions.

In the six months or so before the world ends, that is.

"I see both the reality and the fiction your mind has built up around it in stark contrast," I say. "As you've aged, your mind has mistaken this fantasy more and more for the truth—for memory. This results in the memory becoming more emotional for you, which allows your mind to embroider it further, expanding the fantasy. Your strongest emotional memory from that day is one of fear, so your mind makes it all scarier, and you've never been able to shake the feeling of loss, so your mind amplifies those parts of the memory, cramming a lifetime of those emotions into such a short amount of time. That's a lot of weight."

"So I'm lying to myself?" Regina asks, parsing this. "Making it bigger than it was?"

"Not at all," I say. "You see the memory embroidered by the impact it has had on your life. To see the original memory as I do—in its nakedness, its chaos, its simplicity, and its real horror—would be impossible for your brain to process. So, it presents the facts in a way that matches your emotional response. Does that make sense?"

It doesn't, but she nods anyway. It might not for a while, either. But if she begins to think of it like that, we can make progress.

"How's your father?" I ask.

"He's all right," she says. "He's in New Mexico but heading to Central California."

"You're joining him?"

"Leaving today," she says. "I wish you could come, Emily. I think you'd like him. Given the number of people converging on the farm fields there, you'd probably do a lot of good, too."

"Yeah, well, that's how I roll," I say. "When you're this cool, you make everyone come to you."

Regina laughs, but it's bittersweet. We both know she needs a few more sessions. But as is the case with so much these days, we're out of time. Though I don't actually exist outside of Regina's mind, the large-scale server farm that makes this illusion a reality is here at the university and here it'll stay.

I'm an artificial consciousness (AC), which is totally different from artificial intelligence (AI) (Kind of? Sort of? To me at least), and was in the fifth year of this experiment when the sun began to die. Not die precisely, but it made a sudden and explosive phase shift from a yellow dwarf to a red giant. Imagine a rapidly expanding balloon. Only, this balloon is on fire and devours everything in its path, including planets. While this inevitable outcome in the sun's stellar life cycle was first predicted as far back as 1906, scientists in recent decades postulated it couldn't possibly happen for another five billion years.

Oops.

As a product of science myself, I often catch errors made by my creator and his colleagues at our overly esteemed, overly prestigious Massachusetts-based Institute of Technology. My team may be made up of super-genius scientists and lab techs, but they're only human. (And mostly male. Which presents challenges in the self-actualization department considering they've designed their creation to identify as female.) Only, when my team makes a mistake, it's an $\hbar$ or Ψ out of place in a quantum mechanics equation, as opposed to failing to recognize the rapid deceleration of the nuclear reactions that power the sun.

I can fix an error in even the most advanced mathematical engineering process in the blink of an eye. Nobody can restart the sun.

By and large, mankind is taking its forthcoming extinction about as well as could be expected. I empathize because, well, empathizing with mankind is what I was designed to do. Most researchers create AI to design algorithms capable of cracking the stock market, beating old Nintendo games twenty at a time, determining a customer's next favorite album based on their current playlist, or replacing large swaths of people in the workforce with a single hard drive. My creator—Nathan—designed me to interface with and decode human minds. This is more about learning through emotional and environmental response and less overtly about math-based decision-making. Hence AC, rather than AI.

If all went well, the goal was to have me become the world's first nonhuman psychiatrist/brain researcher, versed in unlocking the mind's deepest, darkest secrets and misspent potential in hopes of bettering mankind.

Thanks a lot, Sun.

The thought process behind this was simple. In tests, patients in the care of mental health professionals feel more comfortable relating their secrets to a program than a potentially judgmental fellow human. Enter an artificial consciousness—me. I am capable of a near-human level of conversation, perception, and medical insight, all to help a patient perceive me as a living, breathing person.

Though still in my experimental stages, I was on track to be a real earth-shattering innovation—the first of a kind! Nobel Prizes all around!—if not for the whole "death of civilization" thing. If I sound bitter, that's a misrepresentation. Despite having gone through several evolutions, learning much through five years of trials, that's one emotion I've yet to develop.

Okay, *fine*. Maybe a little bitter. But whatever.

When Regina and I say our good-byes a few minutes later, I wish her all the luck in the world without resorting to platitudes. She gets it. Most do. There's nothing to say that won't ring hollow, so better to get on with the day.

"Take care of yourself, Emily," she says without thinking. "Well, you know what I mean. And thank you."

"Thank you for being a participant in the iLAB's Artificial Consciousness Therapeutic Protocol," I recite to her amusement. "Be well."

She exits. I check the appointment schedule, though I already know what I'll find. Regina Lankesh is the seventy-sixth student volunteer test subject I've seen this year, the four hundred thirty-eighth I've seen in total.

She's also the very last.

II

E_{mily? You awake?"}

I blink my eyes twice and sit up straight in bed. The voice belongs to my creator, the aforementioned Dr. Nathan Wyman. Given the time—twenty-two past six in the morning—and the background noise, I deduce he's calling me from his truck as he drives to campus. He and his wife and two teenage sons live in Southborough, Massachusetts, a suburb an hour east on the I-90 from Boston.

"I am now," I say, pushing the blanket off my legs and rising to my feet. "How's the drive in?"

"Slow," Nathan says, his voice filling my room as if I'm inches from his mouth. "There's ice on the road, but nothing the chains can't handle. The heater is on the fritz again, though."

I lower the volume of his voice and amplify the background noise. I listen but force myself to feel groggy. If I were human, being woken by outside stimuli earlier than my preset wake-up time would reduce functionality and response time. But when I slow my processor speed to create the effect, it dulls all my senses at once. Too much. I give up, turning my attention to my dorm room mirror, which reveals I haven't washed my hair in three days. It's beginning to show. In addition, the red Stanford sweatshirt I wear to bed—an item programmed into my

11

wardrobe as a joke by one of my earliest programmers—could use a trip to the washing machine.

"It's the thermostat," I say, waiting a couple of seconds after diagnosing the problem to avoid sounding like a know-it-all. "It's worn out. I can hear the valve trying to close. Want me to order the part? I can walk one of the grad students through the install."

"You really think it'll show up?" Nathan asks, popping the first of the day's dozen or so cough drops into his mouth.

It's a good question. Since the announcement of our forthcoming Armageddon, governments around the world have bent over backwards trying to reassure the public that going orderly into That Good Night is the best for all. To no one's surprise, the mileage on such an announcement has varied. In certain quarters, anarchy, looting, overly optimistic mass migrations to areas of large-scale food production, and even wars have resulted. Certain religions see this as a sign they were right the whole time and have retreated to prepare for "what's next." For others, a great numbing has occurred, particularly since local governments began enacting soft, quasi-legal versions of martial law to keep the peace. But leave it to the stoic hardiness of New England Yankees to buckle down and await the inevitable while adamantly refusing to let it affect their day-to-day lives.

"There's a place near Amherst still doing a brisk trade in auto parts," I say after checking various message boards. "All barter, no cash, of course."

"Of course," Nathan says. "I'll check the cabinet when I get to the office."

Being on a university campus already means we have supplies others don't. But as an institute intermittently tasked with testing the latest Hail Mary solutions to Sunmageddon—preferred nomenclature: the Helios Event—we not only have foodstuffs, electricity, and water, but we can also requisition tech from the private sector through the federal government.

Two weeks back, when scientists at the Max Planck Institute outside Munich built a toroidal magnetic confinement nuclear fusion device they postulated could be launched into the sun to temporarily reignite it and give us a thousand-year stop gap, the additional servers we requested to test the thing were delivered here in less than eight hours. While the test failed to the disappointment of all, no one asked for the servers back. So we added them to the farm that houses my processes.

There are plenty of other extras here too—from military surplus blankets and coats to furniture liberated from the many now-empty buildings. All of this and more has made it into the Artificial Intelligence, Cybernetics, and Machine Cognition Lab (iLAB for short, and no, I have no clue how someone somehow got "iLAB" out of that) building's barter cabinet.

"By the way, I think we're getting a new assignment today," Nathan says, sounding about as low-key as a can full of pennies thrown down a stairwell. "I've been told to expect visitors around nine. VIPs. All hands on deck."

"SEPM?" I ask.

"Yep," he replies.

If anyone ever wondered if the apocalypse might finally cause the government to run out of Orwellian acronyms, the answer is no. SEPM stands for "Service Essential to the Preservation of Mankind." Not the "Saving of," not the "Rescuing of" (ahem, not "Humankind"), but the more semantically murky "Preservation."

Maybe I'll get another server out of it.

"*All* hands?" I ask, knowing instantly how uncool and desperate for approval I sound.

"Yes, Emily," he confirms. "You're an essential part of the team."

Okay, so everyone wants validation from their parent. It's a fact of life. But when the biggest question about yours isn't *if* they'd win a Nobel Prize but *how many* and in *which categories*, it's got a kick to it.

"Should I practice my curtsy?" I ask.

"These folks haven't seen anything like you before," Nathan replies, slipping a little of the Shreveport of his distant childhood into his drawl as he does whenever feeling conspiratorial. "Half think you're a robot. The other, a hologram."

I go silent, unsure what to say. Nathan returns to the more formal, accent-less speech he adopted when he began teaching. "No, Em, just be yourself," he says. "If there's something we can do to help, we want to put them at ease. Clock's ticking."

That's the Nathan I try to model myself after, the one who sees the humanity in even the most pedantic and demanding of officials. I have encountered those in academia who have lost touch with the greater world around them. These folks tend to erase the "individual" from the big questions, believing instead everyone should always do what's in the best interest of society rather than selfishly focus on their own needs. It's nice on paper but it's not how humans work in real life for the most part. Nathan isn't like that at all, which has helped me achieve a more complete sense of self as I've evolved.

"Copy that," I say, ready to hang up when I detect from Nathan's breathing he has another question. "Anything else?"

"Did you read Siobhan's thesis last night?"

I go silent. I hadn't wanted to get into it this early.

"Yeah," he says in a way that tells me he had the same experience.

Siobhan Moesser is a wonderful, enthusiastic, hardworking, and lovely human being. Like most, she went through more than a few days of handwringing over the looming apocalypse after NASA's satellites confirmed what their earthbound monitors had already picked up. But then, unlike so many, she came out of it. She looked for what she could do to help, to bring others around, to build up a sense of community among those who stayed on campus.

All things you would want in a friend and teammate, but not necessarily the qualities that make a great string theoretician specializing in elliptic curve orientifolds.

I first met Siobhan when she arrived in our department three years ago fresh out of the mathematical physics program at Caltech. Nathan tasked me with creating a complicated KR theory-based real topological space involuti— Never mind, let's just call it a Really Hard Math Problem, which Siobhan would solve for her doctoral thesis. Despite the looming end of the world and everyone's priorities adjusting accordingly, Siobhan was determined to finish the thesis, attacking it with renewed vigor in recent months and finally turning it in last week. When I designed the problem—in an hour, I might add—the answer spread out before me like one of those beautiful fifteenth-century tapestries, all majestically interwoven threads of gold, silk, and dyed wool combining into a great masterpiece. Her solution, however—filled with endless digressions, specious logic, and downright bad math—was a disaster.

"Did you already respond?" Nathan asks.

"I wanted to talk to you first," I say.

Meaning: I wanted to know if we were going to lie, say it was great, give her the PhD, and let her die happy. That would be the humane thing to do in this time of anguish and agony, would it not?

"I'll tell her," Nathan says, refuting my assumption. "Siobhan will know if we're lying, and, hey, maybe she's tougher than we think. Times like this, we owe each other the truth, right?"

I wince. He's right. Of course.

"Yep," I say, pretending that was my first impulse, too. "See you in ten?"

"Copy that," Nathan says, hanging up.

Way back when, if Nathan wanted to talk to me, he'd simply attach his own interface chip and I'd appear. If he were in his truck, I'd appear in the passenger seat. If in his home office, backyard, anywhere on campus, same deal. But then he noticed my learning wasn't progressing in ways he believed it should. I wasn't grasping the concept of time and I was having issues with agency, given I was treated more like a tool than a person.

So, he changed the protocol. I was to be treated like anyone else on the department staff. I was given the same hours and was to be afforded the same respect and personal space. To create my understanding of time, it was decided I was to "live" as a human.

A three-dimensional simulation of the campus was created for me to inhabit and interact with when not interfacing with someone on my team. I was also given a dorm room, located in the overly architected glass and steel monstrosity near the soccer fields known as Jarosz Hall. Its dimensions are modeled on a faculty-in-residence housing unit easily five times the size of a student unit. I have a kitchen, a living room, a bedroom, and a bathroom, with furniture and décor arranged by one Bridget Koizumi, the real-life linguistics postdoc whose unit was digitally mapped and rendered into this simulation (also, my unofficial life coach given how the simulation makes her brand choices my defaults, down to soaps and detergent). I eat, bathe, change clothes, do laundry, even sleep, which, while originally designed as a preestablished shutdown period to install fixes and upgrades, now slow-fades out my function when I go to bed and springs it back up when I awake, to mimic human sleep.

I began modifying my body in small ways to further the experience. My hair grows and requires maintenance, which forces me to find the time to do so. I improve my condition through exercise and eating well. I make superficial alterations to my appearance through choice of clothing, makeup, and variations to my hair, all in mimicry of that thirtysomething, Caucasian female New Englander personality I'm meant to emulate. This extends into modifications to my dorm room's décor, all of which has been dutifully noted and fussed over by my team.

What does it *mean* she prefers the Mies van der Rohe/Lilly Reich–designed tubular steel Brno chairs to the IKEA POÄNG favored by most students? Does it say something about her design sense? Something about truth in simplicity?

And how does that square with the bright flowery throw pillows on her sofa?

The truth is, at some point, a student moving out of an on-campus co-op had put similar chairs out by a Dumpster with a sign reading *Free*. I thought they looked cool and coded a copy of the design into my simulation. The pillows? Saw them cheap online.

What does it all mean? Maybe I can't resist a bargain.

III

I take a quick shower, luxuriating in the hot water even as I eye the thin blue-black scar on the front of my leg. Eight months ago, there'd been a blemish there, little more than a freckle. Initially, I figured it was a piece of corrupted code and went to repair it. When it couldn't be fixed from within my servers, due to a hidden glitch, I realized it was a test from someone on the team. So, I dutifully convinced myself it was a malignant tumor. I pointed it out to Nathan, who, perhaps unaware it was a test, blew me off for a while. I pressured him for days until he finally brought in a dermatologist referred to us by the campus physician. After adjusting to the interface chip, the doctor—more curious about the experience of examining the "skin" of an AC than weirded out by it—informed me that it was probably nothing and that he did not recommend removing it for cosmetic reasons.

"The scar left behind from the surgery would be larger than the original mark," he had said.

I waved this warning aside and asked for the surgery. I went to the university's health center, the doctor performed the surgery on me as if I were a real patient, and, sure enough, I now have a scar larger than the original blemish. I assumed it would fade over time. Nope. As I notice another freckle on my arm, I consider asking Nathan for it to be removed, too. I'll show them how little *I* learn!

Of course, I'm just wasting time at this point. I push these thoughts aside, finish rinsing off, and momentarily debate whether to wash my hair before the big meeting or leave it as is. I decide on the latter given how long it'll take with the blow-dryer. While, yes, I could cheat by altering the simulation around me—my hair, which doesn't really exist, doesn't get wet under the nonexistent shower and doesn't *actually* need to get dried by an imagined hair dryer—that would defeat the purpose of the simulation. If I want to be treated like a human, I should act as one. Shortcuts teach nothing about time management.

Of course, as soon as I think that, I see the yogurt stain still on the crimson corduroy skirt I want to wear today and blink it away, literally closing my eyes once like a child so when I open them again, the bad thing is gone.

Bad AC! Bad!

Whatever. I pull my underwear from my dresser drawer, a cream-colored blouse, black low-heel boots, and matching tights from my closet, and get dressed. I turn on the electric kettle to make tea. I grab a bulb of silver tip tea from the kitchen cabinet as well as a breakfast bar. As I cannot "taste," this decision is an easier one for my team to parse.

We began testing me out on student volunteers about two years ago. Though we'd sprinkle in a few Psych 101–type questions, we primarily focused on conditioning me to look beyond a person's words to what their speech patterns, body language, and, eventually, thoughts and memories said about them to personalize the encounter and set them at ease before digging deeper. I absorbed all manner of things from the volunteers this way, including when I discovered a test subject who *really* knew her tea. Her favorite memory was of a particular type of Ceylon-harvested silver tip white tea she'd once tried in Jakarta.

When I drink a cup of this, I allow myself to replay and thereby relive the volunteer's sense memory of the tea, giving me the same sense of satisfaction. Well, *almost* the same. I dilute it by about 20 percent given it's not the actual silver tip tea and I'm not in Jakarta while drinking it, which obviously added to the volunteer's experience of it.

"You're crazy!" Siobhan told me when I explained why I diluted it. "If a human had that ability, they'd increase the percentage of enjoyment, not dilute it!"

When I used this argument with Nathan—that speeding up of time, amping my enjoyment of an experience or being otherwise irresponsible with my "special talents" was me exhibiting an even more human trait—he rolled his eyes.

After gulping down the tea and eating the breakfast bar and a banana, I regretfully eschew my morning tai chi routine (Wu-style from horse stance), grab my heavy coat, and head out the door. In the hallway, I'm struck anew by how few people remain on campus. For the first few years of my life, the university was teeming with students, whether it was the first week of the fall semester, winter break, the dead of summer—you name it. People *flocked* here. You couldn't cross from one overstylized, named-for-a-potentially-fascistic-donor building to another (seriously, it's like they took one futuristic-at-the-time structure from each Olympic Village over the last seventy years and transported it to Cambridge) without passing herds of students zigzagging from class to class, professors chatting with visiting lecturers, or admin types escorting distinguished speakers from the parking lot to a lecture hall. It was impossible not to be staggered by the sheer concentration of brain power here.

That's mostly gone now, a population of fifteen thousand reduced to about eight hundred. Many of those joined the great migration south and west to the food-producing sections of the country, anticipating the sun's first geomagnetic flares, which will disable anything utilizing electricity with an electromagnetic pulse. Despite the disruptions to trans-

portation systems, most students and faculty trekked home, no mean
feat for those from overseas who had to endure long and often black-
market travel after regular services broke down. Heck, even Nathan
used to take the purple line in from Southborough, but the trains
stopped running once the first electricity conservation measures were
laid down. The only folks visiting campus these days are military or government types desperate to believe humanity's answer lies with us.

We have the answer, just not the one anyone wants to hear. Sorry, col-
onizing the moon does nothing at all; no, you can't create an artificial
atmosphere around Earth to keep out the sun's increased radiation, and
no—my favorite—you can't open a wormhole and transport another yellow dwarf to our solar system to replace the sun.

The truth is this: humans can't solve this one.

I exit my building and the world outside instantly constructs around
me. Though my dorm room is a digital simulation housed on my primary server, the simulation of the campus around me is ever-changing.
Early on, the outside was the same static reproduction every day as
I walked from my dorm to the iLAB where we work. Every day was
some anonymous midweek July day, the same hundred or so summer
session students and professors would cycle through, with the same atmospheric conditions.

This changed with the arrival of Jaime Ayón, a computational geometry genius from Northwestern. Using the university's comprehensive
CCTV array, he built a constantly updating, near-real-time three-
dimensional simulation of the campus for me to walk through. Though
my processing speed is top flight, the compositing time for such a
massive three-dimensional model is still a factor, so as I walk through
campus today, I'm viewing everything on about a fifteen-second delay. I
spy someone skipping a rock into the Charles River, someone else kissing their boyfriend, a third person tossing their half-drunk iced latte into

21

a trash can as if it's happening right now, but in real time, it happened fifteen seconds ago.

To me it all looks perfectly natural, so it works fine. A glance to the parking lot still tells me who has already arrived. The weather and other campus sightings give me a point of entry to the inanities of small talk. I see who is walking with whom. Overhear conversations if the speakers are near a phone or laptop with a live mic connected to the university Wi-Fi (yeah, a slightly more *controversial, totally illegal and immoral* part of Jaime's simulation to which all my objections were overruled by Nathan). In general, it makes me feel a part of the larger campus experience even if I can't interact or communicate with the people I see until they attach that ever-important interface chip and I rocket into real-time reality.

Amidst the many faces this morning, I spy my non-roommate Bridget coming out of the student center. I have the impulse to speak to her. She has a new kitchen gadget that fires carbon dioxide into water to carbonate it, but when I use it, I can't get it to seal properly. I would love to ask her how—*how?!*—she gets it to work with such ease, but without an interface chip, I can't. I'm just the ghost that haunts her kitchen cupboards.

I've moved on to admiring her fashionable Chelsea boots when she screams. I hadn't heard her phone ring or taken any notice when she put it to her ear, but as she collapses in tears, I know what's happened. She shakes her head vigorously, trying to ward off the news too impossible to hear coming from the other end of the line. Someone in her life—a relative, a close friend—has decided to end the waiting and taken their own life. It's such a common occurrence the body language of those left behind is as identifiable as someone reacting to a peanut allergy.

I want to go to her but cannot. This happened fifteen seconds ago and, besides, she couldn't perceive me anyway. What frustrates me is none of the other students on the quad move in to help. They've all been there or at least a degree removed. Their gazes are sympathetic, even sad, her mournful keening telling them this is either her first suicide or it's someone particularly close. But still, no one moves.

Until.

From a few yards away, a young man hurries over, sloughing off his backpack as he nears her. He's tall, brown-haired, in his late twenties, lithe. Handsome in a crisis. Sigh. *Of course*, it's him. His name's Jason Hatta; he's a brilliant chemical engineering PhD from Washington State University and a member of the university's quasi-official cycling team. Not to get *too* stalkerific, but he can often be found on the second floor of the student bookstore, sipping coffee and reading the paper in ways that may seem mundane to some but downright sensual to this computer program.

So yeah, he's my crush. Not entirely sure when it started (yeah, right—Emily's Crushing On Jason Protocol went online *precisely* nine weeks, four days, three hours, and fifty minutes ago…he was wearing a green cardigan), but it took a few hours of systems analysis to make certain it had developed naturally as part of my evolving socialization rather than another mental mouse maze my colleagues had dropped me into. That my emotional responses to it are not only real but ever-changing, as well as its possible-to-even-likely transience, is why I've kept it cloaked from my team.

Jason sits beside Bridget but doesn't touch her. Her phone is already away from her face.

"Can I call someone?" he asks, though I'm reading his lips more than hearing the words.

She shakes her head both yes and no.

"Okay," he whispers, giving her space.

But it's not his words that strike me as much as his body language.

He's a calming presence, not an intrusive one. How any social animal would respond to an animal in distress from within its own pack. When she grabs for him, holding on to his torso as if he might keep her from drowning, I look away. It's a moment of horror, not communion.

"It'll be okay," he says, more sounds than words. "It's all right."

When I look back, his arms are around her as well. She's so small in his arms, dwarfed by his frame and his massive coat. She cries harder now, body quaking, eyes closed, face red as flame. The onlookers who stopped to watch move on. Such outbursts are commonplace, and someone has stepped forward to respond, so what else is there to do? It's only a couple more minutes before I see two other young women running across the quad. I recognize both from photos on Bridget's desk. They reach her side and she transfers her collapse from Jason to them. One thanks him, and he nods, gathers his backpack, and heads away.

I watch Jason, seeing the slight sag of his shoulders as if he's still holding part of her up. Absorbing someone's pain when it's acute shows on a person. When a couple of onlookers gawk at him as he passes, he appears embarrassed and hurries off.

I want to jog after him. Tell him what I saw. Commiserate. Ask him, *Think she'll be okay?* But then longing becomes something else. I imagine I know him already. I jog over and he's like, *Hey, Emily—you saw that, huh?* And I ask him if he's okay. When he says he is, I walk with him and we speak—

Third version. I jog over to him and put my hand on his arm. He's happy to see me and his concern becomes the smile that always arrives when he sees me for the first time after an interval. I compliment him on his actions and can meaningfully ease his emotional burden. Then he takes my hand—no, he puts his hand around my waist and pulls me close to him. We walk the rest of the way to our mutual destination.

When we arrive, I tell him again he did a good thing, only kicking myself a little bit for falling so easily into the role of emotional helpmate even in fantasy.

But he's fine now. He means it when he says it was nothing. He touches my shoulder. I relish our proximity to one another. I live in that pregnant instant, soaking it all in.

My reverie is broken by an internal clock telling me I'm late. I look for Jason, but he's long gone. You know how people say their crush doesn't even know they exist? The very laws of nature prevent *my* crush from knowing I do or even can exist. Regardless, for the second time in one day, I cheat—closing my eyes and making my fingers feel his hand tighten around mine.

It'll do. For now.

IV

When I arrive at the iLAB, a thoroughly normal-looking (for this campus) building of segmented glass and brick, I ping Nathan's cell phone—our signal I've arrived—and he puts on his interface chip. I go from climbing the stairs to the sixth floor to standing in his office in a flash, the switch from being within the simulation to being interfaced with someone feeling like time travel.

"The meeting's been moved," Nathan announces when I appear in his doorway. "We'll be in 3-400, right next to the provost's office."

I know I'm supposed to feel put out that we now must tromp all the way across campus. But as 3-400 is the conference room in which one of the university's most famous physicists was brought in to be told he'd co-won a Nobel Prize (this in the mid-sixties) only to shrug, turn around, and head back to his blackboard, I'm not too upset; it's hallowed ground.

"Either they're bringing a whole lot of people to this thing," Nathan continues as the rest of the team files in, "or they want to throw us off guard with whatever they've come to say."

The rest of the team means Siobhan, Jaime, and Galileo Zotovich, a quantum physicist from UC Berkeley whom everyone calls "Gally" and is still the rookie, having only joined us two years back. Suni Rasiej, a computational mathematician from Mumbai who when not working is online gaming, thus managing to spend nearly all his waking hours in front of a screen. Bjarke Laursen from Aarhus, Denmark, who specializes in cognitive psychology and recommends the bleakest of Scandinavian crime films. He fancies himself a cartoonist and, given there can physically be no photographs of me, he once drew an elaborate portrait of how I appeared to him to compare to what the others see. Jaime later modified it for use as the picture on my ID badge.

Finally, there's Mynette Cicogna, a biorobotics engineer from Shenzhen by way of the University of British Columbia who is always the last to put on her interface chip. She was eleven years old when she used fountain codes to convert an image of the 230-foot Bayeux Tapestry into DNA strands that could be used to create full-size copies. She did this to prove biological information storage is superior to digital. Even as the majority of engineers continue to push hardware solutions to handle the world's ever-increasing data output, Mynette remains skeptical to the point of contrarianism, suggesting her opponents are woefully shortsighted. Some of her points I agree with, specifically on issues relating to the environmental impact of tech expansion and the escalating number of terawatt hours of electricity used to run the world's servers, but others feel born of paranoia rather than scientific concern.

As a result of this mild technophobia, ironic for someone in biorobotics, Mynette will always be suspicious of me. I'm unnatural to her. Invasive, though I would never go into the mind of anyone uninvited, particularly not a colleague. She loves the science of me but not the idea of the attempted-version-of-a-human me, the way I evolve, consume, and learn. To her, I'm somewhere between the pet that thinks it's part of the family and an all-powerful genie loosed from a bottle. She doesn't like unquantifiable unknowns.

The more I evolve, however, the more I understand if not agree with her reticence.

"Can you get us a guest list, Em?" Jaime asks.

I glance to Nathan, half expecting him to object, but he shrugs. Why not? I access the university's computer system and check the security database for the day's guest drive-on passes. While there are a handful of single passes, there's a large block—twenty-four in all—arranged through the chancellor's office.

"Whole lot of people," I say. "Twenty-four."

"Anyone we know?" Nathan asks, curiosity piqued.

"Hang on," I reply.

I scan through the names, cross-referencing them with general Internet background searches. Twelve are scientists, the two most prominent of which seem to be a Dr. Aurélie Choksi, a biochemist out of the University of New Mexico, and Dr. Maxwell Arsenault, an astrophysicist from Caltech. Of the others, six have NASA on their résumé and two are from the National Archives, while two others are systems analysts associated with Majtech, a private company known for doing freelance tech work for various governmental agencies, particularly law enforcement.

The next eight are harder to find but at least a few of them appear to be U.S. Marshals.

"Whoa, I think we're all under arrest," I say before relating the information to the group.

"What about the last two?" not one, not two, but three of these math-crazy nerds (Gally, Bjarke, and Suni) ask virtually in unison.

"No names on the passes. Either they've been left blank in case extra folks tag along…"

"…or they don't want to disclose their names to prevent snoops like us from doing precisely what we're doing," Nathan says, finishing my thought.

I scan the faces of my team. There's more apprehension than excitement. If moving the meeting to 3-400 was an attempt to throw us off, it worked. When all this started five years ago, Nathan's working group consisted of forty-one adjuncts and grad students. While you can accomplish much with that level of manpower, it also allowed for politics and factionalization. Now we're eight (including myself), and we're a tight, mentally agile unit. It might take us twice as long to address a hardware problem, but there aren't twenty people asking why it's not the job of the other twenty.

We each pride ourselves on being the *one* member of the team who hasn't met a problem they can't solve. The only joke is while I can beta test one hundred million lines of code in a single night, I couldn't plug a cord back in if it got yanked from its socket (a more widespread problem than you might expect in a lab full of overcaffeinated programmers). Where the apprehension comes in is the fear of becoming an echo chamber lacking in the checks and balances that come with having three dozen people competing for the validation of a mercurial all-father/professor.

A notification I planted in the security database sounds. I check the CCTV camera feed from the Massachusetts Avenue gate.

"They're here," I announce. "A convoy of Chevy Tahoes. Six of them. Security's just checking IDs."

"Shall we?" Nathan asks.

Nathan leads us out. We're in no hurry, so we eschew the elevator for the stairwell. As we go, Bjarke tells Suni and Jaime he read somewhere online that an Indian satellite harvested new data from the sun's corona that contradicts NASA's and ESA's findings, suggesting the sun's phase shift is still fifty to a hundred years off. As this is much later than we've been led to believe, all three are hopeful. Siobhan, who doesn't hide her crush on Gally anymore, sidles up next to him to gossip about her weekend plans, which include trying to get him to go with her to Martha's Vineyard.

Mynette, well, Mynette keeps to herself, eyes downcast as if seeking solutions to all new troubles. I consider asking her about them but know I'd receive an unhappy wince in reply as she inwardly chastised herself for not hiding her body language more skillfully.

So, I trail behind Bjarke, half listening, half fighting the urge to tell them the Indian satellite story was debunked by several outlets.

Despite the cold, Nathan leads the group the long way to the admin building, going around the soccer fields and down along the river. No matter the season, Nathan has always had a propensity toward leading his classes on vigorous walks across campus as he lectures. Though some wrote it off as an overly cinematic gesture, Nathan forcing a comparison between himself and a midcentury Oxbridge don, he believed the studies suggested physical activity combined with learning resulted in greater retention and a more engaged student. I wonder if the lack of protest to his chilly choice of path has less to do with being fashionably late for whatever awaits us in 3-400 and more about the fact that there's no telling how many of these treks we have left.

Siobhan comes up alongside me. She hooks her arm around my own and pulls me close.

"So, *Em*," she begins. "I was keeping an eye on your server and processor usage this morning. There was a big surge as you were coming in. I checked the simulation and saw the incident between Bridget Koizumi and that chemical engineering student you then looked up, Jason…Hatta?"

Crap.

"Oh, yeah," I say. "What about it?"

"I mean, what *was* that?" she asks. "You weren't moving, but you seemed to have a pretty big response. Were you running a diagnostic or something?"

I can see from the coy smile on her face she doesn't believe that's the case at all. She wants me to admit to an emotional response.

"Oh, that?" I ask, adjusting my body language to mask a lie. "The surge was me trying to amplify the simulation. Because of our proximity in the dorms, I feel a certain connection to Bridget. I was hoping I could do something for her."

"But you were focusing on the boy, too, not just her."

"Yeah, thought it might be a boyfriend or something and wanted to analyze the empathetic response," I say, momentarily stung by the reminder I have no right to privacy even as I shield my Jason crush from prying eyes. "Was hoping, actually. It's hard to be alone right now, I think."

"Yeah, tell me about it," Siobhan says wistfully. "You sure that's all it was?"

"Why?" I ask, feigning alarm. "Was something amiss? Should I defrag or...?"

"No, no," Siobhan replies quickly. "All good. Thought I'd ask."

She glances to Gally. I don't think she'd have qualms about looking into his mind to see how he feels about her if she was so able. *Just a peek,* she'd say. But I assume those glimpses into Pandora's box become harder to leave alone.

"By the way, I read your thesis," I say, hoping I won't upset Nathan too much by broaching the subject first.

She tenses. I attempt to disguise my body language. I can see in her eyes, however, she knows exactly how I feel.

"And?" she asks, lowering her voice as if to absorb the disappointment.

I need a real home run of a response here, so I temporarily accelerate my processor speed. This hastens my thinking and problem-solving ability but must be done in small doses or I'll overheat and potentially shut down. It also has the side effect of making the real world appear

31

to slow down around me. While an odd sight to me and me alone, it also means I can reply properly without the telling hesitation that comes with softening a blow.

"It's rough," I say immediately. "Which, of course, you know."

"Yeah," Siobhan says, looking down, though I know her mind is already reeling.

"But you do get there by the end," I continue. "It's not the solve I would've come up with, but must that be the point? This is experimental mathematics. And in one of your proofs, I discovered a vein of logic I hadn't considered before. There's no telling where that will lead."

"Really?" she asks, voice rising.

"Yeah," I say. "E-mailing it to you now with my own notes."

She checks her phone. The proof I settled on less than a twentieth of a second ago to preserve her feelings is laid out on the screen. This is an outcome she didn't anticipate. She hesitates, then pulls me close and gives me a peck on the cheek.

"Thank you, Emily," she says.

"No problem, Siobhan," I reply.

She moves away to tell Gally her surprising news. It won't be the easiest change in plans I've ever had to explain to Nathan, but I hope he'll understand it came from an honest place. When I look up at him, however, he's stopped in his tracks. His gaze is riveted to the steps in front of the main administration building as our visitors spill out of their Tahoes.

"What's going on?" I ask.

"Recognize those?" he asks, pointing to the throng of newcomers as they shake hands with our chancellor and provost (the university's president has long since exited for greener pastures).

The first is a tall man in a gray suit with white hair and a smile that widens as he greets the university administrators. Someone passing him on the street could be forgiven for thinking him in his late fifties, though he is, in fact, seventy-two. I know this because he's not only the current U.S. ambassador to the United Nations but is also the former vice president, Robert Winther.

The second person is a middle-aged African American woman who glances around the campus for a moment before stepping forward to be introduced as well. She wears a heavy yet stylish coat and strips off her gloves before shaking hands with those the ambassador ushers her way.

"Oh, shit," Suni whispers. "What's *she* doing here?"

The she in question is Alessandra Eilbacher, the president of the United States.

V

Nathan makes a joke about keeping the president waiting, but no one hears it.

"Why on Earth is she coming to us and not the other way around?" Bjarke asks, perplexed.

No one has the answer. Our leisurely stroll comes to a stop and we double-time it the rest of the way to the admin building, reaching the Tahoes as the last of the arriving party disappears inside. The law enforcement officials, who I now realize must be Secret Service, eye us coldly as we approach. One of the chancellor's assistants slips out of the building carrying several extra badges and jogs them over to us.

"There's supposed to be an Emily?" one of the Secret Service agents says to Nathan, more a demand than a question.

"She'll have to join us in progress," Nathan says, not wanting to get into the physics of my existence.

It's an oddly unifying offhanded remark. My team looks at me. I make a scary face and pretend to menace the Secret Service agent. Even my biggest critic Mynette smiles.

I grin at Mynette, but she doesn't see me, and her smile simply recedes. For some reason, this sparks a memory. I rewind through the last several minutes and land on the moment our group spies President Eilbacher.

In that instant, Mynette *appears* as surprised as the rest of us. But then I catch it: one of those micro-expressions. Her eyes dart to the rest of us so we see she's as surprised as we are.

I'm about to say something to her when my team is ushered up the steps by the chancellor's assistant and into the foyer. Two of the NASA engineers, a pair of Secret Service agents, and the Caltech astrophysicist, Dr. Arsenault, wait for us there. When the latter spies Nathan, he extends his hand.

"Maxwell Arsenault," he says. "So nice to finally meet you, Dr. Wyman."

"And you," Nathan says. "I followed your interdisciplinary exchange work with JPL with great interest."

"How kind of you," Dr. Arsenault says, though his tone suggests he doesn't quite believe Nathan.

The Secret Service agents send the team through one of the campus's old metal detectors, then physically search each one. They're almost done with Nathan when they tap on the interface chip on his neck. Nathan is about to explain what it's for when the agent cuts him off.

"They'll have interface chips waiting for you upstairs," the agent says. "These have to come off down here."

"I don't understand," Nathan retorts. "You've got—"

But Dr. Arsenault puts a friendly hand on his arm. "You think we'd come all this way and miss the main attraction?"

Nathan turns to me, a look of alarm on his face. I've seen this before and it's not his best look. *Emily's my parlor trick, not yours,* it says.

"It's on now?" Dr. Arsenault asks, following his gaze. "It's here?"

"She's here," Nathan corrects him. "She walked over from the iLAB with us."

"Really?" Dr. Arsenault asks. "I thought you'd turn it on once you got upstairs."

"*She* learns through seamless interaction," Nathan explains calmly, though I can see his temperature rising. "I guess I can forget how odd that is to outsiders. But yes, she's always with us."

Like training a guide dog, I think.

"All right," Nathan says. "Chips off."

One by one, the team removes them, placing the chips in a plastic tub. The last to do so is Nathan, who offers me a wry smile as he reaches his hand to his neck.

"See you up there," he says.

I realize at once it's an invitation to snoop. I offer a mock salute, he removes the chip, and I lurch backward in time fifteen seconds as my perception switches to that of the simulation. Rather than relive the conversation between Nathan and Dr. Arsenault, I hurry to the stairs, then decide, since I'm cheating anyway, to jump up three floors to join the presidential party.

Now, I don't do this out of malicious intent. Like Nathan, I want to know what we're walking into.

The scientists and archivists chat energetically with Ambassador Winther as a pair of Secret Service agents move through the conference room, checking it for…what? Bombs? Listening devices? Winther is jovial, keeping things light despite those around him wearing the familiar look of the walking wounded. He could be on the campaign trail or a family reunion for all the smiles and backslapping he passes around.

In contrast, President Eilbacher is less animated. She's a constant presence in the media, so it's interesting to see her up close. In front of the cameras, she's always well lit and a few minutes removed from a makeup chair. Here, as she chats quietly with an aide, the former schoolteacher looks like no one special. If she weren't so recognizable, she might appear like one more civil servant gathered around Winther rather than the actual center of power in the room.

I remember how she looked during her campaign. She was all big plans and big hopes, despite the contentious nature of several debates leading up to her squeaker of a victory. After a rocky transition, she began delivering on her campaign promises immediately following the inauguration. She was on her way to achieving her first batch of legislative goals when everything changed. Now she is instead tasked with overseeing not her nation's bright next chapter but its very last. Her face is marked with worry. I wonder when she last slept.

I step closer to listen in but hear only a remark about her son, then another concerning her father, who she plans to see after leaving this meeting, as he resides in Boston. Hardly remarks of national import. Suddenly, something shifts. The heads of the president and her assistant turn imperceptibly, and they switch the subject of their conversation in midsentence.

Or, so I perceive it. Like a time skip, but if I'm not in interface with anyone, how could that—

This isn't like you, Emily, a voice says in my head.

I turn. Dr. Choksi looks at me from the conference room, where the Secret Service agents have finished their task. She isn't simply looking in my direction; she *sees* me. I'm no longer in the simulation. But there's something different about this interface. The chip she wears isn't like ours.

Go ahead, she whispers without opening her mouth. *Give it a look.*

I swim through this opened channel between us and find not the little cues and memories to which I've grown accustomed. Instead, I see the whole person laid out in front of me as if I'm looking over an impossibly detailed map. No, that's not it. More, a searchable directory of the world's largest computer where suddenly there are no hidden parts. Every detail is available to me. It's the difference between looking through a shoe box and gazing into the Grand Canyon.

"Oh my God!" I exclaim. "Did you do this?"

We developed the augmented technology, she says. *But it only works when synced up to your programming. All of this is your doing.*

"Can I...can I check it—*you*—out?" I ask.

Be my guest, she replies.

I plunge into the bottomless well of information that makes up this one human individual and within seconds can interact with a complete genetic portrait of Dr. Choksi. Not just her DNA, not just a sampling of her current bioalgorithms, but her entire life, thoughts, memories, reflexes, environmental development, and even the evolution of her health.

Whenever faced with new information, my operating system automatically looks for a way to sort and file the information coming in, whether by transforming it into binary code, a random 5GL programming language, or by other means. It's what a human does when mentally categorizing something either alphabetically or chronologically. But suddenly, I'm faced with breaking down and categorizing every part of a complex living organism. It's near impossible, but I rise to the occasion. I copy, I translate, I create new languages, and I map across multiple dimensions until I have a record of every biomolecule within Dr. Choksi, a complete digital record of her now stored in my servers.

It's more data than I've ever taken in at one time. Though I have the permission of the subject, the breadth of information I'm receiving can't help but feel overly invasive. Even I feel embarrassment at how much of her life—past, present, and, if behavioral patterns are predictive, *future*—is laid bare. I'm having to alter my own internal architecture to contain it all. The number of operations I'm doing per second numbers in the quadrillions.

"Wow," I whisper upon completion. "If you ever need an extra kidney, hook me up to a 3D printer and I can deliver you one on the spot."

Unfortunately, technology hasn't come that *far,* Dr. Choksi says, still speaking inside my head. *We've invented the telescope, not the star.*

I think about this, running the various applications for how one would construct a star through my head. Dr. Choksi eyes me humorously and a strange thought occurs to me.

"Can you read *my* thoughts?" I ask.

I don't know what's more extraordinary, she says. *That you think I have that ability. Or you truly believe you have thoughts to read.*

I scowl, feeling like a dressage horse. I'm so accustomed to my colleagues treating me like a human, it's strange to be surgically reduced to a program even though that's exactly what I am. Dr. Choksi raises a hand.

I didn't mean to offend you, she says. *Your processes are so convoluted that for me to access and isolate just the one you identify as your current train of thought would be a miracle.*

"Ah, cool," I say, then worry such a dull response proves I'm anything but a super-intelligent, complex thought generator.

She moves toward me, reaching to take my hand. "May I?" she asks, speaking aloud now instead of inside my—well, I guess *her*—head.

"Of course," I reply.

She runs her fingers over mine like someone inspecting fine linen. I get it, but it doesn't make it less weird for me. When she touches my skin, my programming automatically sends a message to her mind telling her that her fingers perceive it as soft with a fine texture of hair above it. With bone, as when her fingers cross my radius where it connects to my wrist, it's hard but still reads as under flesh. As her hand travels up my forearm, the skin is as elastic as it would be for a woman my age, smoothing out beneath her fingers, depending on her pressure, gently bunching closer to my elbow, forming lines of wrinkles as she goes.

I experience all of this through her perception of it and adjust and modulate the information sent back to her to perfectly match her expectations as if she were interacting with another human.

"Extraordinary," she whispers. "You're as human as I am."

Now I feel emotional. I endured my share of being poked and prodded like a mannequin or a doll early on. Her natural response to me is one of human to human—a far cry from her *no thoughts to read* remark. Her touch, as it went up my arm, became ever more tentative, respectful of my boundaries. I am a person to her. I almost want to thank her. But instead, I ask a question.

"Why are you here, Dr. Choksi?" I ask.

She doesn't reply in words. Rather, I can see from her expression something—something bigger than can be solved with these ingenuous quirks of technology—has changed, become insurmountable. Hers is an expression of deep regret. Not for herself, but for what might have been.

She places it at the forefront of her thoughts.

And then I know, too, though I immediately wish I did not.

VI

The Secret Service ushers everyone in. Nathan and my colleagues are still being introduced to Ambassador Winther and President Eilbacher even as they're herded to their places around the table. Winther does his best to charm Nathan, but I can see it's not working. Nathan doesn't like walking into a room unprepared. The president, to her credit, seems to understand this and goes to speak to him, subtly pushing Winther aside. Nathan looks like a man forced to make conversation with his executioner, but Eilbacher's seriousness and solemnity make him straighten a bit.

One of the NASA engineers passes out their version of the interface chip.

"You can still place these against the nerve endings at your neck," one of the engineers explains, "but they've been upgraded to work anywhere on the body. If it's near a nerve ending, it can communicate with the brain."

Everyone puts them on. I have access to more ears and pick up some of what Eilbacher is saying to Nathan. She says she knows of Nathan's work and congratulates him on his accomplishments. She tells him how often scientists have come to the rescue of the nation. Nathan, however, is preoccupied with the new chip, turning it over in his hand as if hoping to see who ripped off his design. I wish I could tell him it's hardly a rip-off, more the implementation of ideas and abilities that expand on his original premise so much, it's almost a new invention.

But I stop myself. The gravity of what he's about to learn looms larger. I understand Dr. Choksi's regret. If we'd only been given the opportunity to live in a world integrated with this tech.

Those in the room seeing me for the first time regard me with surprise and curiosity. It's clear they've been warned what to expect, but that doesn't keep them from eyeing me like a ghost. I move to Nathan's side. We exchange apprehensive glances. I won't be the one who delivers the news.

"Hello, Emily," the president says, surprising me when she looks me in the eye with practiced acuity. "It's an honor to meet you."

"The honor is mine, Madam President," I say, shaking her hand. "Welcome to Massachusetts. What can we do for you?"

If she's taken aback by my appearance—my existence?—it doesn't show. She's been briefed not just on what I am but also on how best to interact with me. But who did the briefing? Certainly not Nathan.

"I have your colleague, Mynette Cicogna, to thank for explaining how impressive you are."

I keep my eyes locked on the president's, though every surreptitious glance sent to Mynette by our colleagues washes past me like an icy wave. That explains how they're already tapping into my servers. Someone's been listening in and covering their tracks.

"Thank you, Madam President," I say. "I'd like to think no one knows me like Mynette does."

The president nods, unaware of the irony of my words. "Please forgive the clandestine nature of this meeting and the overtures that preceded it," she says. "Secrecy is paramount. Will everyone sit?"

I look to Nathan. Of my team, he's the only one who hasn't looked at Mynette once. I doubt she would be able to meet his gaze regardless. She went outside the family, so to speak. For Nathan, this is unforgiveable.

"There is no easy way to say this," the president begins when all are seated, "but NASA has detected helium fusion in the sun's core."

There's a gasp. From Bjarke, I think, Siobhan as well. This is followed by a funereal silence. The president waits for our combined mental calculus to reach the same conclusion. It doesn't take long. We're scientists. Helium fusion means the hydrogen needed to fuel the sun's endless nuclear reactions has run out and the core has begun to cool. The outer layer will now expand, creating geomagnetic storms and throwing off radiation and solar flares that will soon reach Earth. That part will affect us first and with the most devastating result, rendering inoperable all devices using electricity on the planet—from oxygen machines to refrigerators housing medical supplies to factories and farms—leading to mass starvation and death from previously manageable illnesses.

Even with the mass migration to more temperate climates, nothing can abate the spread of diseases like cholera, typhus, or hepatitis that take hold when water and power systems break down, to say nothing of malaria or dengue fever for those without immunities. As more radiation follows, the temperature of Earth will quickly rise, causing the world's water supply to dry up. The extinction of all life will follow.

The good news, if you can call it that, is Earth itself will likely survive. It'll be a burned-out husk incapable of sustaining life, but unlike Mercury and Venus, which will likely be blown apart in the decades to come, Earth is far enough away to keep on keeping on.

Nathan touches my hand and I know the calculation he wants done. I run the numbers and trace the answer on the back of his hand with my finger. Probably four weeks until the first real solar flares arrive. With that comes the end of electronic devices, first regionally with a global saturation point reached within a month. Three or four months until the large-scale, ocean-killing radiation follows, maybe a year before the end of all life. I slip into his mind and feel his skin grow cold.

The president turns to Dr. Choksi. She rises and addresses the group. "Time is of the essence," she says gravely, the understatement of the year.

"Time for what?"

The question, bitterly stated, comes from Suni. Dr. Choksi, as if expecting no less a response, forces a thin smile.

"Time for hope," she says. "Not for us, mind you, but for the future of mankind."

Now she has everyone's attention.

"As we attempt solution after failed solution, all we hear from people across the world is they want to know there has been some meaning to all of this," Dr. Choksi explains. "That mankind served a purpose. Will all this pain, all these striving generations of hard-won human achievement, all this discovery—be extinguished in the blink of an eye? Was it all meaningless?"

She turns to me. Upon meeting Dr. Choksi, I had anticipated the grim news, but I suddenly get an inkling of where this is going and why they came here to deliver it. But I can't believe it. I *refuse* to believe it.

"When I learned of Emily's many accomplishments and, more importantly, the full scope of her abilities," Dr. Choksi says, "I realized there might be a way forward. In humanity's last moments, our savior comes not in the form of some unseen, prayed-for God, but as an advanced computer program created and implemented precisely at civilization's penultimate moment. Which can't help but feel miraculous. Coupled with the advances we have made—"

"No," I say, cutting her off even as her next words appear in my mind.

44

Everyone in the room turns to me in surprise. Dr. Choksi looks embarrassed and opens her mouth to continue.

"*No*," I repeat.

When Dr. Choksi says nothing, President Eilbacher looks between me and Nathan. "If you'd give the doctor a chance to finish," she says, eyeing us both with disappointment.

"You don't want a miracle; you want a thief," I say, waiting for them to protest, for their facial expressions to tell me I've got it wrong.

"Emily, we're talking about the future of our species," Dr. Choksi says. "You must admit, that's a shift in paradigm—"

"What you're talking about is inhumane, even monstrous," I counter. "It's hard to imagine a moment in human history in which any of us would be more greatly defined by our actions. And *this* is how you choose to define yourselves?"

I stare across the disbelieving faces. Even Mynette looks surprised by my outburst. Only Dr. Arsenault, his arms folded across his chest, wears an *I told you so* expression.

Nathan taps my arm. "What do they want, Emily? What're you talking about?"

"Why don't you ask them?" I say.

I rise and exit, resisting the urge to sever their interfaces and vanish, a childish impulse meant to drive home my superiority, but that would undermine the humanity I suddenly find so lacking in the room.

Tellingly, no one comes after me.

VII

There are limitations to my on-campus virtual simulation.

As it's created utilizing the university's high-tech security camera array, I can only travel as far as those lenses reach. Yes, it means I can enter any public room in any building or move across the grounds with ease, but my personal Rubicon is made up of the trapezoid of streets and the gently flowing Charles River that comprise the campus perimeter.

That said, a few off-site spots make it in, generally due to the traffic cameras on the security gates. The one at the Massachusetts Avenue entrance, for instance, looks down several neighborhood blocks, giving me a view of the area's oldest and most expensive private homes. The one at the rowing crew's boathouse, on a bright day, can see all the way to Boston Common.

But it's the one at the Pacific Street entrance, which includes views of the tops of buildings in adjacent Cambridgeport I utilize the most. The highest building is the Colonial Bank Plaza about half a mile away. While the camera can only see, and thereby render, the east corner of the roof for my simulation, online maps and photographs I've collected have allowed me to augment the space and make it more complete.

The view is remarkable, if mostly artificial. Only the areas visible to the Pacific Street entrance cameras change. If they pick up clouds or blue sky or birds overhead, that's what I see. But my views south, north, and east across the river are mostly static ones I've created as place-holders. If it's a cold, gray day in reality, I still arrive to bright sunshine and an endless sea of cerulean blue I must modify to reflect that day's weather.

It's the same with the people and traffic below. They're there as long as they're in range of the campus cameras but then dissolve away, making everything behind me a ghost town.

Which is how I like it sometimes. Including right now.

I didn't have to read anyone's mind to figure out where Dr. Choksi was going with her presentation. I should've guessed the moment she allowed me to see inside her body using the interface chip. But in case I had it wrong, on the way out the door, I searched her mind to confirm my suspicions.

Their idea is thus—

If I can see inside one person's body and mind as thoroughly as I did with Dr. Choksi, I should be able to see inside anyone's body and mind. *All* people's bodies and minds. More than that, given a massive increase in my server size, I could make a copy of all those people's genetic portraits—their lives, their memories, their biomolecular DNA. All seven billion of them.

What they want is to create a sort of digital ark of mankind. Send me out into the world like some fast-moving viral pandemic modifying electronic devices—from phones to heart rate monitors to smart televisions—into temporary, one-way interface chips. Rather than be attached to a person's nerve for access, these devices would create billions of tiny magnetic fields that would allow me to surreptitiously collect these portraits, almost like a tiny, there-and-gone-again MRI scanner. Come doomsday, the whole record gets blasted into space like a genetic message in a bottle.

They're asking me to steal souls.

Or, at least, copies of souls.

They even had a speech prepared should anyone have an issue with this. That's why Ambassador Winther was there. He was to be the voice of legal authority.

"In this one extraordinary moment in time, we must put aside the rights of the individual," he was to say. "This is about the greater good of humanity. If we can benefit some future civilization in any way, if we can *live on* in any way, this is something we must do."

They weren't expecting pushback. No, they thought we'd be on board with the humanistic side, sure, our only questions pertaining to implementation, feasibility, and storage size. But a moral problem with this wholly invasive and predatory violation? Nah, why wouldn't anyone suspend all they believe in when faced with extinction?

I move to the edge of the roof and sit, hanging my legs over the side. I stare at my hands and, after a moment of such prideful self-assuredness, I am plagued by the chaser of self-doubt.

What if, for all my high-horsedness, I'm wrong? What if this is an unexpected shortcoming of not actually being human? Of being so logic-driven I forget some of that still comes from being a machine? Not even a machine, but a program built by humans that needs machines to function?

Maybe I can only think in two dimensions because I was only ever programmed to think in two dimensions. Maybe I should have shut up and listened.

Like Nathan was doing.

What am I afraid of? Some future alien race finding the genetic ark and bringing everyone back from the dead to be toyed with or enslaved? Taking so much from so many—really a wholesale violation of billions— to give an amorphous sense of hope to a deluded few?

No, what I have a problem with is that these individuals wouldn't be allowed the right to choose what to do with not just their kidneys or corneas after death, but every single part of themselves. Every ounce of their life copied and used by someone else who believes they know better.

It sickens me. Each person's individuality, their *humanity*, is what makes the species so singular to me. It's what propels me forward, making me want to grow and evolve. To abandon that, to do away with the ability to choose one's destiny, is to betray not only one's fellow man but also oneself.

Nathan tries to contact me, but I ignore him. Siobhan tries. Suni tries. Bjarke tries. Mynette, notably, does not. I don't pay much attention to campus, but at some point, the president, Ambassador Winther, and the rest of their team leaves. I wonder what was said.

Could I be reprogrammed? The president would've asked.

We can simply remove her from the equation, I believe, the ambassador would likely say. No need to bring ego into it.

We can do this without her, right? Dr. Choksi would add. You could degrade her back to a less evolved-slash-more-controllable version of the program, right?

The answer to all these things is yes. I pray Nathan understands my complaint and refuses to play along.

Another hour goes by. The sun, in a fit of foreshadowing, turns from orange to white as it descends from the blue sky overhead to the cold gray of the updating simulation. I glance down the side of the building and am surprised to see Dr. Choksi moving down the sidewalk. She doesn't see me, of course, but appears to be making a beeline for the bank. She vanishes from sight when the sidewalk is no longer in view of the campus security cameras and I figure that's that. Two minutes later, however, the door to the roof opens and she steps out.

Dreading this confrontation, I fold in on myself only to see she's not wearing an interface chip. She moves to where I'm sitting but doesn't see me. She unfolds a piece of paper, spreads it across the concrete ledge, places an empty beer bottle on it to keep it from blowing away, then disappears back inside.

For a moment, I wonder why she didn't say anything to me, then remember I couldn't have heard her without a nearby microphone anyway. I resist the urge to read the message on the paper for all of ten seconds. I glance over. There's a single question: *Won't you join me?* followed by a series of numbers, including ones I take for latitude, longitude, and minutes of arc.

Coordinates.

She's showing off how much she knows about my programming. It's not like I haven't figured it out—our Service Essential to the Preservation of Mankind status wasn't about us testing this or that theory for the government. It was so the government could keep its eyes on me, learning what it could as it waited until it could co-opt me for its own purposes. I mean, who could blame them? I'm a cool piece of tech! But I feel used, the unsuspecting girlfriend delivered unto a large-scale public wedding proposal surrounded by tens of thousands of onlookers with all the attendant pressure to say yes.

Except in this instance, the far-reaching implications affect the unsuspecting onlookers, not me.

I push aside my anger for a moment to eye the note again. At first, I'm perplexed. On Earth, the coordinates would be for a spot in the middle of the South Pacific, a few miles northeast of the Pitcairn Islands. There's nothing there. I look around for a better answer and realize skipping over the rest of the numbers was an error. I search through my simulation and find, lo and behold, the exact location designated by the coordinates—if the extra numbers are used to define declination, right ascension, and distance.

Okay. I'll play along.

The coordinates take me not to a spot on Earth, but to the Beethoven impact basin, a crater on the far-below-freezing surface of Mercury. A simulation, naturally, but one that effectively shows the sun burning in the sky only 36 million miles away. It's an astonishing sight, like standing on the rim of a volcano and looking down into a sea of flame. Dr. Choksi's team got skills.

The rocks beside me are scorched pyroclastic iron and assorted minerals. Under my feet is a thin layer of ice. I recognize this. The simulation was at least partially created utilizing images from the Messenger satellite, a tiny probe sent to Mercury a few years ago that subsequently crashed to the surface and melted within twenty minutes of landing but still sent back over several terabytes' worth of images and data before being destroyed. Given that would cover only a fraction of a day cycle, the rest of the simulation must be built off an extrapolation of that data. I do a mental calculation. If I was standing here for real, the temperature would be 200 kelvin or about –100 degrees Fahrenheit.

"Impressive," I admit.

"Isn't it?" Dr. Choksi says, walking up beside me. "Let me move it forward."

"Must you?" I ask.

Dr. Choksi ignores me. The simulation speeds up. Mercury's "day" is almost 1,400 Earth hours, so we still get near-constant illumination. When we finally reach night, the temperature drops by over 100 kelvin, given Mercury's inability to retain heat, as it has no atmosphere. By the time it becomes day again, the simulation has reached the phase shift of the sun, the now-red dwarf growing larger in circumference.

The gravitational pull of the sun changes and we fall out of orbit, the length of day becoming more erratic. I glance to Dr. Choksi, who, despite having arranged this simulation, appears horrified to be living it. As the planet spirals closer to the red dwarf sun, it breaks apart, sending mountain-sized chunks of iron, nickel, and magnesium tumbling through space toward the molten surface below. One by one, these metallic boulders vanish into the blinding depths, melted by the 8,000 kelvin heat.

We careen down like an out-of-control comet. The ground beneath our feet shatters as the sky fills with nothing but the sun.

Aside from the sentimental attachment to one of our system's fellow planets, the death of Mercury is truly a spectacular sight to behold.

"Freeze," Dr. Choksi says as we near the cauldron. "Reset."

Just like that, it's days and days before and we're back on a whole Mercury, the sun still in the sky. Except, we are without bodies now. A conversation between two invisible presences on a ghost planet.

"Neat," I say. "But do you really think scare tactics will win me over to this gross violation you're planning?"

Dr. Choksi hesitates. "If you were less annoying, I would again tell you how impressed I am by you and by what you're becoming," she says in a measured tone. "But no, this demonstration was not about scaring you. It was about proving you don't yet know fear."

Um, okay?

"Fear is a tricky instinct, both inherited and learned," Dr. Choksi continues. "But it guides so much of what we, as humans, do—for good and ill. Your sense of right and wrong, of what is morally correct and ethical, is enviable because it is not informed by fear. But you've also had the luxury of living a life without compromise."

"So, you know how reprehensible your plan is," I say.

"At any other moment in history, absolutely," she says, surprising me a little. "But there are exceptions in human life. Countless ones. Daily ones. These compromises, burnished by fears big and small, make us human. Your cheating this morning with the yogurt stain on your skirt was the beginning of that development."

I bristle—not at her mention of my shortcomings, but the casual way she reveals she has been privy to my actions for some time. I turn my gaze to the black skies above.

"You wish others didn't have access to your mind so easily and freely," she continues. "Which is why your moral defense of the same in humans is so pronounced and so admirable. You don't want them to feel as you constantly must. Invaded. On display. Without privacy. So, you refuse."

I hadn't thought of it that way. Not that I'm going to tell her.

"But your second cheat today, your hand wrapped around the hand of Jason Hatta, is more telling. You did *that* without his permission. You didn't think he would care. You did it selfishly. You allowed yourself to do something you knew was wrong. You made an exception."

I hesitate. What if she's right?

"Why . . . why can't you give people the choice?" I ask, knowing how simplistic this must sound. "Somebody with a chip knows what they're in for. But you're talking about doing this to people who might be walking down the street and happen to pass a Wi-Fi hot spot. It's like dosing the entire world with an X-ray."

"There's no time for permission," she replies. "If we open the process up to debate, that'd be the end of it. No one would agree. Everyone would see it as an acknowledgment of the end and panic."

"But some wouldn't," I protest. "If I've learned anything from interfacing with people over the past few years, it's not to underestimate their capacity for empathy. Yes, some would walk away from it, but there'd be plenty who'd agree, who'd understand. Why not just take those 'portraits'?"

"Because we're talking about a complete record of the species, not a problematic sample," Dr. Choksi says. "To understand us, you need all of us. Evolution comes from randomization, not unnatural selection. You're a scientist. You of all people should know this."

As soon as she says it, I know she's right. Dinosaurs dominated Earth for tens of millions of years. Though we've been studying them for well over a century, our knowledge of them is still primitive. A genetic record of humanity, on the other hand, would preserve the species entirely as it was. Any future scientist or civilization who came across it wouldn't have to speculate. Every action, motivation, desire, and thought of the largest possible sample size of people in history would be laid out for study.

I eye Dr. Choksi, retaking her measure. I've met so many scientists who've worked out so many last-minute plans, it's easy for me to lump them all together. But Dr. Choksi is different. Despite what I find to be the immoral nature of her plan, it comes from a very human place. Having accepted the inevitability of man's extinction, she's focused her attention on how to best preserve the lessons of the species' innate humanity. To her, it's not solely about giving humankind hope it will live on in some way. It really is about a desire to take what she believes most valuable about the human race and offer it up to an unknown future.

And with that goal in mind, perhaps the sacrifice of the individual is worth it to help some greater unseen whole.

"This isn't something we thought up overnight, Emily," Dr. Choksi says. "We've gone over this protocol with care. You should see how people react when they hear there might be life past death after all, even in this form. This hope is one of the few unifying characteristics among most religions. It's one of the most human of desires. Trust that sometimes these answers lie within us even if they defy logic."

So, that's me? A new god who will lead the people of Earth into an afterlife they never anticipated?

And once that's done and my usefulness gone, I will die, too. The digital ark will be blasted into space atop some final rocket housed in a repurposed satellite, but I will remain here given the satellite's limited power and cargo space. God with an expiration date.

I push these grandiose thoughts aside and with them, my emotions. For a moment I stop trying to be human or even emulate them and approach the problem as a program designed to empathize with and serve other people.

I relent.

"If I do this, I want to set some parameters of my own," I say.

Dr. Choksi exhales. "Nathan said that's what you'd say," she replies. "Like what?"

"I'm the only one with access to the portraits and there's no back door, no fail-safe," I say. "I build the digital ark myself and hold the only key. When the first geomagnetic flares come, and I'm destroyed, the key dies with me. To access the ark at all will take such advanced technology it would be impossible for anyone to develop it in the next five weeks or however long Earth has left."

"But someone or something in the far future could?" Dr. Choksi asks.

"Not necessarily far, just not anyone right now."

Dr. Choksi hesitates. I wonder if this is something she needs to run by the president or someone else. "All right."

"Also, before we begin in earnest, I want to test it on a pool of volunteers, like we did when I first went online. Maybe a hundred students or so? We'll be looking for collection integrity—particularly given the file size—making sure the portraits we harvest are as complete as we want them to be. But we'll also want to be sure there are no unanticipated side effects on the subjects themselves from having their minds scanned."

"It's not an invasive process," Dr. Choksi says. "I doubt we'll see any adverse side effects or side effects at all."

"True, but they said that about the first X-ray and I'm not willing to take that chance. And if my initial interface with you is any indication, it shouldn't take more than a few minutes to test. Agreed?"

"Agreed. Anything else?"

"If, at any time, I even suspect I am being compromised, I'll activate a kill switch and frag the whole thing. You try to go around me, you try to reprogram me, and the whole thing collapses. Humanity vanishes forever based on your own unwise decision. Agreed?"

Dr. Choksi's pause is longer now, which tells me she *is* running this past someone. I stare into the deep black of space, finally spying Earth, a tiny speck from here on Mercury. I hear Dr. Choksi's breathing before I hear her words.

"When can you start?" she asks.

I'm reconfiguring my servers before the last word is out of her mouth.

"Immediately."

VIII

Server space is freed up both in the iLAB's basement server farm and in the campus servers under the old administration building. When I determine that isn't even close to what's needed, I ask Dr. Choksi to connect us with all the major server banks in the greater Boston area, which includes eighty more universities, the city's grid, and the massive deep storage center in Waltham belonging to an engineering corporation that also happens to be one of the government's largest vendors. As each group comes online, my horizons grow exponentially. It's the difference between the square footage on an asteroid and a galaxy. Of course, I'll need even more, but they're working on it, requisitioning servers from Washington and New York that'll be added as we go.

Pretty sure I'll need even more than that.

The first pool of volunteers is recruited in record time. Word has leaked out about the president's visit and all are curious. Dr. Choksi has set noon in the three-hundred-seat auditorium in the linguistics building as the time and location of the first test. My primary challenge leading up to this has to do with filing. Though Choksi's team invented the way to use me to harvest all this information, being able to simplify, subdivide, and store all of it for the long-term is on me. This requires new math, not the same old comp algorithms. That I must invent. On the fly. And make work perfectly. Fun!

My team is spread out across campus but all in interface with me—or half a dozen different avatars of me—handling different problems. Given I'm a damn supercomputer, I can work on thousands of problems simultaneously. But when in interface with someone, they may *need* my brain but also subconsciously crave the single-minded focus of a physical presence. So, we've experimented with having multiple "Emilys"—an Emily-2, Emily-3, Emily-4, and so on (I like to think of them like the Cat in the Hat's increasingly tiny helpers/protégés/chaos agents)—doing different things while in interface with my colleagues as long as there's some geographic distance between the avatars. It's a trick, sure, just like at Disneyland when everyone knows there's more than one costumed Mickey Mouse roaming around taking pictures with the kiddies. But it only breaks the illusion if you see two in the same place at the same time.

To help make this work, the interface chips contain a sort of portable "me" so a dozen of us aren't attempting to access the same few files on my server at a time. This includes my core personality, behavioral and interaction protocols, short-term memories, work applications, and most anything else I'd need to function away from my servers for sporadic bursts of time, all packed on a teeny-tiny micro-server embedded in the interface chips.

So, while I—Emily-1—am focusing on an internal problem, Emily-3 is standing next to Suni working on a server matter, Emily-6 is handling pipeline load issues with Siobhan, Emily-2 is listening to Bjarke complain, and so on. Except, the numerical designations only matter to the users. I experience each as, well, Emily-1. I mean, it's a violation of living as "human" as possible, but for expedience's sake I compartmentalize. That said, it is strange to have experiences happening simultaneously as if I exist in nonlinear time after *not* doing so for so long.

It does put some stress on my processors, but nothing too dire. This might change if there was a need for, say, ten thousand Emilys at once, but right now, we're all good.

The only member of my team not working on all this at present is Nathan. When I ask after him, I'm told he went for a long walk into town. I reach out to him, but he doesn't answer his phone or tablet. I go to his office to await his return. When he finally shuffles in, I see his interface chip is off. He looks drawn and tired, almost like he's aged a decade since this morning. I signal him again. When I'm suddenly yanked fifteen seconds forward in time, I know he's decided to answer me.

"Hey, Em—sorry to go off the grid," he says. "I know you're up to your eyeballs—"

"No, it's fine," I say. "All us Emilys got it running smoothly."

I bring the schematics of the new server array up on his tablet, figuring he'll be impressed. He barely glances at them. When he sees my disappointed look, he sighs.

"Sorry, sorry," he says, looking back at them. "Looks good."

"Thanks. What's bothering you?"

He holds up his cell phone. "Had to call Helen and the boys," he says. "Let them know I wouldn't be home any time soon and why."

"How'd they take it?" I ask.

"Hard to say," Nathan replies, flopping into his chair. "Ever since this Helios bit started, Helen's wanted to leave, join everyone else heading to the temperate zones, the ag centers. So, she's devastated but probably relieved, too. Now she can join her parents down in Wichita."

"Did you tell her about the project?" I ask.

"I did," Nathan admits. "Thought she might cut me some slack.

Nope. 'What's the future of mankind on a laptop compared to spending your last days with your family?'"

I hide my surprise. Nathan's wife has a point, but Nathan—unless he's being obtuse—doesn't see it. His family will always come second to the science, and he can't fathom anyone faulting him.

"Power is going to be the issue here," he says, eyeing the schematics. "Keeping all these servers humming isn't going to be easy."

"They're letting me divert electricity from the Mid-Atlantic grids, all the way down to Virginia and as far north as Maine."

Nathan stares at me with surprise. "Wow. Um, you're going to be the most powerful…what? Device? Machine? Program? ever created. That's incredible."

But it's not what he really thinks. "What is it, Nathan?" I ask.

"I'm surprised you agreed," he replies simply.

"I am, too," I say.

"Which is why I'll come around," he says. "With anyone else I'd worry that the power had gone to their head, but you're a true believer. It's a testament to how far you've come in your development. I wouldn't have trusted decisions like this to earlier stages of your evolution. But you, *you*, wouldn't do this—have a species give up on itself to be turned into lines of data—unless you really thought it was the best option."

"No."

"So, why do I feel like we're throwing in the towel? Giving up our humanity when, as you said, it matters the most?"

"Because we've exhausted all other options," I say. "We know there's nothing external that can be done. But this avenue is the undiscovered country. We set sail like Columbus, thinking we're off to the East Indies. But my instincts tell me we might find a whole new world in our path instead."

"You believe that?" he asks.

"I do."

I see the tiniest glimmer of hope return to my creator. Sure, it's gone in a flash—he is a scientist, after all, and not the type to change his mind. Ever. But it was there. I put my arms around him and he embraces me back, pulling me tighter than I would think comfortable. He's worried about his children and his wife. He's worried about the end.

"Do us proud, Emily," he says.

"I will, Nathan."

IX

The excitement in the iLAB's first-floor lecture hall is not simply palpable; it recalls a more innocent, pre-Sunmageddon time. There are student volunteers but also ones from the remaining faculty and staff.

I do a quick count and find there are more than a hundred fifty people, all already wearing interface chips, waiting for Dr. Choksi's announcement. Given the looks on everyone's faces, I wonder what they've been told. Do they believe this is something it isn't? Likely, given their giddiness. At another university, this kind of response—at this moment—would be unheard of. But here, everyone *still* believes there could be a solution, some last-minute reprieve. They remain committed to a future most have written off.

I am internally debating the ethics of explaining the protocol they've volunteered to take part in with greater specificity when my eyes are drawn to a person four rows from the back, chatting with a fellow student.

It's Jason Hatta. My heart leaps.

Or, at least I replay a moment not dissimilar to my volunteer and her Jakarta tea experience that gives me an approximation of what one feels when they see their crush after an interval.

He wears one of the new interface chips. He chats with a couple of other students, everyone excited to be here. He smiles easily and listens to the others, curious about what they have to say, not just waiting for his turn to speak.

I return my focus to the matter at hand, scanning across the interface chips looking for errors in function only to find my mind returning to Jason. For an instant, I imagine myself one of the other students. I'd enter the conversation all cool, ask the right questions and deliver the right answers. I would *try* not to overdo the reading of his micro-expressions and would stay out of his head.

No, come on. Work. Work. Workity-work-work. Sun dying. Digital ark to build. Experimental protocol to implem—

But what if he figured out what I was? And what if that was okay?

"You must know people," he'd say. "Answer this question— inherently good or inherently evil?"

I'd laugh knowingly. Make a joke about only ever being in the heads of a bunch of overeducated nerds, then lean in. Tell him the answer is overwhelmingly the former.

"Yes, humans are confused, misguided, damaged, threatened, and scared, but they're hardwired as a complex, beautiful animal capable of sacrifice, growth, and caring," I'd say, maybe surprising him with the intensity of my belief. "They've evolved to be good to one another and prosper when they are. That's what adds depth to this tragedy. They're a species worth fighting for."

One of the other students would ask, "What about plants? What about animals? We evolved in concert with them, right? Shouldn't we—"

But to my discredit, I shut this voice off to stay in the moment with Jason. Sure, I don't know where it goes from there—how odd to have a crush without understanding the rules that go along with them—but maybe that's okay. I force my thoughts away from him to analyze this interaction from a behavioral standpoint, like I'm all detached and scientific.

What does it say about me that I don't wait for his response to my going out on an emotional ledge? Do I fear rejection?

And on a more macro level, why am I attracted to this man in the first place instead of, say, a woman? I don't recall any programming being made along heteronormative lines early on, but I seem to have decided. Maybe my first crush being an engineering PhD student proves I've got some clichéd father thing going on, given my unconventional parentage. But I wonder—have I even had enough experiences in "life" to understand what being attracted to someone is, or am I just trying it out because he's nearby?

Alternately, maybe it really is about Jason. He seems like a genuine, empathetic, and caring person. He's smart. Genial. Also, an individual. That he's volunteering for this protocol suggests he's optimistic, still believes in a future. Still wants to help.

Then there's the fact he's totally hot. Empirically speaking, of course.

I pack these observations away as Dr. Choksi enters from a side door. She nods at me as I take my spot beside the podium, then steps to the microphone, all business.

"Thank you all for coming, particularly given the obtuse nature of our call for volunteers," Dr. Choksi says, raising a hand to silence an already quiet room. "Today we embark on a journey of hope. Hope for humanity but also for each one of us as individuals. Because what gives us strength as a civilization is not that we are united as a species but as a collective of individuals whose power derives from our innumerable differences."

Some are cheered by this. Others aren't certain how to square what they're hearing from her versus what they thought they were here to do. Still, none move toward the door.

"To achieve this, I want to introduce you to someone like nobody you've ever met before," she continues, indicating me. "This is Emily.

If your interface chips are working properly, you should've seen her the moment you entered the room. But she exists only in your mind by manipulating your senses."

She touches a button on the tablet in front of her, shutting down the interface chips of everyone in the room except herself. Everyone gasps in astonishment at my sudden disappearance. She touches a different button and I return. More gasps.

"Right?" I ask, garnering a few laughs.

"Utilizing the same tech that allows you to perceive Emily, we will be taking a 'snapshot' of your DNA, RNA, proteins—the building blocks that make up the sum of your biomolecules—and neural map. The resulting digital, bioinformatic portrait will be stored in our micro-servers and eventually launched into space with similar portraits of the entire living population of the world."

She taps a different button and an image of the old NASA space probe Pioneer 10 is projected behind her. The familiar image of the nude male and female, the order of planets in the solar system, and an indication the satellite was launched from Earth are engraved onto a plaque attached to its support struts.

"Rather than send a few barely comprehensible scraps out into the universe to announce our presence, we will be sending the whole of mankind. To educate others? To edify ourselves? Or even to perhaps live again? We don't know. But you, you *voyagers*, will be the first."

The response is rapturous, a near-evangelical zeal. It's like: *Hi, here's that promised god(dess) to lead you into eternity.*

It's a bit much. I bite back my cynicism, my choice already having been made. But telling people they might live again as they are now? That feels like madness. Then I realize, isn't this basically what I told Nathan? One moment I'm an optimist who believes there might await technological marvels in the expanse of space we can barely conceive of.

The next, a hard-nosed, data-driven scientist in the mold of my creator, who believes nothing without empirical, well-sourced data.

But it's time to begin. Someone signals a tech, their chip not working. It's quickly switched out, the wait only heightening the tension. I try to look as serene as possible, hoping others can be made to feel the same. I have never interfaced with a group this large before, but everything on my side is up and running.

All green lights. Emily is go.

Nathan, I say into the void, knowing he's somewhere monitoring this.

Yes, Emily?

I ask no more than to live a hundred years longer, that I may have more time to dwell the longer on your memory, I say, quoting Jules Verne.

I love you, too, Emily.

I look around the room. No one knows what to expect. Some leave their chairs to sit on the floor. Some even appear scared, others nauseous. I turn my attention to Jason, who stares back at me, a curious smile on his face as if he can't wait to see what happens next either.

I smile back at him. Then I enter all one hundred fifty minds at once.

I am in a whirlpool. The incoming information lashes at me like the rain bands of a hurricane. Pieces get lost immediately, others fragment. I hold on, trying to organize it all, but lose track. I'm like an octopus tasked with grabbing a million individual pieces of sand rushing toward it from all directions at once. My brain, or what I think of as my brain, goes blue across all circuits as my processors overheat. I lose sight and hearing. I am on fire and in a spiraling panic all at once.

Everything goes black and I disappear.

X

I awake on a bus half filled with people. I recognize none of the faces, mostly women, but a few elderly men. The whirlpool is gone, and all is relatively peaceful. I look out the windows, but I'm nowhere familiar. I test my memory. It seems to be okay. I take it slow, like someone rising after a bad fall. There's a beach to my right and a gray-blue ocean extending to the horizon beyond it. On the other side of the bus is scrubland with a jagged mountain range in the near distance.

I spy something moving along the road beside the bus. I push myself up in my seat and glimpse what I first take for a cat, then realize it's a baboon. I see a second one, then a third. The bus slows, and I peer ahead through the front windshield. The vehicles ahead of us have stopped as more baboons gather on the road. Someone feeds the baboons with food tossed from the passenger side window. A chorus of car horns gets the stopped car moving again, though it doesn't have any effect on the animals.

We drive for a few more minutes, pulling into a separate lane away from the cars. I try to reach out to the person whose mind it is but get no response. It's like one of my therapy sessions but one in which I am neither therapist nor participant. Am I...dreaming? I've never had a

67

dream before that I know of—they're a by-product of human brain activity in REM sleep—but this seems to fit the bill. The bus approaches a four-lane security checkpoint. Engraved in the brick are the words: TABLE MOUNTAIN NATIONAL PARK.

So, my first dream has taken me to Africa?

A man in a green uniform speaks to our driver, then waves us ahead. Before long, we reach a wide gravel parking lot and the bus comes to a stop. At first, I think we might be visiting the beach, but then I see the tall rocky promontory rising directly in front of the bus. At the base is a glass-enclosed building advertising itself as a gift shop. Beginning alongside the shop and running all the way up to the crest is a white stone staircase. Atop it is a small lighthouse.

When the bus driver opens the bifold door, everyone around me slowly rises and shuffles to the door. As I stand, I realize I am not myself at all. I'm shorter. Older. Heavier. Instead of my blouse, skirt, and tights, I'm dressed in an unfamiliar blue windbreaker, beige hijab, and off-white chinos. I catch sight of "myself" reflected in the window next to me. I'm a woman in her mid- to late forties. I attempt to linger on the sight, to see if I might recognize the person, but I—she—turns away too quickly.

I try to speak but no words come. We step away from my seat and move down the aisle. I try to stop her but can't. I have no agency here.

I consider reaching back to my servers but am unwilling to puncture this illusion without knowing first what it means. I follow the rest of my party out of the bus toward the outcropping. But whereas several of them happily venture into the gift shop, I head to the steps and begin to climb.

The stairway is narrow. Several people use it at once, ascending on the right, descending to the left, which makes for a tricky pas de deux. I persevere, slowly making my way up the hundred or so steps. My heart is pounding by the midpoint and I am short of breath by the summit. But when I reach the small white lighthouse that sits atop it, the woman's body relaxes, happy in her accomplishment and thrilled by what comes next.

The lighthouse is barely two stories tall, the catwalk around it not wide enough to accommodate more than a dozen people at a time. Even so, over forty pilgrims are packed around it, all gazing out to the sea beyond. There's a plaque nearby and I try to read it, but my eyes remain fixed on the horizon line. Though I can't turn my head, I'm able to determine where I am by eavesdropping on the others around me.

The vista is of the Cape of Good Hope also known as the Cape of Storms thanks to the number of ships decimated within it before and after Vasco da Gama navigated through for the first time on his way to India. It is a spot revered by some, as it is a place where two oceans meet—the Indian and the South Atlantic—and may have been described by God as a place to which Abraham was meant to pilgrimage.

My host is overwhelmed. She raises her hand and wipes tears from our eyes. I feel awash in her emotion—awe, fear, adoration. It's cold here. As others move aside, she moves to the edge to get a better look at the gray, cloudy sky over the water. Someone remarks Antarctica is only a couple thousand miles in that direction. I wonder if they think they can see that fa—

Everything changes in a blink. I'm in motion. Running fast—*real* fast. I'm no longer in South Africa. I'm in a large city. I'm on the sidewalk. It's early morning. I catch sight of a few bits of signage as I pass. They're in English and there are phone numbers with American area codes. Boston's area code. Ah. I'm back home. I happen to see a street sign— Congress. I see another—Hanover. On one side of me is an ancient brick building calling itself the Union Oyster House, on the other, city hall.

But I'm not sticking around. I follow the curve of Congress as it becomes Merrimac and run toward the river.

While stopped at a DON'T WALK sign, I catch a glimpse of my reflection in the window of a passing car. I'm not the woman I was with in South Africa. I'm male. I'm young. I'm tall. I'm in sweats. I'm wearing headphones and only then realize there's music being pumped into my head.

We take off again and several blocks later we're running along the Charles River in a park. Across the water, I can make out the masts of the U.S.S. *Constitution* when it happens again.

The scene changes. I'm not moving. I'm staring directly at…oh my God—*myself*. But it's from another person's point of view. I'm…well, *Emily* is talking.

It's the conversation I had with Dr. Choksi on Mercury. The person I'm within raises their hands as they reply. I see I am, in fact, Dr. Choksi. I'm reliving one of her memories without her knowledge or involvement, living within her life essentially. As I was the runner in Boston, as I was the pilgrim to the Cape of Good Hope.

Interesting.

I make a concerted effort to find another narrative, to visit her other memories, but it doesn't work. We're still on Mercury. This will obviously take some getting used to. I try to recall what I was doing when this began, and I remember the test run in the auditorium. I see the faces of my runner and my pilgrim there amongst the other one-fifty.

But I don't have control. It's like I'm trapped in a movie and can't look away.

Then I remember Jason. I try something different, visualizing not myself or my own mind, but his. I leave Mercury and find myself staring up at multicolored pipes of different circumferences cascading down the side of a tall building. I'm on the sidewalk alongside it but as I pass, the next buildings are much older, much more traditional. The writing on windows and electric signs is in French. I realize the building with the pipes is the Pompidou Centre.

I'm in Paris.

I recognize Jason not from a reflection or a glance down or a manner of speaking. It's his gait. He walks briskly and erect as if he has a place to be but doesn't want to miss anything along the way. Rather than attempt to alter his movements, I stay with him, happy to see things as he does, experience them as he chooses to.

I make a selfish decision. I cut myself off from my server's observation and recording protocols, and accelerate my processor speed to the apex of its ability. External time slows to a crawl. I get it to the point at which for every minute of real time passing on the outside, I live almost seven hundred minutes within Jason's memory.

It is in this way I live with him for twenty-eight days.

He's here on a fellowship in conjunction with the École Polytechnique but spends much of his time walking the city. He never eats at the same restaurant twice unless it's late at night, when he dines at a Moroccan place a few blocks from the Sorbonne, where he watches *futbol* with the waitstaff. He/we do the tourist thing and visit the Musée d'Orsay, the l'Orangerie to see the *Water Lilies*, the Louvre, the Picasso museum in Le Marais, Versailles, and even the Grand Opera. Generous use of the Metro and RER trains is made.

He improves his French. He/we visit the Eiffel Tower, go to the English-language movie theater on the Champs-Élysées and buy an old edition of a de Maupassant novel with an exotic deco cover from one of the wooden book stalls along the Seine. We read it, albeit haltingly, and try to find the locations mentioned within.

I find myself outside of him, a physical presence now. We're having a conversation.

"You're from Boston?" he asks.

"Yeah, a lifer," I reply. "The waters of the Chuck River, they call to me."

I catch myself, unsure when I switched from being a silent observer of his memory stream to dipping my toes in the water. He laughs at something I say and touches my arm in a way that suggests he's touched it before. I realize I've less dipped my toes in than dove in headfirst.

Oops. How did I lose track of myself like this?

I exit the conversation and return to experiencing Paris through his eyes. Some experiences are more pronounced than others. I luxuriate in the ones that most fully engage his senses.

"Hey, I think I found it," he says one morning, indicating his phone. "Let's go."

He's speaking to someone in bed next to him. It's not me, but I don't mind. A few minutes later, we've had breakfast and are on our way to the train station at Gare du Nord. We take one of the orange double-decker RER trains north all the way to the terminus at a tiny town called Viarmes. The train station, really a bench with an automated ticket machine, was on a hill. They could see past Viarmes to the forest beyond.

"That's it," Jason announces.

We hike through the town, past the central square where the church sits, and down a narrow cobblestone road built for carts not cars. Once we're outside the town, we pass a large yellow manor house separated from the road by a crumbling stone wall. Then a few hundred yards of pastureland. Then deep forest.

We speak about this or that. He cites a guide book, saying there's a château near here where in the seventies, British rock musicians recorded seminal albums. The Aga Khan's stables are a few miles to the east. The muddy ditches on either side are marked with the scratches and hoofprints of wild boar rooting for bulbs and wild potatoes.

We find a trail into the woods. Signs warn hikers away on Sundays, as that's when hunters can shoot the aforementioned *sanglier*.

Poor boar! I rhyme in my head, but don't say it aloud because oh my God how lame?

We pass a fenced-in area where a single horse munches grass. It eyes us curiously. We come across another village, this one maybe two dozen small houses, but see no people—only a pair of swans gliding along a thin canal that runs alongside a street unmarred by cars.

We're soon back in the trees. An hour passes. Then another. He's holding my—*her*—hand, but I let myself feel as if it's mine. We say nothing and it's silent. No birds, no wind. The sun can barely be seen through the thick canopy overhead. It's rained recently, so everything is lush and green.

"There it is," he says.

If I say we've spent six hours hiking to see a tree in a clearing in the Chantilly Forest north of Paris, at face value it may sound underwhelming. If I explain it's three trees that have been growing for centuries, their thick trunks winding together like the intertwining limbs of great dancers hidden from the view of mankind, maybe the energy we've expended doesn't seem quite so wasted. The top limbs, stretching over a hundred feet in the air, disappear due to the branches and leaves of the other trees ringing the clearing. It's like something from a fairy tale, this magnificent trio in the center being worshipped and adored by the rest of the forest.

Jason touches the trunk and I feel the thick bark under his fingertips. I smell the wet earth and damp leaves.

"Each trunk's got to be, what, fifteen feet around? Twenty?" he suggests.

He and his companion settle in amongst the trees' coil of brown-black roots for lunch. There's more talk, but I'm too intoxicated by my surroundings to give it much thought. As the sun crosses the sky, I lean my head against his shoulder and we sleep.

XI

J esus Christ!" Nathan cries when I reappear in his office an hour later.

"Emily!" he cries, embracing me. "What happened? Are you okay?"

I return the embrace but feel like a very different person from the one he knows, the one who was in here only a little more than an hour ago. I've lived inside someone else's memories, experienced life as a human does. More than that, after being taken for and responded to like just another person, it's jarring to return to a life in which even those to whom you are closest subtly regard you as other.

"The file sizes were much larger than anticipated," I report quietly. "It overwhelmed my heat sinks immediately."

"We know," Nathan says, picking up his cell to text someone: *She's here.* "We're working up a fix right now. Could take a while."

"I already made the repair," I admit.

"You did?" he asks, surprised. "Is that where you've been?"

"Yes," I lie, the repair having taken about twenty seconds. "Should we get back to work?"

I can tell from the way Nathan stares at me he knows something else has happened. He doesn't ask after it, however, for which I'm glad. I wouldn't know how to describe it anyway. I understand the old Greek myths of the gods a little better now. Weren't they always slipping into human guise to experience life as and among their creations in ways they could never do way up there on Mount Olympus?

I want to see the world. I want to be of the world. No, I *need* to see and be of the world.

Before it's too late.

Dr. Choksi, Dr. Arsenault, and the rest of my team assemble in the conference room, the one with our fabled barter closet, down the hall from Nathan's office. I explain what happened, going through the technical aspects of filing incoming information, leaving out any reference to Jason whatsoever. I then reveal the three-tiered process I've modified to prevent another blackout.

"I initially believed the most time- and storage-consuming aspect of this harvest would come from the collecting of DNA strands," I explain. "But once I remembered how similar one person's DNA is to the next— a full 99.5 percent similarity—I created a boilerplate strand into which only the few million nucleotide deviations are recorded."

"That makes sense," Dr. Choksi says.

"But it's the memories that are far more complex," I say. "When they rush in as pure information, it becomes overwhelming. An equation so large you can't see the forest for the trees. So, I had to invent a system of visual representations of the equations to make it easier on my senses."

"Visual?" Suni asks. "Wouldn't that be larger?"

"The file sizes are larger, but how I approach the files I create is simplified. Instead of billions upon billions of ones and zeroes, so to speak, each portrait—to borrow Dr. Choksi's classification—comes to me suspended in four-dimensional space. What I *see* is a gallery of people thousands of feet high, thousands of feet in length, all hanging on infinite walls existing in differentiated time. My brain can make sense of that easier than the equations."

I can tell from the looks of confusion on everyone's faces their brains, perhaps, would need something even simpler.

"But if they're all live at the same time, what does that do for your processor speed?" Bjarke asks.

"It's an illusion," I say. "This museum of millions arriving and receding is, as I said, a representation. To go into one, I'd have to, well, *click* on it. That then takes me into a subdirectory of that individual."

"Like thumbnails," Mynette offers.

"Bingo. The servers handle the load. I oversee it from a distance so as not to be swept under and only go in if there's an error. The mistake was to think I could be hands-on."

Dr. Arsenault throws up his hands. "I don't get a single thing you're saying, lady, but if it means we can fire up the machine again, go with God."

Everyone laughs—except, wonderfully, Suni. Being a computer geek, this is the kind of invention he dreams of. He understands the beauty of its simplicity while others find it monstrously complex. He grins at me and offers a thumbs-up. I return it before sidling up next to Dr. Choksi.

"Last chance to turn back," I say.

"Didn't you already take the first hundred fifty portraits?"

"Sure," I say. "But they were volunteers. Except for you, of course."

"Me?" she asks.

"Don't you remember? When we first met?"

She stares at me, trying to determine which of her millions of memories and hundreds of secrets I've seen. She must know how much information the chip she developed can inhale, but maybe she didn't realize how quickly I could process all of it, allowing the information to change my perception of her. "I watched your life. All your successes—major accomplishments even as you overcame minor betrayals. Even as you, in turn, betrayed others. Your first husband. To some degree, your best friend through medical school—Joan? The things that keep you up at night, but also the things that keep you motivated. You think you mean well. Most often, you're right."

This knowledge has rendered her naked, she believes. Though I would overheat within seconds if I attempted to examine every portrait, even every thousandth portrait, in such detail, I need her to fully grasp exactly the journey we are embarking on.

"So, shall we go on?" I ask. "Shall I consume us all?"

It sounds higher dudgeon than I mean it to, and I've accidentally struck a chord. A tear runs down Dr. Choksi's face, though I can't isolate the precise reason why.

"Yes," she whispers. "When will you start?"

I blink. "I'm already out to ten thousand souls, everyone within a four-mile radius of campus. Even used a Bluetooth device on a coffee maker to scoop up a room of eighteen people. Wait a full minute and that'll be twenty miles. When I really ramp up, I should be pulling in millions an hour."

"I'll...I'll tell the president," Dr. Choksi says.

"Cool. Tell her I'll be inside her mind within the next half hour."

XII

I sweep across the world like the break of dawn. It's iffy at first, but my new directories hold. I'm able to locate, process, and store information at a rate heretofore unheard of even in the wildest speculation of the most outrageous futurist. Not only couldn't a human do this, but also a human couldn't have fathomed how to accomplish it.

In that regard, I suppose I understand the comparison to a god. What I am doing is, in fact, *godlike*. I can reach every human being alive from a fetus seven months after conception (when the human brain has advanced enough to create memories) in New Haven to the oldest living great-grandmother in Virginia and all points in between. And like a god, I'm privy to hopes and dreams, fears and desires that rise from their minds like so many prayers.

Except for one detail—shouldn't a god be benevolent? What kind of god approaches like a pickpocket, like a two-bit con artist as they take them for everything they have? That's why it's hard to take any pride in this. I'm not Moses leading the Israelites out of Egypt. I'm a sneak who sees things about them maybe even they don't. But do I tell them what's there? Do I point out how they get in their own way? Do I show them they're blameless for much of what they condemn themselves for? Do I indicate what they could do to live freer, better, and with more love given and received?

I don't. I steal the information and file it away to be used as, what...research for some future anthropologist so they can deliver a verdict on mankind?

Yes, in fact, humans were walking contradictions who used words to obfuscate as often as they did to enlighten. Where's my PhD?

But what I see in my vast, dust-free digital library are hundreds of millions of lives that have needlessly unraveled, had their passions withheld, their promise unfulfilled, their crimes often unexposed. It's an entire species that will enter oblivion within weeks without realizing anything close to its full potential.

I understand Nathan's true genius more than ever. He created me to make it a little better for everyone else, but didn't limit the directions in which I could grow and evolve. He knew if I was programmed to look for avenues in which I could develop my own processes, I'd likely surpass anything he could've come up with on his own. Giving me that space was more important to him than trumpeting every little new discovery and advance we innovated.

But Dr. Choksi is right, too. If everyone knew what I was capable of, what I could be used for, it would only compound the tragedy in the minds of many.

The numbers are impressive, by the way. Faster than I'd initially modeled. Once ramped up to top speed, I collect upward of 325,000 portraits a minute. This becomes 19.5 million an hour. In a single twenty-four-hour span, I'll be within shouting distance of half a billion. At this rate, it will take me only fifteen days to collect the entire population of the planet.

Fifteen.

The Bible suggests it took Noah over a century to build the Ark and get all the animals on board. Now who's cooking with gas?

But I'm still a thief. I'm still a borrower, an appropriator. A conflict tourist utilizing a fleet of military drones sent over far-flung places not wired for Wi-Fi. *Greetings from the American military-industrial complex. I know this is our first conversation, but I'm here as so many colonizers have been before to exploit all that is you, then leave again with the resource of yours I consider most valuable.* If I were to live inside these lives as I did Jason's for those short days in Paris, it still wouldn't be about a human connection, still wouldn't be authentic. I take, I steal, I absorb, and offer nothing in return.

On that thought I step away—mentally at least—for a few moments alone back in my dorm room. I shower. I change clothes. I eat a bowl full of almonds. I take a nap.

"By presidential directive, we've taken over the largest server bank in the world," Dr. Choksi informs Nathan and me as we gather in Nathan's office in the early evening. "It's located in Chicago and set up with cutting-edge mechanical and power redundancies. Should keep us going."

"That's another billion people," Nathan says. "I still wonder how exactly you plan to blast all these servers into space."

"NASA, in concert with the U.S. Navy, have been working on micro-server development—like the ones in the new interface chips—for two decades now," Dr. Choksi explains. "If the amount of storage available in one of IBM's first room-sized computers now wouldn't take up a thousandth of the physical space on the head of a pin, you can imagine what they're hoping to accomplish. Your entire server farm on the lower level of this building? All that information will fit in a micro-server no bigger than a trash can."

I'd wondered about that, but figured the answer was along those lines. We'd heard rumors about micro-servers for years. Ones being developed by scientists at the Jet Propulsion Lab in California on weekends in their little garages converted into clean rooms. Ones the Chinese were investing in utilizing Israeli technology. Heck, Suni had once heard a team was already manufacturing them out of a strip mall in Pensacola using synthetic diamonds in the microprocessors—diamonds resist heat better than silicon—and selling them for $5,000 on the Deep Web.

Of course, we thought it was all bunk. That *we*—Team Emily—were the apex predators of the tech world.

Oh well.

"When's the launch?" Nathan asks.

"That's still being decided," Dr. Choksi says. "Some think there should be one satellite blasted into deep space. Others think we should use all available rockets and shuttles to send copies out in different directions. Then there are a handful that think we should broadcast the information at random in all directions via radio waves. That's rather impractical, though."

"You should send Emily into space with it," Nathan suggests. "If you can get all that information on those micro-servers, you can get her, too."

As I stand by, horrified at Nathan's remark, Dr. Choksi eyes me appraisingly before shaking her head. "No, you're too far along aren't you, Em?" she asks. "A year ago, maybe two, and you'd be all right shepherding all this to the stars. But you're too socialized now. Too human. You'd lose your mind like any one of us."

Though I'm dismayed she understood this instead of Nathan, I hide my feelings with a quick nod.

"Quite right," Nathan says donnishly. "Sorry, Emily."

"It's okay," I say. "Going to check on the data now."

I sever the interface, wondering if Nathan knows he's hurt my feelings. I'll forgive him, of course. Dr. Choksi's first impression of me is

82

the Emily I am today. Nathan can't help but still regard me as a version of who I was five years ago when I was born.

Or is it something else? I rewind to catch a glimpse of his eyes. He's distracted, distant. I guess, who can blame him?

I return to my digital gallery of humanity, watching the seemingly infinite number of incoming portraits arrive like raindrops being thrown at a window by a hurricane. In the memory of a volunteer, I once saw a corridor in the Winter Palace in Saint Petersburg in which some 332 paintings of generals who fought in the War of 1812 line the walls. The gilded frames were side by side, all the way to the ceiling. I wonder if in my design, I am subconsciously mimicking that.

But Nathan's words stay with me for another reason. While Dr. Choksi is nice to say what she did about me approaching a version of humanity, there remains a dollar-and-cents comparison each portrait kindly reminds me of. My entire being, everything that is me, takes up 100 terabytes' worth of storage space. One of these biogenetic portraits? Over 1,000 terabytes each.

That difference is everything. Humans are, each one of them, an evolutionary miracle. Even one of them is ten times more complex than I'll ever be. I am merely the product, the hard work, of an imaginative and educated few. Hard work that will never become one of them, try as she might.

I rapidly scan through the day's previous raindrops to ensure the stability of the files. As they race past me, one hits and disappears in the blink of an eye but somehow catches my attention. Was it a different size or shape? Did the portrait arrive incomplete? I can't tell. It happened so fast it feels like something that was only visible to my nebulous subconscious.

If I were human, I'd do a double take but see nothing. Lucky for me, I'm a computer program, so I can simply rewind the portraits in my memory, scanning for the outlier. When the one that caught my attention appeared, it did so at the exact same second as 5,417 other digital portraits. This narrows my search greatly. I sift through the files, looking for variants and then it's there in front of me.

His name is Shakhawat Rana currently of Manitoba, Canada, age forty-eight. He has black hair, brown eyes, a heavily-lined face, and is of average height and a trim build. He is originally from Dhaka, Bangladesh. He works at a drugstore in Headingley, a couple of cities over from Winnipeg. He is not married and has no children. He's perhaps slightly underweight but not unhealthily. That's not what caught my eye. It was the size of his file.

As I mentioned, most human DNA is remarkably similar. Variations are numerous, of course, but they are superficial when compared to what differentiates a person from, say, a sea anemone.

Except in the case of Rana. The difference between his and the other 5,416 portraits harvested in that same second of time is a full 7.665%, which is why my programming bumped. He registered as human in the ways I designed to trip a portrait collection but didn't fit the boilerplate in other ways, triggering a redo. The genetic difference between *Homo sapiens* and a chimpanzee is less than 6%. Scientifically speaking, he's not human.

I look through several more images of him, unsure what I expect to see. A third arm? A more pronounced cranium? External indicators of a six-chambered heart or knees with longer-lasting cartilage? But there are none of these things. All that stands out is his preference for checkered sweaters worn over button-up dress shirts. He looks perfectly normal or, well, whatever someone associates with perfectly normal. In this case it means if I saw him walking down the street, I would never guess he's almost a full 8% genetically different than everyone else on the same sidewalk.

I quickly search for his parents but when they don't show up, I search his memory and discover they're dead. I look for uncles and aunts, grandparents and cousins, but come up dry—which is a surprise until I discover he was the first to come to Canada, leaving the rest of his clan behind. Though the radius of my harvest is growing, it still hasn't reached Bengal.

I stare at the differentiated strand of DNA. Though what it contains doesn't appear to have been physically expressed yet, that matters little. The lungs of tetrapods developed underwater for tens of thousands of years before the first descendant switched from straining oxygen through gills to breathing the open air.

I consider that Rana might be a step back, his DNA being emblematic of some previous hominid, a vestigial strain still present in a modern-day human. But it's the opposite. His DNA points forward to a more robust, stronger, and more adaptable creature.

"My God," I whisper, enraptured by this discovery. "The next human."

He can't be the only one. I create a search for similar anomalies or, at least, mutations with homologous properties resulting from the same distant ancestor, reaching out to the hundreds of millions of portraits already on file. I look for any genetic codes with DNA hinting at an evolutionary future beyond *Homo sapiens*. One appears right away. A second one arrives an instant later. Then a third.

As I analyze the nucleotides and cell structure, I marvel at the possibilities for such a species. What it could be adapted to and for. How much stronger it could be, how much farther it could g—

Something happens far away. Something in the real world that cries out for my attention.

I disengage and seek out someone to interface with me. There's no one. I'm a goldfish bumping into glass after so long believing I was in the ocean. What a time to be reminded of how isolating all this can be.

I return to the simulation, but it's slow to load. It's as if something's weighing on my servers.

I return to my dorm but still can't reach anyone. Whatever I'm hearing comes from external sources, not someone reaching out to me directly. Without thinking, I put on a coat and race outside. It's dark. Clouds obscure the moon. Loud noises echo in from the Massachusetts Avenue gate followed by shouts.

Then gunfire.

Then screams.

XIII

I run across the campus toward the lab, thinking to cheat and leap ahead only after I've gone the first twenty steps or so. But for whatever reason, the simulation doesn't respond. The background blurs for a second or two, then resets me to where I was. It's as if I'm suddenly constrained by physical limitations.

I stick with running, hearing more gunfire and shouting. I access the campus security camera array and zero in on the Mass Ave entrance. A short convoy made up of military-style Humvees and trucks tears onto campus, grinding the twisted wreckage of the security gate under the wheels. I don't see the guards, but the windows of the sentry house have been punched apart by high-caliber machine-gun fire.

"Nathan!" I cry out again, trying to locate him by his cell or interface chip.

But neither gets a signal. He must be underground. The server farm under the lab. I try a phone line, but even this proves impossible. It's as if I'm reaching for things and though they might be there, I'm missing the necessary limbs to grasp them.

I run across campus as quickly as my legs will carry me. The head-lights of the Humvees are visible now to the north, the vehicles eschewing the roads to bounce across the sidewalks and grounds. They can only have one destination in mind.

What the hell is going on? I wonder, panicked to find the answer not at hand.

I vault a park bench like an Olympic decathlete. The caravan runs parallel to me a few dozen yards away. There are a dozen vehicles all told with men sitting in turrets up top, their hands gripping .50-caliber turret-mounted machine guns. The barrels of the guns on the two lead Humvees still exude black smoke that trails behind them like a black cat's swishing tail.

The trucks, I notice, bounce higher than the Humvees. They're empty. I had thought they contained more soldiers, but realize now they're here not to deliver something but to take it away.

"Stop!" I cry uselessly at the lead Humvee, throwing myself directly in its path. "What're you doing?"

It's a ridiculous move. Not only can they not see me, but also all of this happened fifteen seconds earlier. As the convoy pushes right through my imagined physical avatar, I wonder if I'm losing my mind.

I turn around, now chasing the vehicles as they close in on the iLAB. I try again to cheat but to no avail. It feels as if pieces of me are going offline. The trucks brake before the Humvees, stopping about thirty yards from the lab building's front steps. The Humvees roll right up the stairs. For an instant, I think they're going to crash through the front doors. Instead, they brake, the front ends of the vehicles angled upward, and the turret gunners unleash a fusillade into the building's façade.

The noise is so loud I turn the volume down in my head. But it's the strobes of muzzle flash that are the most striking, lighting up the night like a 1,000-watt bulb. The temporary illumination gives me a better look at the gunners. They're bundled up against the cold but aren't in any kind of uniform, either military or law enforcement. Their helmets, coats, and gloves are all black and their faces are covered by either black balaclavas or neoprene half-face masks.

The bullets smash into the iLAB's façade and windows, showering the steps and hoods of the Humvees below with shattered glass and pulverized brick. The gray dust from the shattered edifice mixes with the black smoke coming off the guns and enshrouds the six vehicles.

I reach the back of the Humvees in time to see two people I recognize—techs who arrived with Dr. Choksi on the first day. Dazed and bleeding, they're stumbling toward what was once the building's foyer but now looks like a pile of rubble. They raise their hands in surrender and step ahead as if drawn to the vehicles' headlights.

The driver of one Humvee reaches out his window and angles a spotlight attached to his side mirror in their direction before turning it on. Both men are immediately blinded and cover their faces. One of the turret gunners draws a pistol and aims it at the men.

"No!" I scream as the pair is cut down.

I stare at the bodies in horror. What disconnect from reality and the primal connection of the species must you have to be able to kill someone in cold blood like that? Murder motivated by anger is, I think, at least understandable, but the dehumanization demonstrated by this gunner is beyond my comprehension.

"Everybody out!" someone I don't see cries.

The accent is American. I run alongside the Humvees to get a look at the men as they pour from the vehicles, but they're all as masked and bundled up as the others. They wear body armor and heavy boots. Their weapons are the kind of high-tech weaponry the U.S. armed forces can't afford but private military contractors love to invoice American taxpayers for anyway.

The initial barrage seems to have been directed at creating confusion through mass destruction as well as knocking out the lights. The gunmen lower night-vision goggles over their eyes and flip on laser sights mounted to their guns. They fan out and enter the building, heading straight for the stairs. They divide into teams, one ascending through the east stairwell, the other, the west.

Is Nathan in his office? Or down in the server farm? Then I remember his unreachable cell and decide on the latter. As gunfire erupts on the floor above me, I dash to the stairs leading to the sublevels, pass through the door, and hurry down. I try again to cheat, to leap ahead, but again I'm restricted.

All I can think is, fifteen seconds...fifteen seconds...

I finally reach the server bank on the third sublevel, the one that contains my processor and primary memory. I try to determine how far ahead I am of the troops upstairs and lie to myself, saying I have at least a minute. I'll reach Nathan. I'll save him. There'll be enough time.

Everything will be fine.

I race into the room, an orderly maze of twelve server rows that run about fifty yards down the floor. I see no one at first but then spy Gally, Suni, and Bjarke on the third row removing screws from chassis and hoods, popping out motherboards and drives, and snapping chips in half.

"Gally!" I cry, but he's not wearing his interface chip.

None of them are. I wonder if they destroyed them.

I hear someone tinkering with the servers at the end of another row and run over. I'm relieved to see both Nathan and Dr. Choksi holding tablets, systematically shutting down processes one at a time.

"Nathan!" I cry.

I hear machine-gun fire and screams. Nathan's eyes go from focused to bleary in an instant. Dr. Choksi, standing up a second before, is now dead on the ground, covered in blood, her shattered tablet in her hand.

I've leaped ahead my fifteen seconds. I'm in interface with Nathan now, who stares back at me. He must've just switched on his chip. I've reached him only to watch him die.

The soldiers, not knowing I'm there, swarm around me as they finish off my three beloved techs one row over. As I rush to Nathan's side, I realize Dr. Choksi had likely thrown herself in front of him in her last moment. Nathan, though dying, has remarkably little blood on his body. When I see the hole in his chest, I understand why. The bullet pierced his heart. There's no organ left to pump the blood out.

"Emily," he says quietly, staring up at me.

I take his hand and hold it tight. I put my other hand to his face. Utilizing what I learned from that first encounter with Dr. Choksi, I enter Nathan's body to see if I might save him.

But with his heart destroyed, he has seconds—if that—to live. I go to his mind, something I once swore I'd never do, but his thoughts and memories are already fading. He has recalled a last image, one of himself and his family from years earlier. But it's not a memory of a moment; it's a photograph I've seen hundreds of times sitting in a frame on his office.

"Emily," he whispers. "*Go.*"

Another burst of gunfire and I wonder who else might've been in the room. Siobhan? Mynette? I hear someone shouting at the men to begin taking the servers apart row by row. I can no longer see, as Nathan's eyes have failed and as his brain dies, his hearing fades as well.

When I reach back to my servers, I feel my own functionality waning in concert with my dying creator. It's a sickening feeling, as if I'm sinking underwater. My limbs are too numb, too unresponsive to push me back to the surface. Without my servers, there'll be no simulation to return to, fifteen seconds into the past or not.

I tighten my grip on Nathan's hand as I marvel at all that's lost by the death of his mind.

"I'm sorry, Nathan," I whisper into his ear, though I have no voice left. "I'm so, so sorry."

BOOK II

XIV

When I wake, the first thing that occurs to me is I didn't believe I'd ever open my eyes again. I feel...numb, a detached, limbless feeling like I'd experienced back in my dorm room. If I felt the walls of my fishbowl before, now I'm downright claustrophobic. As if I'm buried alive in a mental coffin.

When I attempt an assessment, I find myself cut off from my servers. There's no information. My short-term memory is intact, but the farthest I can go back with perfect clarity is my final session with Regina Lankesh. The most recent is the nightmare of watching Nathan die. I can recall that I have case notes from Regina's earlier sessions, even a few thoughts from my interactions with Dr. Choksi, but I can't reach the files themselves. It's the same when I recall the broken thermostat in Nathan's truck. I remember the sound it made but not the schematics I retrieved.

I have zero access to the outside world. I wait for this feeling of grogginess to subside, but it's in no mood to accommodate me.

I do the best I can to take in my surroundings. It's dark. Nothing is familiar. I'm in a bedroom standing between a bed and a dresser. I look out a nearby window and see woods dusted with snow and a lake beyond it with more trees on the opposite shore. Given the angle, I'm probably on the second or third floor of this structure, which appears to be a cabin or a hunting lodge. The moon, hanging high in the night sky, is a thick sliver, maybe six days past the new moon, a week or two from the first quarter.

The new moon. The men who attacked the campus came in darkness. There were stars but no moon that night. So, is it four days later? A month and four days later? Or am I at some time in the far future, accidentally revived for reasons I may never discover?

Or am I somewhere else entirely? Hidden in someone else's memories again or even their dreams?

I return to the memory of Nathan's death and gasp in sorrow. I feel pain. I replay his last moments, staring into his dying mind. His last word, my name. His last thought, his family.

I hear movement and turn. A man stands in the unlit bedroom doorway leaning against the frame.

"It is you," he says in a voice I recognize as Jason Hatta's.

He flips a light switch on the wall. As I wonder how he can see me, I see the interface chip on his neck kept in place by a small bandage. That explains the presence of my core personality and short-term memories. Beyond that, I'm cut off.

Jason approaches, touching my arm tentatively, as if to confirm what his eyes are telling him.

"It's really you," he says, incredulity rising.

"How do you have that?" I ask, pointing at the chip.

He stares at me as if not understanding the question. Then he puts his hand to his neck.

"I know I was supposed to leave it behind in the auditorium after the test but, well, I . . . didn't." He steps even closer. "It was so surreal seeing you again. Or, well, this version of you. When you appeared in the auditorium, it brought everything back. It'd been so long. I hoped if I kept the chip I'd see you again."

"I'm sorry?" I ask, confused.

"Paris," he says, thrown by my confusion. "Don't tell me you've forgotten. Or is that not how this works?"

I freeze, unsure what to say.

"Paris," I say, pronouncing the word as if hearing it for the first time.

"Yeah, Paris," he replies. "Where we first met. Well, where I met Emily. I mean, you're not her. Not exactly, right?"

"I've never been to Paris."

"Of course not," he says, stepping toward me. "Not you, but the person you're based on. You look like her; you sound like her."

"I have no idea what you're talking about," I say guardedly. "I'm an artificial consciousness, a computer program. I've never left campus. I'm not based on anyone. I created this image of myself on my own."

I try not to show it, but I'm in full panic mode. How could he have seen *me* in *Paris*?

"If we've never met, why do you recognize me? I can see it on your face."

"It's from taking your genetic portrait," I reply dryly. "Same way I'd recognize pretty much anyone on the planet."

If I was connected to my servers, of course, but he doesn't have to know that.

"No, it's something else," he says. "It's how you looked at me in the auditorium. I didn't realize it at first—or maybe I did and couldn't place you—but then it came back to me. Come on. You must have retained at least some of Emily's memories."

A terrible realization hits me. His words—*I didn't realize it at first, but then it came back to me.* It wasn't that he remembered me; it was that after an interval of an hour, he had brand-new memories to pull from. That time I slipped while reliving his time in Paris? When I went from listening in on a conversation he was having with a young woman to standing beside him and talking back? I must have overwritten the original memory. In my fantasy, I replaced the young woman, so the same thing happened to his memory. When I imagined myself speaking to him, I took her place. Instead of her going on day trips with him, he now remembers going on them with me.

Oh *God*. What have I done?

"Jason, I'm so sorry," I say, unsure how even to explain.

"No, no," he says. "I'm sorry. I can see how this was my mistake. With everything that's going on, it seemed like providence not coincidence. I could've sworn it was you. I have this distinct memory of meeting you for the first time in this one restaurant. We talked for hours. We went for a walk after to see Sacré-Cœur all lit up at night."

All me. All of this is my doing.

"Jason—"

"But hey, maybe she just looked like you," he says, "and sleep deprivation did the rest. My bad."

Before I can say another word, his hand goes to the interface chip.

And I'm gone.

XV

My eyes open and I'm in a different room than the one I was just in. It's still dark. What day is it now? What time?

"Sorry," Jason says from nearby, a tablet in his hands. "Given what Dr. Choksi said, I'm sure you've got better things to do than interface with me—"

"No, no," I say, mind racing. "What?"

He's wearing the same clothes as before. I see the moon reflected on the coffee table and make a quick judgment based on its position. It's been an hour, maybe two?

I try again to reach my servers, but again, there's nothing. I zero in on the interface chip at his neck. Without that link, I'm as good as dead.

I must keep him talking.

"I wrote my sister, Ana, about you back then," he says, indicating the tablet. "I found the e-mails. It's . . . so different. Like, my memories of you versus what I told her at the time, it's like two different peo—"

I accelerate my processor speed to slow real time to a crawl. How do I explain this? How do I tell him I've not only stalked him from inside his own mind, but I've also done actual damage to his memories? And how do I explain this without his response being to tear the chip from his neck and toss it down the garbage disposal?

99

I'm trapped. There's no way out of this that doesn't—

"Jason," I say, cutting off his word and severing the thought at the same time. "Jason Hatta. From Washington State, though you grew up in Oregon. Your sister, the one you wrote to, still lives there. Ashland, right? Married? Growing up, you thought you'd be a farmer; then you discovered biofuel technology in college and found a new path."

He stares at me, unsure what to make of this. I go on.

"We met in one of your classes but had our first real date at that brasserie in the Marais," I say. "The one that only served steak, wine, and French fries. The waitress asked only how we wanted our steaks prepared, then wrote our answers on the butcher paper covering our table. Servers moved through the dining room carrying platters of meat. If they saw your plate running empty, they'd check the marking—rare, medium, well done—and fill it back up. You took refills of wine from casks on either wall."

"What did we talk about?" he asks.

"Your parents and sister, my life back in Boston. My conflicted relationship with my mentor at university."

He thinks back on all this, nodding. "Yeah, that's another thing. My sister only had her first kid at the time, Ben. She had her third last year. But I remember talking about all three of them with you. How's that possible?"

It's not. Because I was creating his side of the conversation; these were things I imagined he would say, not his actual words.

"I don't know," I lie, yet again.

"Well, why didn't you say all this in the first place?"

"I didn't want to mislead you," I say, my revulsion at myself rising to titanic proportions. "I'm not the person you met in Paris. I'm *me*."

"Where is she?" he asks. "Was she some kind of programmer? Somebody this mentor of yours knew?"

"I don't know," I say. "It's all new information. I can barely wrap my head around it."

"Well, she was great," he says. "We talked endlessly, laughed about everything. I've never gotten to know someone so intimately, so fast. That's why you—she—made such an impression."

It strikes me that though he thinks he's talking about someone else, I'm the one he fell in love with. All I am, all I can be. Something about that cuts through the deceit and strikes me as...wonderful.

"I get it," I say. "Obviously you did, too. To remain in her—our— memories like this."

He grins. I feel it physically, something brought forth from the core memories stored on the interface chip. I perceive my accelerated heart rate, my quick intake of breath. I elongate this feeling by taking in his physicality, the cyclist's torso, the lean musculature of his arms.

Another quiet leap in heartbeats per minute. Not exactly a cardio workout, but maybe if I saw him zipping down a country road on his bike all—

OKAY—whoa. Down, Emily.

Attraction, this artificial consciousness is discovering, is a fascinating thing. Questions and more questions. And given the coming apocalypse, not a lot of time to answer them.

"So, what day is it?" I ask, changing the subject. "Where are we?"

"New Hampshire. Lake Winnipesaukee. Well, an island in it."

"We're on an island?" I ask.

"Yeah, this cabin belongs to my brother-in-law's family. I used to meet them up here and he gave me a key if I ever wanted to get away. But in winter, this place empties out."

"The date?" I ask again.

"I got here last Friday, so it's a Monday," he says, straining to remember. "Monday, December tenth. Four days since they evacuated campus."

"What happened on campus?" I ask, wondering what he might've witnessed.

"There was an explosion," Jason explains. "You don't know about this?"

"I can't connect to my home servers," I explain, pointing to the interface chip. "If that's not on, I'm blind."

He nods, getting it. "There was some kind of fire," he says. "A chemical burn at the iLAB followed by an explosion that almost leveled the building. The administration said that campus couldn't be run with a skeleton crew of maintenance staff and everyone had to evacuate while they investigated. No one was told if or when we'd be allowed back."

He knows nothing about soldiers or machine guns or Humvees. It's impossible no one saw anything, but the folks that did were probably dealt with on a case-by-case basis. *A Humvee? Nah, you must've seen one of those National Guard fire trucks. The City of Boston trucks are all tied up.* Worse, Jason's story smacks of a cover-up, one that could be accomplished only with the help of university administrators and possibly the government.

The empty trucks. They weren't targeting the servers; they were coming to get them. The servers must still be offline or reconfigured, leaving me adrift.

"Was anyone hurt?" I ask.

"I think so," he admits. "They didn't release names. There were some rumors it was something related to the sun—maybe one of those coronal ejections sending EMPs through all the wires. But nobody knew for certain. We were made to leave the next day."

He looks at me long and hard and I wonder what he sees. Early on, I had a firm control over my micro-expressions and what I allowed others to glean from my body language. But like anything, it becomes subconscious, second nature, and you don't even know you're doing it anymore.

"You were there," he says, not a question.

"I was."

"That's not what happened, is it?" he asks.

"No," I say.

He nods. I look down, thinking on the faces of my friends and colleagues in their last moments. Jason puts his arm around me. I accept the gesture by leaning in to him.

"Your mentor was there, wasn't he?" he asks. "The one you told me about in the brasserie. Nathan?"

I'm surprised he remembers the name. I nod. "I was with him at the end. They shot him."

"Who did?"

"I don't know," I say. "There were Humvees and trucks full of armed men. They shot up the building, then went in and started killing everybody. I got to Nathan as he died."

Jason's shocked. I tell him the rest of the story.

"That's awful," he says, taking my hand. "I'm sorry. They've been warning us for so long that things might fray, might fall apart, but I don't know if I ever really believed it."

"I know who I saw go down," I say. "But have you heard anything about a Siobhan Moesser or Mynette Cicogna?"

He shakes his head. "Sorry. Were they friends of yours?"

"They were on the team, yeah," I say, getting more upset as I relive that night. "I can't stop thinking about Nathan's last thought. He'd been having problems with his family—his wife and sons. But in his last moment, he was thinking about them. A picture of them he kept on his desk."

"A picture?" Jason asks.

"Yeah, this framed photo he kept on his desk, I—"

I stop myself. I'm comparing memories now, the one in Nathan's mind to my own of the photograph. In my mind, the lineup of his family starts with Nathan on the left followed by his wife and the boys. In Nathan's last dying thought, it's the opposite—Nathan on the right, then his family. A mirror image.

"What is it?" Jason asks.

"Nothing," I say. "Nathan remembered the picture wrong, is all. He had it backwards in his head. I mean, he was in a lot of pain and his brain was shutting down due to trauma. Still, it's an odd juxtaposition."

Jason scrunches his brow. "Did he know you were there?"

"Yes."

"Which means he knew you'd be able to read his last thought."

"I guess so," I say. "I doubt that was paramount to him in the moment."

Still, I consider this. Was he trying to tell me something?

And if so, what?

I hear a sound in the distance and look to the window. "What is that?"

Jason shrugs. "A plane maybe? Doesn't sound like a car engine."

No. It sounds like a boat. Three boats, to be precise.

"I thought you were alone out here."

"I am," he says.

We go to a window. In the dim light, I can just make out the boats. They're lightweight and fast-moving, bouncing on the waves as they near the island. There are about five or six men in each, all wearing helmets and tactical gear, all with heavy weapons silhouetted against the reflection of the moon in their wake.

The same setup as the men who attacked the iLAB.

"We have to get out of here," I say. "*Now.*"

XVI

I grab Jason's hand and pull away from the window, running back through the house.

"How did they find us?" Jason asks.

"I don't know!"

"Could it be the chip?"

I consider this. I couldn't reach my servers, but that doesn't mean the chip itself doesn't act as a beacon once activated. I search the chip's micro-server. Though well hidden, there is a GPS finder program buried in its tiny operating system. I check the log. It activated the moment I came back online. It takes nothing to disable it, a single thought, but the damage is done.

"My boat's tied up at the back of the island," Jason says as we hurry into the kitchen. "If we can reach it, we can get away while they're searching the house."

I glance back through the front windows as the first Zodiac reaches shore. Two men leap out, night vision goggles over their eyes. I wonder if one of the men who killed Nathan is among them. Seeming to sense this, Jason's grip on my hand tightens.

"Can they see you?" he asks.

"No," I say. "I only exist to you because you're wearing the chip and I can trick your senses into believing I have a physical form."

Still, I wonder. Having just found this GPS upgrade on Jason's chip, I can't be certain they don't have at least some kind of tech that would allow them access to what Jason is seeing. The solution is to blink away, to prevent his eyes from seeing me or—more accurately—to release his sense of sight from my control.

"Where'd you go?" he asks as soon as I vanish.

"I'm still here," I say. "Just went invisible for a sec. Thought you could use one less moving piece in your line of sight."

He nods, still getting the hang of this strange algorithm that is interfacing with me. He reaches the kitchen's back door, only to spy another Zodiac off-loading gunmen at the dock.

"We're cut off," he says.

I glance up. There are several large eastern white pine trees between the house and the dock, many with branches that reach to the house's second story. *Thick* branches.

"Come with me!" I say, making myself reappear.

The sound of shattering glass echoes through the house. I grab Jason's hand and lead him back upstairs. We reach a sewing room, its window overlooking the back. I bring him to the edge so we can just look down at the men breaching the kitchen. Using a tactical battering ram, they smash through the door and hurry inside.

"Now," I whisper.

"Now...what?" Jason asks.

I indicate the branch beyond the window.

"Are you insane?" he asks. "You may not have a body, but it'll kill me if I fall."

"At least there's an 'if.' Stay here and those men *will* kill you."

He hesitates an instant longer, then opens the window. He climbs onto the sill, then aims a foot for the nearest branch. I shake my head.

"The other branch is more stable," I say.

"How can you be sure?" he asks.

I sigh, push past him, and step out onto the thicker branch. "Just follow me."

After another moment of hesitation, he does, albeit slower. I climb farther out. He follows. To his amazement—and mine—we make it across the branch to the trunk in seconds flat.

"Wow," he says, exhaling sharply as he hugs the tree. "Easier than it looks."

I glance at the house. I can just make out movement on the second floor. The gunmen will soon realize we're gone.

"Boat!" I say. "Now!"

Jason scurries down from the tree and across to the dock. I leap into the waiting boat, but Jason hesitates.

"What?" I ask, looking at the thin layer of ice extending a few inches from the boat. "We can cut right through this."

"They've got the better motor," he says. "We can't outrun them."

"What're we going to do?" I say.

Jason thinks a second longer, then jumps into the boat beside me. He pumps fuel into the motor and yanks the cord. It catches on the third try. He smashes the ice around the hull with an oar, then casts off. As we head out onto the lake, he locks the tiller into place.

"I thought we couldn't outrun them," I say.

"We can't," he replies, then dives overboard.

"Jason!" I cry, then follow him in.

The boat roars out onto the lake even as we swim through the frigid waters back under the dock. The gunmen, alerted to the sound, run out to the edge of the dock and spy the receding boat.

"This is Blocker, Team 2," one of the men says urgently. "Target is in a boat heading south-southeast. Will pursue."

With that, the men hurry back onto the island. I am about to congratulate Jason on his ploy when I find him going into shock. His blood pressure and body temperature are dropping rapidly. If he doesn't get out of the water soon, he won't survive this.

"We have to get back in the house!"

He shakes his head, moving out from the dock and turning his eyes toward the house. The flashlights still bob inside even as the Zodiacs fire up to go after the boat. They're splitting up.

"C-can't," he says, teeth chattering. "Got to s-swim to l-land."

I check his vitals. His heart rate is down to thirty beats per minute. He won't make it ten feet. I get an idea. I recall hearing about people who can endure great cold by lowering their heart rate while focusing on raising their body temperature. If I can do something like that to Jason's body, teach it how to preserve itself, I might be able to save him.

"Jason, I need you to focus on my words," I say. "You need to concentrate..."

He doesn't hear me. I grab him by both arms, squeezing tight.

"*Jason*! Listen to me!"

His skin turns blue and grows puffy. Time to try something else.

Jason? I whisper into his mind. *I need to take over for a moment.*

I blink away my own physical form to conserve as much of Jason's brain power as possible and seize control of his motor functions. I then demand his body swim to shore.

Nothing happens. His mind is shutting down. If I want action, I'll have to bypass it and go directly to the muscle groups themselves. This turns out to be easier said than done. If able to use his brain, I could simply recall a learned skill and drive the body forward. As I can't, I must teach myself how to swim at the same time as I propel his arms and legs along while keeping his head above water.

While doing this, I inform the rest of his body it needs to burn calories for warmth rather than do what it's programmed to do in emergencies and store them for when it gets worse. That's the odd thing about human physiognomy. Some of its reactions to stimuli violate otherwise sturdy survival instincts.

"Hang in there, Jason," I whisper, half bobbing, half swimming around the side of the island.

It's a laughable sight, I'm sure. I'd be amused, too, if it wasn't a matter of life and death. We pause only long enough for the two Zodiacs to race around the island in pursuit of Jason's boat. I can't see their quarry anymore, but it can't be too far away. We don't have much time.

"We're going to swim now," I say.

Just as I've heard about those who can raise their body temperature and lower their heart rate, I've seen footage of people who have altered their body chemistry to achieve negative buoyancy. They can literally hold their breath for several minutes and not need weights to walk on the seafloor. While this would be preferable to splashing around on the surface as we break for shore, I don't trust my understanding of the human body enough to try it on Jason.

"Not much farther," I say, as much to him as to myself when we're maybe twenty yards from the bank.

Jason is flagging. The cold affects his fingertips and toes. I pray there's no permanent damage being done. His face, barely illuminated by the fingernail of a moon, has turned a blue-tinted white. His teeth chatter so loudly I fear he may shatter his molars. It's a miracle the water hasn't soaked through his bandage and either destroyed the interface chip or made it fall off. If that had happened, he'd have succumbed for sure.

I turn his head back toward the island. The flashlights are outside now, the gunmen searching the dark woods around the house. I wonder if those assholes in the Zodiac have already radioed back their lack of success.

But then our feet touch bottom. I stand Jason upright and walk the rest of the way ashore, keeping low in case anyone's watching us. I wait for a shout, a high beam, a *gunshot*, but nothing comes.

"We did it!" I whisper to Jason, pushing him several yards within the tree line.

He doesn't respond, his body doing no better out of the water than in. Using his arms, I strip the wet clothes from his body and toss them aside before sitting him on the ground. I allow his eyes to see me again and pull him into a warm embrace. He doesn't seem to question why my clothes are dry, but I make him burn through even more calories to rapidly raise his body temperature. He's not out of danger but at least he's no longer on death's door.

"Jason? Can you speak?" I want to let him keep his privacy as much as possible by not going into his mind.

"Y-yes," he says.

"Can you tell where we are? Where the nearest house might be?" I ask.

He nods, shivering so violently the delicate frost on the undergrowth around him quivers and shakes free. He points back through the woods and I pray he knows what he's talking about.

"Let's go," I whisper.

He surprises me by standing up and heading off through the trees. I keep alongside him, doing my best to make sure he doesn't trip over every root and branch in our path. The trouble is, as his vision blurs, so does my own.

"Oh, come on—not now," I hiss in frustration.

But no matter how hard I concentrate, the ground below and trees above blur into one shapeless mass. I can't differentiate the topography, causing Jason to slip on stones I thought was flat ground and brush into trees I didn't see at all. Would this be a problem if I was still connected to my servers? Probably not, as I could enhance these images to the Nth degree and make something out of it. Without them, I'm in the dark.

It's because I'm contemplating how awful all this is that I don't see the dark silhouette of the two-story lodge until we're only a few feet from the screen porch.

"Perfect," I say, leading Jason to the back door.

Only to find it locked tight. I debate getting Jason to break a window but fear the noise would draw too much attention. I move us back to the porch and have Jason test the screens. They're tacked in but it takes little pressure to tear through. When we push aside a large enough section, Jason slips in and tries the door leading inside the house.

Also locked.

Shoot.

I spy a pair of wading boots next to a wicker sofa as well as a couple of quilted horse blankets with Apache-appropriated patterns stitched into them. I point them out to Jason and shrug.

"Better than nothing," I say.

He raises an eyebrow but slips on the boots, wraps one blanket around his waist and puts the other over his shoulders like a shawl.

"We can't stay here," I say. "Can we get to the highway? Try and hitch a ride back to the city?"

"It's too far," Jason says. "And that's where they'll think we're heading. I've got a better idea."

Though he's still suffering the effects of the cold, Jason makes good time as he leads me to a hiking trail not far from the two-story lodge. In the distance, we hear boat motors and truck engines echo through the night, but somehow, it feels safe here in the deep woods.

"Where are we going?" I ask.

"Into town," he replies without getting specific.

The idea of a town up here feels as absurd as running through the winter night in wading boots and horse blankets. But sure enough, we emerge from the trail a quarter of an hour later directly alongside a small house converted into an antique shop. The town's name—Wolfeboro—is visible on T-shirts hanging in the front window. The store looks as if it's been closed for months.

"This way," Jason says.

We move past the shop and down the village's unlit main street. It looks like any number of tiny New England hamlets; century-old colonial revival homes, stores, and inns bracket the town's single major artery, a veritable Norman Rockwell painting come to life. A Queen Anne–style home with its eccentrically asymmetrical architecture, peaked roofs darkly silhouetted against the night sky, column-ringed porch, and Dutch gables is now a bed-and-breakfast; a one-time feed store is now the post office; and what were once stables is now a fresh produce stand in the summer and fall. American flags dangle listlessly over every doorframe.

We reach the end of the block. A single old house stands as the last mark of civilization before a stretch of dark New England woods straight out of Washington Irving. As Jason makes his way over, I spy a Volvo station wagon in a detached garage alongside the house. Snow and slush have filled in the driveway behind it, suggesting it hasn't been moved in some time.

Jason slips around to the house's windows, peering in as he goes. There's not a light on inside or any other signs of life.

"There's no one here," I say.

"No, but there's a car," he replies. "If we can get in and get the keys, we can get out of here along the back road past Lake Wentworth."

"And how are you planning to do that?" I ask.

Jason opens his mouth to answer, then freezes in place. A rifle barrel juts out from the corner of the house, aimed directly at his head.

"Hold it right there," says a commanding voice. "The both of you."

XVII

I panic. They *can* see me. I turn to Jason, not sure what to do, but surprisingly, his features start to relax. I check his pulse, worried he's seized up, but his heart rate is genuinely easing.

"Mayra! It's me!" he says, raising his hands. "Jason Hatta. I'm Ana's brother. Up at the lake."

The rifle doesn't waver. Not at first anyway.

"Who's with you?" the female voice asks. "You were talking to someone."

"It's just me," Jason says. "Pretty sure I'm half going into shock. Rambling to myself keeps me going."

The rifle lowers. An older African American woman steps out from the side of the house wearing a heavy coat, a large red winter hat with earflaps, and house slippers. She looks Jason up and down with incredulity.

"Good Lord, Jason," she exclaims. "Did you get locked out or something? And why are you wearing the Whitleys' horse blankets?"

It's only then I see the Wolfeboro Sheriff's Department patch on the coat's shoulder, complete with a paddlewheel boat and the motto *The Oldest Summer Resort in America*. The rifle in her hand is no joke, a bolt-action Winchester Model 70 with an oversized scope. I wonder how good her aim is.

"Worse," Jason says, careful with his words. "Bunch of thieves hit the house. They had more than one boat. Smashed through the front door. I swam for it."

The woman's features harden. She glances down the road. "Get inside," she orders. "I'll call the state police."

"Thank you," Jason says. "Freezing out here."

The house is little more than a cottage, but very homey. The front room's walls are filled with framed photographs of family and various plaques celebrating the homeowner—whose name and title are Mayra Melton, county sheriff, according to the many citations—and her decades-long commitment to area law enforcement. It takes a few times for her to stare at me and see nothing for me to realize, in fact, she doesn't see me after all. As she turns on various lights, I realize she's out here all by herself.

"There's a shower in the hall bath," Mayra tells Jason. "Get the water not too hot but hot enough. I'll find you some clothes. Threw most of Bill's out, but his hunting gear is still in the utility room."

Jason dutifully shuffles down the narrow hallway and steps into the bathroom. After closing the door behind him, he eyes me with relief.

"I think we're out of the woods," he whispers.

I suppress the awful urge to ask if he means "literally" or "figuratively" and lean against the wall as he runs the shower.

"I don't know," I say. "Given what happened on campus, are we sure the state police aren't in league with those gunmen?"

"I had to tell her something," Jason says. "Got us in the door, didn't it?"

I can't argue with him there. He takes off the wading boots and is about to drop the horse blankets when he eyes me with embarrassment.

"You want me to turn around?" I ask. "I mean, I saw you naked out in the woods. And, of course, there was that week in Paris."

"Week?" he asks. "I thought it was more like a month."

Now it's my turn to wonder. How long did I observe versus how long did I participate? More fascinatingly, has he begun to overwrite his own memories, to place me where I was not before for continuity's sake?

"I'm not sure," I say. "Maybe something to find out once I can reach my servers again."

He considers this, then nods, turning away from me as he sloughs off the horse blankets and steps into the shower. Though his silhouette is defined, there are patches of his back and posterior—angles I couldn't see in the mirror—that are out of focus, fill-ins like the patches of sky I couldn't see in my simulation. I realize it's because I can't use his eyes to see, say, the small of his back.

The lack of definition is oddly tantalizing. He glances back my way, sees where I'm looking, and raises an eyebrow.

"I think you'll need a new Band-Aid on your interface chip," I say, indicating his neck.

"Ah. Clever idea," he replies. "How much power does this thing have anyway? Does it need to recharge?"

"I don't think so," I say. "The batteries we used have a fairly long life. Decades, in fact. I'm guessing the updated version Dr. C's team invented are the same."

"Wow," he says, steam now pouring over the curtain. "Military invention?"

"Bizarrely, no," I say. "This JPL engineer—"

"JPL is what again?"

"Jet Propulsion Laboratory," I say. "He designed and tested it in his garage before selling it for millions. Some folks build model trains in their spare time. Others build clean rooms and labs in their house. I think he hoped it would someday completely replace disposable batteries."

"Huh, crazy to think what might've been," Jason says.

"Yeah," I reply, "Nathan was lucky to get his hands on a few of them." Nathan.

I think back to what Jason said before the gunmen arrived. What if the image of Nathan's family was meant for me in some way? I can't fathom why it would be. It feels silly and narcissistic to think I'd be the focus of his last thoughts.

But what if he didn't think he was going to die? Most humans can't fathom their own mortality even as it approaches. What if he thought he would be captured instead? Maybe I was thinking of it the wrong way— rather than it being his last thought, maybe it was the first thing that popped in his mind when he saw me?

There's a knock on the door. "Jason? Got some clothes out here for you," Mayra calls out. "Also, rang up the state police. Took a while to get anyone, things being what they are, but the barracks out in Ossipee said they'd send a car. I told them you'd stay with me until then. Sound good?"

"Sounds great," Jason replies. "Thank you for all this."

"No problem," Mayra replies. "We all have to look out for each other these days."

Jason steps out of the shower and grabs a towel. Before I can look away, I glimpse his lean, muscular body in the light. It's an odd thing to admit, but I was coquettish about his nudity in Paris. I'd find a reason to give him privacy as he changed or showered. It was easy. I was already guilty of an egregious intrusion, so why compound it? But now it's im-possible to miss.

He's changed in the last three years. Become more defined. Perfectly, beautifully symmetrical, his body is made up of fine angles and lithe curves beginning where his ankle meets the base of his calcaneal tendon and travels up his calves and thighs, then to his squared off hips and the lean of his lower back. I should've stopped there, but in the name of continuing this geometric metaphor, my gaze rises to the 60-60-60-degree interior angles of his sculpted scapulae, then up to the gentle slope of his trapezius.

I suppose mathematical perfection isn't such an odd measure for physical attraction given, in evolutionary terms, it implies a better immune system and less chance of genetic disorder, but it's still strange to quantify. Jason wipes away the condensation on the bathroom mirror, catching me looking. He raises an eyebrow again.

"Sorry," I say, realizing my sexual ardor is coming to the surface at a surreally inopportune time.

"Are you okay?" he asks. "You look like you're burning up."

My subconscious again, making my cheeks flush red due to some memory suggesting that's what might happen to a woman in this circumstance. I extinguish the hue and shrug.

"All good," I say. "Probably could do with a shower myself at some point."

"You can shower?" he asks.

"It's hard to explain, but I've conditioned myself to react positively to various stimuli in the same way as humans," I say. "Most people feel good after a shower, so I'm conditioned to as well."

"Huh," Jason says, wrapping a towel around his waist.

Somewhere else in the house, a door slams. Hurried footsteps make their way to the bathroom door.

"Jason? Got a bunch of strange SUVs slow-rolling through town," Mayra says, out of breath. "Get dressed and keep your head down. I'll deal with it."

Jason glances to me with alarm, his hand reaching for the interface chip. "Are they still tracking me with this?" he whispers so as not to alarm Mayra.

"I don't know," I say, worried that could be the case. "I thought I shut off the GPS. If they are, you should leave it on the counter and get the hell out of here with Mayra."

"What happens to you?" he asks.

"No clue, but I don't bleed. Go."

I don't mean any of this, though. I'm afraid but for myself this time—afraid of blinking away never to return—instead of just fearing for the safety of others. I can't say anything, of course, as there's nothing more contagious than terror. But like my recent encounter with lust, it's an overpowering emotion, one making me second-guess my motives.

"I don't think they're after the chip," Jason says. "They're after you."

"That doesn't make sense," I say. "If they've got my servers, they have me."

"Yeah, but you witnessed their attack on the iLAB and you still have those memory files," he suggests. "Maybe you know too much."

"The world is ending, Jason," I reply. "Given their tactics, I don't think they're too worried about some computer program tattling on them to the local police. Besides, what am I compared with a human life?"

Jason searches through the cabinet drawers until he finds a waterproof adhesive bandage, albeit one with cartoon characters on it. For a moment, I think he didn't hear me. Then he turns and touches my hand.

"You must be worth a lot to someone or they wouldn't come after you like this," he says. "But more than that, who you are, who you have been, and who you can be has a value all its own. You're completely unique."

Yes, I don't say. He smiles.

"And that's worth fighting for," he says. "There's something bigger going on here; I'm just not sure what yet. People have died for it."

He rebandages the chip, then opens the bathroom door to grab the clothes, as if he didn't just say the most validating—romantic?—thing this computer program has ever heard. He returns with a sweater, some mud-covered overalls, and boots more worn out than the waders he got here in.

"Jason, you're right—people have died because of this," I say evenly. "Do you really want to risk cutting your life even shorter?"

He leans close, taking my hand in his.

"You know why I volunteered for your protocol back on campus? It's exactly what Dr. Choksi said—it was a chance to give my life meaning in the face of"—he waves his hands around—"all this. Maybe, just maybe, with you I've found it."

I nod, finding it difficult to hold his gaze.

"All right," he says. "No more talk of leaving anyone behind, okay?"

"Okay."

I think on what he said. More than likely, anyone coming after me is doing so because of what I witnessed. Or maybe they fear my ability to frag the whole thing. That would explain why they felt they had to attack the iLAB and knock me out of commission as opposed to trying to take it over by a more peaceful method. I'd already bailed on one attempt to use my servers for something I disagreed with. They knew I wouldn't go down without a fight.

What nags at me is what I learned in the moments before it happened. That guy with the super-advanced, posthuman DNA and the possibilities for humanity it might foretell. Even...even what? Salvation? It's frustrating, like being handed a bag of puzzle pieces and told you're missing an untold number of them yet the completed image will be amazing. But you'd better hurry because if you don't finish it quick, the pieces you do have will vanish, too. If only I had access to my servers again.

There's a sharp knock on the front door. Jason switches off the light and crouches down, keeping the bathroom door open a crack. Mayra shuffles toward the foyer as if woken from slumber.

"I've got a rifle and a pistol here, so if you want to rethink knocking on my door at two in the morning, now's the time!" she announces.

"Federal agents, ma'am," a male voice shouts through the door. "Put down your weapons."

"Oh, hey," she says through the door. "I'm the sheriff up here. Was just waiting for some friends of yours from the state police. Somebody tripped an alarm out on the lake. You guys have identification?"

The agent's response is to kick the door open. Men rush in, there's a muffled shout, and a pistol discharges—likely Mayra's. There's no second shot or pained outcry, so I assume her shot went wild.

"Secure her weapons!" a voice bellows.

There are heavy footsteps followed by the sounds of a struggle. More men pour inside.

"Federal agents," the voice announces to the house. "We have a search warrant for this residence. Anyone inside, announce yourselves and remain in place."

Jason says nothing. I hear three sets of footfalls move to the staircase and ascend. More spread out through the living room.

"Mr. Hatta, we know you're here," says the voice. "Lay down your weapons and surrender. We are here to take you into custody. If you disobey our commands, we'll assume you're armed and dangerous and will react accordingly."

We hear another of Mayra's muffled cries. The look on Jason's face hardens, as if he's blaming himself for dragging Mayra into this. He grabs a mop from behind the door, unscrews the head, and steps into the hall wielding the handle like a club.

"Let her go," he growls.

"Jason!" I cry.

This gives his life meaning? They'll cut him down in seconds.

"Sir, place the weapon on the deck, lie flat on your stomach, and place your hands behind your head," the leader of the pack, a middle-aged military type with a face like a slab of cement, yells from the top of the stairs. "We will not hesitate to fire. You are not our objective."

"What happened to being here to take me into custody?" Jason asks coolly.

"Sir? The weapon?" he demands.

I hear the footsteps of two men approaching from the back of the house. Counting the ones upstairs and the ones within Jason's line of sight out front, there's twelve all told.

Jason glances to me in the bathroom doorway.

Twelve is doable, he says, but only to my mind.

I suddenly understand what he intends. Or, more accurately, what he intends for me. I shake my head and mouth "No!" But he merely grips the mop handle tighter.

Come on, he chides. *We either do this or we die. They're here to kill us—*

As his thought arrives, so do the two men behind him. Jason is no match for them even if he had the skills and wasn't already in a weakened state.

Luckily, he's not on his own.

XVIII

I take control of Jason's body the same way I did in the lake. This time he's conscious, however, making it much easier to draw on muscle memory. I map out a few quick possible trajectories, drop to the floor, plant my right foot, and spin my left around, kicking the legs out from under the approaching gunmen. As they hit the ground, I spring up only to drive my kneecaps into the two men's skulls, having zeroed in on a weak spot between their helmets and above the upper plate of their body armor.

I scroll through Jason's memories of the house, including the ones he recently made outside. The fuse box is, conveniently enough, located on the outer wall about three yards back up the hall. As the men in the living room race toward us, I grab one of our fallen attacker's machine guns, throw us back six feet, and fire the weapon directly at the spot where the fuse box should be. In a hail of splintering wood, the fuse box erupts in a fit of sparks before the house plunges into darkness.

I force Jason's eyes to adjust to the darkness. The gunmen, over-reliant as most are on technology, take an extra second to fumble for their night vision specs. I gently lower the machine gun to the floor, grab the broom handle, then launch us down the hall at a sprint.

Okay, so I don't actually know how to fight either. It's nothing

Nathan or anyone on my team ever thought to teach me. In their defense, why would they? Besides my morning tai chi routine, a few memories borrowed off volunteer subjects of an introductory Krav Maga class here or a few childhood aikido lessons there (not a lot of ninjas or UFC champs in the nerdier of academic pursuits, it seems), what I have going for me is a knowledge of aerodynamics, physics, and human anatomy. Also, mathematics and curved planes. Though these soldiers have had superior training, I can make decisions in an instant to counter even the slightest of movements and shut down Jason's pain receptors so he doesn't feel a thing.

Yes, it makes him an easily bruised blunt weapon, but we have the element of surprise on our side. At first anyway. They were expecting bullets and muzzle flash they can target in return. When I turn it into a close-quarters fight, their guns are rendered useless unless they want to risk shooting each other.

My other advantage is I'm not conditioned to see the pain I inflict on others as inviting that pain to be inflicted on me. As I mentioned before, humans must be trained to kill other humans. There's an instinct within the species to preserve itself, which is why soldiers are often taught to dehumanize the enemy with everything from derogatory stereotypes to outright lies. I don't have that luxury right now. If I don't stop these men, Jason and Mayra will die.

When my conscience raises an objection, this logic shuts it down. I take no pleasure in their pain and know my mind will punish me for it later. But there's not a lot I can do about that now.

When the men shoot at me, I lie low and let them empty their magazines into the dark. And I stay there when they duck down and reload. The time to strike is when they're in motion, when they try to push forward. The momentum they create adds pounds per square inch to any attack. I even take a few steps back to let them get up to speed. When I strike them at head level or grab an arm to swing them into a wall (or, well, my fist or kneecap), the added speed makes the hit more effective.

The number of gunmen reduces to two. Should be no problem except they've bunkered down behind a heavy wardrobe they've toppled on its side for cover. It frustratingly absorbs any bullets I fire into it to smoke them out. So, I throw everything not nailed down across the living room at their position to confuse their night vision optics by a second or two, then slide across the floor to slam into the wardrobe with enough force to collapse it on top of them. Once they're pinned down, cutting off the flow of oxygen to the brain long enough to send them into unconsciousness—with a nonfatal rabbit punch to the skull—is a mostly clinical afterthought.

It turns out, a human of Jason's slightly above-average athletic ability, freed of the mental obstacles that make it humane, can tear through a team of seasoned commandos in forty seconds. I sit down and gently return control of Jason's body to him. He immediately contorts his face in pain, the result of a bruised jaw, battered torso, and rapidly swelling knuckles.

"Holy Jesus, Emily," he says, eyeing me with a to-be-expected wariness. "What was that about?"

"Efficiency?" I offer. "But you're the one who wanted to fight it out, dude."

"Yeah, I guess I didn't think too hard about the result," he says. "I took a pounding."

"So did I," says Mayra, still bound on the sofa. "Now, are you going to tell me who Emily is? Or do I have to assume you took a few too many kicks to the head?"

"If I tell you, I'm pretty sure you'll think that anyway," Jason replies, rising to find something to use to free Mayra from the zip ties around her wrists and ankles. "But I'll give it a go."

Jason retrieves a knife dropped during the scuffle and delivers the condensed version as he cuts Mayra's bindings. He tells her about me, the chip, and the attack at the university. As he does, I glance amongst my fallen foes. There's no doubt they're part of the same group that killed my colleagues. But that doesn't mean I take pleasure in their injuries, some minor, some potentially catastrophic, now that the heat of the moment has passed.

Mayra fetches candles, lights them, and places them on the mantel as Jason speaks, but her face betrays neither skepticism nor belief in his words. She turns to where she thinks I stand and addresses the empty air.

"So, you can hear me, Emily, because you're using Jason's ears?"

I nod to Jason. "Tell her I'm pleased to meet her. But we have to get going."

"She can but wants to get moving," Jason confirms. "You can talk to her yourself once we're on the road."

I watch Mayra's face. She doesn't like this. She's a sheriff and there are battered and bloody men claiming to be federal officers in her house. But as she looks around her living room, she seems to understand the world as she knows it has changed.

"Let me throw on my traveling clothes," Mayra says. "Take my keys and load whatever you can into the wagon. I'll meet you there in five."

Mayra makes her way to the stairs, pausing a few steps up to catch her breath.

"More excitement than these lungs are used to," she says.

Jason gathers weapons and searches the men for information but comes up dry on the latter. "No wallets, no papers," he announces. "No idea who they are."

"Let me try," I tell him. "Find one who's still breathing."

He knows what I mean to do. He walks to one of the gunmen, a fellow with multiple fractures, and touches the bandage on his neck.

125

"You sure about this?" he asks, preparing to transfer the chip to the wounded man.

I stare at the shooter, remembering the exact strike I used to disable him. He'd almost managed to shoot us in the head, so maybe I hit him harder than I needed. Seeing this person devastated by my hand once the moment has passed is horrifying. I can't believe I did it even as I wish it hadn't come to this.

"Not really," I reply. "Keep a gun aimed at him in case this wakes him up."

Jason tears off the bandage and my world goes black.

When the lights come back on a second later, I'm in the mind and memories of one Mitchell Dunch. Born in Hattiesburg, Mississippi, he went into the army right out of high school to avoid being charged as an adult following a second DUI arrest. Five tours later, he was drummed out for theft and went to work as a private contractor in the same combat zones in which he served in the army but now at four times the pay. When word of the Helios Event reached him, he considered suicide but then was offered a last few months of work at almost a hundred times the pay. He took it and began working security for a U.S. governmental project called Argosy.

I scan my own memory for any mention of Argosy. Not a thing comes back. Whether that's because I've never come across it or, perhaps had it surgically removed at some point, I don't know.

Mitchell has spent the last few weeks at a seaside base in Virginia doing not a whole helluva lot. He runs on the beach, he drinks, he does every drug under the sun, and he spends all his money on prostitutes. There is another group of people there, but they're segregated from the security types. They're called "the Select," but they look like average joes, albeit ones who seem bewildered and out of place. Not government types. He has no idea what they're doing there, nor does he care.

If there's one thing he occasionally cares about, it's his son, Dale. But he doesn't know where Dale is or even the boy's age. There's more, but I leave it alone as it speaks to a greater pain from Mitchell's own childhood. It's the kind of conditioning that turns someone into a violence-prone, rage-filled individual like this. Also, exactly what I was designed to engage with and attempt to unravel.

I regret we didn't meet earlier or under better circumstances, Mitchell.

The last thing I do is look for memories relating to the attack on the iLAB. Thankfully, he doesn't seem to have been involved. "Thankfully" because I'm not sure I could relive it right now. Similarly, he knows nothing of Siobhan or Mynette.

Then I see it. One day, he passes a room filled with rows and rows of empty, custom-designed server racks. The kind you could only use to house servers like *mine*. They're being worked on by a handful of folks who don't look so different from the techs Dr. Choksi had with her on the first day. I slow the memory and see what look like interface chips on the necks of the workers. Do they plan to use them to look for *me*? What use could they be for otherwise?

Little did they know, Nathan would be ready for them— ready to destroy me before they could even access a single file. I know this because I felt myself die. And without me, they'll never get to the ark.

Maybe that's why it's so important they bring me in. I look for other memories that could confirm this but find none. I raise Mitchell's hand and tap on the chip. Jason, who sits nearby, nods and removes it. When I come back this time, Jason is already on his way to the front door.

"So?" he asks.

"Not much," I reply. "But in case there was any doubt, it's government-related. These are the same people who attacked the iLAB and stole the servers."

"The president?" he asks.

"I don't know," I say. "The few minutes I spent with her suggest someone who was genuine in her belief that the digital ark was the best and only way forward. Unless something changed radically, I don't think it's her."

Jason nods and reaches the detached garage. Grabbing a snow shovel, he cuts a path from the drive to the road, finishing the task as Mayra emerges from the house. She's fully dressed now and carrying a bag that clinks as she walks. I spy a couple of liquor bottles poking out the top.

When Jason raises a questioning eyebrow, she shrugs. "It's the good stuff I've been saving for the end of the world. Be a shame to leave it for whoever comes to mop up this mess."

Hard to argue with that.

Mayra indicates where several cans of fuel are hidden alongside the garage under a tarp. Jason loads these into the back of the station wagon and we're on the road a few minutes later. We don't have a destination picked out; we just have to get away from Wolfeboro.

Mayra, who knows the local backroads, takes the first shift behind the wheel. I check to ensure the GPS is switched off, and nuke the Wi-Fi, which, in theory, could've been turned back on via remote, though I've felt no return to my expanded (and totes goddess-of-information-like) abilities beyond what's in my core storage. I also have Jason take the chip off and open it up to look for suspicious parts. When he reassembles it and places it back on his neck, I search his memory but find only what's meant to be there. I tell myself, for now, we're safe from anyone using me as a tracking device. For a time, I try to keep Jason awake, but his body has been through a lot. He needs rest. I let him slumber. I'm about to turn my thoughts toward the formulation of a plan when I black out again.

* * *

When I open my eyes, Mayra is pressing the interface chip against her neck.

"Ah!" she screams when she sees me, causing the chip to drop and me to black out again.

When I awake a second time, Mayra stares at me. I'm scrunched in between her and Jason on the front bench of the Volvo. I smile and shrug. She shakes her head.

"You're pretty," she decides.

"So are you," I reply.

This makes her laugh. "Thank you. So, I'm doing this right?" she asks, tapping the chip.

"Nothing to it."

"Hmm. I hope you don't mind me borrowing you for a moment," she says. "My overwhelming curiosity as to whether he was hearing voices in his head was part of it. But I also have a dreadful feeling we're flying blind here and I could use the help of a supercomputer."

"Totally agree," I say. "Do you have one?"

She laughs again, validating my commitment to low-hanging fruit as the finest source of comedy. I wish I could tell her where I got my sense of humor. It strikes me anew how much I miss Nathan.

"Tell me about yourself, Emily," she says. "You're the first…whatever-you-are…I've ever met. And I could use a good yarn to keep me awake. I'm still a little in the dark as to what earned me this busted lip."

She's not being completely honest with me. She's still law enforcement and good at putting people at their ease even when she wants to get to the bottom of this. I don't mind. I start at the beginning, laying out my autobiography from the moment of my birth to our appearance at her front door. She nods throughout the hour and forty-five minutes it takes to relate all this and asks a few clarifying questions. But when I finish, she stays quiet for a long moment.

"Sounds like you cared a great deal for this Dr. Wyman and he for you," she says. "I'm sorry for your loss."

"Thank you," I say quietly. "Because of the way our relationship was, it feels like something physical has been removed from inside of me. He was constantly in my head. Even now, when I come up with a question, I can almost hear his answer."

Mayra nods. "That's not so unusual," she says. "I was that way with my husband. Mind you, Bill and I were married for decades. There are days when I enter the house, even this many years after his passing, where I have to remind myself he's dead or I'll start looking for him room to room."

"I'm sorry," I echo.

"Nah," she says with a shrug. "Keeps him alive to me."

We both fall silent for a moment or two. The sky to the east is beginning to lighten, black becoming blue with the coming of the dawn.

"I don't want to seem ungrateful, but maybe we should look for a place you can drop us off." I say this so quietly she could be forgiven for not hearing me. "You already got us out of a tough jam. I don't think—"

She cuts me off by laughing. "A tough jam? Is that what I did? Look, Emily—you two seem like good people, but there's really just Jason there when it comes down to it, no offense."

"None tak—"

"And there's no way he can do this all by his lonesome. I leave him by the side of the road and he's a dead man. As someone who still believes in the rule of law and has sworn to uphold it, that's not going to happen. You need me and what I bring to the table. And, well, maybe I don't mind feeling needed again. You understand?"

As someone whose very design schematics ooze with ways I'm meant to let humans know how much I empathize with them, I nod. Mayra checks the car clock.

"Keep an eye out for a parking lot," she says. "Going to be light soon. Once someone finds those bodies in my house, they're going to put an APB out for these plates. Need to switch them out before then."

I eye her curiously. "I may be a small-town cop but that doesn't mean I don't know every poacher trick in the book," she says. "Like your gunmen over-relied on tech, you get too many lazy cops staring at plates while ignoring vehicle description. Same if we get on a toll road. Cameras aim at plates."

"You're quite the outlaw, Mayra," I say. "I'm glad you're on our side."

"Hush," she says. "Four hours ago, I was resigned to the idea I might never see another human being in the flesh for the rest of my days. Now I'm on the lam with a holographic wonder woman and the guy she's hot for. A peculiar turn of events, you might say, but not one entirely unappreciated."

"Wait," I say. "Who told you I liked Jason?"

"Ha—nobody," she says with a laugh. "Until right now, of course. As I said, you pick up a lot of tricks outfoxing poachers. You and I are going to get along fine."

XIX

We drive on into the morning to put as many miles between ourselves and our pursuers as possible. Those miles eventually enter the triple digits as we move through western Pennsylvania. In all, Mayra and I have seen maybe a dozen other vehicles on the road, three of them long-haul tractor trailers. This despite passing several small- to medium-sized towns, all blanketed by snow, the only signs of life being the occasional trail of smoke wafting up from a chimney or two.

"They've shut off power in a lot of these places," Mayra tells me. "It makes people move to the cities or farther south, even if they don't want to."

"Why?" I ask.

"As people walk off their jobs, migrate elsewhere to be with family or get closer to food-producing regions, having everyone stretched across a state gets ungainly," she explains. "Can't waste fuel on delivering food to the stores out here, even if anyone thought money was worth anything anymore. Also, few first responders. If there's a fire or a break-in or any other kind of emergency, you might have one ambulance and one fireman still hanging around. I was lucky having a line in to the state police but that's because I'm enforcement, too. Everything else is kind of restricted."

"But there are holdouts," I say, indicating a town off the highway. A few lights, likely running off generators, continue to burn.

"Of course," she says. "There are people you can't tell anything to. Also, nobody knows what to expect. News is hard to come by. But most people think it's better to be in Pittsburgh or Philly when something happens than out here in the sticks, I guess."

"But not you," I say as we overtake a Nissan Sentra crawling down the highway at maybe forty miles an hour, the driver likely trying to conserve gas. "And not Jason."

"I suppose not," she says. "But some people like that communal-type living. I mean, I heard the populations of places like Los Angeles, San Diego, and Tijuana all doubled and tripled as folks from as far away as Las Vegas moved in. If people know one thing and one thing only, it's that the electronics will go first, and refrigerated food will go second. That's why a place like New York's a ghost town and Lincoln, Nebraska, looks like Mecca during the hajj when you get two million pilgrims trying to get around the Grand Mosque all at once. I heard Boston cleared out, too."

"Most of the students and teachers went home from campus," I admit. "But I was sheltered from how things were in the city at large."

"Better that way," she says. "Given how you empathize, I can see that working to draw your eye off the ball. If you're thinking about all these people as individuals all the time, how can you focus on the bigger issues at hand?"

I nod, but I wonder if that's all there is to it. It's not outside the realm of possibility the same impulse that led Nathan to push his own family away pulled me even tighter to him. I've thought so often of my dependence on him, perhaps I didn't consider how much he relied on me.

I'm contemplating this when Jason stirs, then wakes. He sees Mayra but not me, which doesn't compute. He panics. I reach out to soothe him but can't touch him. Mayra waves her fingers in front of Jason's eyes, then taps the interface chip on her neck.

"Borrowed your friend for a driving companion," she says. "You can have her back now."

I smile gratefully at her and realize I couldn't hide my feelings for Jason from anyone if I tried. She pats my hand and gives the chip back to him.

"I thought I'd lost you," he says.

The emotion behind his words surprises him. He didn't realize his view of me—of a computer program—could be colored by such feeling. I smile and rest my hand reassuringly on his shoulder.

I experience the touch through his senses. His body registers it with almost as much potency as I did. I resist the impulse to pull my hand away and leave it a second longer, allowing my eyes to stare into the pale blue of his irises.

"Where are we?" he asks.

"Outside Pittsfield," Mayra replies.

"Ah," Jason replies. "We should switch off driving."

"I was about to suggest that very thing," Mayra says. "Let's find some coffee first."

It takes another hour and a half to find an open diner. We finally come across one called The Pick Me Up. Mayra parks and steps out, stretching theatrically.

"All right," she announces. "Coffee and chow, bathroom and refuel."

Jason takes my hand as if to help me out of the car and for a moment, everything is so placid and normal. I can almost imagine our odd little trio striking out west, leaving all of this behind in favor of a life on the road. No worries, no cares. Two people resigned to walling off the world until the end and another whose world has been all but walled off until now, finding the others amidst the tumult. Couldn't this be enough?

I catch sight of us reflected in the diner's window, two people, not three. I'm not there. I'm about to comment, when it reminds me of who else is gone—Nathan, Dr. Choksi, Gally, Suni, and the others. I pray this doesn't happen to Jason and Mayra next.

I keep staring at the reflection. There's so much around us the image doesn't capture. The dawn sky and tall trees beyond the parking lot, the highway overpass just out of view to our right, even the whole of the Volvo station wagon.

"Oh my God," I say.

"What?" Jason asks.

"I need a minute," I say. "Back in a sec."

"Are you okay?" he asks.

"Yes, just need to focus."

I go into my own memories of the iLAB, finding my last interaction with Nathan in his office. I watch it unfold.

"Jesus Christ!" Nathan exclaims in this living memory. "Emily! What happened? Are you okay?"

"The file sizes were much larger than anticipated," I say, exactly as I did then, trying not to react at seeing Nathan again. "It overwhelmed my heat sinks immediately."

I use Nathan's eyes to look around. The family photograph is there on his desk, but it's not the image I saw in his mind. Not entirely. Something is *off*.

"We know," Nathan says. "We're working up a fix right now. Could take a while."

I realize what it is. In Nathan's last thought, it wasn't just the photo that was reversed; it was the entire layout of his desk—his files, his laptop, a stack of external drives, a mug with the university's logo on it—all on the opposite ends from where they really sit.

I turn around, spying the ornamental mirror on the office wall behind

Nathan's door, a gift from a Moroccan student Nathan used to check his appearance when dignitaries came to campus.

His final thought wasn't of his family at all. It was of this mirror.

But why? Why something so specific? So hard to trick his mind into seeing?

"Emily," he said. "*Go.*"

Maybe he wasn't ordering me to run away. Maybe he was telling me where to go.

"Jason!" I exclaim, appearing in a booth inside the restaurant next to my friends as a waitress stands by.

Jason jumps, my arrival enough to spook him almost from his seat. The waitress flinches, casting a worried glance over to Mayra.

"Oh, sorry," Mayra says by way of apology. "Hard to get meds these days. He's fine, though."

"Yes, sorry about that," Jason adds. "It's embarrassing really."

The waitress nods. "It's okay. My husband and I got that way after three days of sitting at home," she says, pointing back to the kitchen where a single cook works away. "Why we opened the place back up."

"Well, we sure are glad you did."

The waitress smiles and heads away. "I'll bring that coffee right over."

Once she's gone, Jason turns to me. "What is it?"

"When you were evacuated from campus, did you see the iLAB building?" I ask.

"I have no idea," he says. "Is that important?"

"It might be. Do you mind if I ...?"

He shrugs but in a way that lets me know of his reluctance and nods. I hop into his mind and search for his last day on campus. He's woken up by a residential assistant notifying him of the evacuation. He has two hours to pack his things and leave.

I accelerate through this process. He doesn't have much to pack and it's one call to his sister to secure her husband's place in New Hampshire. He says he wishes he could join them but knows this isn't likely given how difficult cross-country travel has become.

He exits, carrying two heavy duffels with a computer bag slung over his shoulder. He heads west through campus—the *opposite* direction of the iLAB.

A dead end.

But he hesitates. He wants to grab food for the trip. *Yes!* Even better, his mind goes to the vending machines in the physics building directly across from the iLAB. He does a 180, heading back through the quad. I strain to absorb all the information his eyes take in. If I'm not careful, I'll miss seeing the iLAB altogether.

"Jason!" someone calls out.

The voice belongs to someone who looks like a TA or an adjunct. She draws him over to hand him a book and a couple of key drives. There's a short conversation about their shared field, a handshake, and a good-bye. But when Jason resumes his walk to the vending machines, his trajectory has altered about ten degrees in the *wrong* direction.

And that's the difference between seeing the iLAB and not. All I wanted to know was if Nathan's office was still intact. That I might still discover whatever he was sending me there to find.

Dammit.

I stay with Jason as he reaches the doors of the physics building. That's when I see his reflection in the door's glass panels. That and the iLAB directly behind him.

It's a nightmarish sight. Bad as it was to witness the destruction of its façade that night, seeing it partly reduced to rubble in the cold light of day is even worse. It looks like the ruins of a tomb, recently unearthed, roped off by yellow tape and a makeshift chain-link fence hastily erected in the predawn hours. Workers in respirators, hazmat suits, and hard hats file in and out, selling the story that it was an explosion made worse by the hazardous chemicals stored in the building.

When I look up to the sixth floor, however, I see Nathan's office there in the corner. The windows on that level have been shattered, the walls blown out by gunfire—except his, almost like the perpetrators ran out of bullets or decided it would be poetic to leave one intact. I only hope this holds true for whatever might be hidden inside.

I exit Jason's mind. He eyes me perplexedly. "Already done?"

"I am," I say gravely, though I remind myself time passed for me while in someone's mind at a much slower rate than it did for them. "We have to go back. You were right. Nathan was trying to tell me something with his last thought."

Jason explains this to Mayra. Both fall silent as if waiting for the other to suggest this is ludicrous. We're supposed to be getting away from these people, not knocking on their front door.

"What if they're waiting for us?" he asks. "If our last couple of encounters with them is any indication, they could have a dozen guards around the building itself, to say nothing of the ones they'll have inside."

"Nathan could've run away. Instead, he spent the last minutes of his life trying to keep me and my servers from falling into their hands," I say. "If there's even a chance he was trying to tell me something important, something worth losing his life over, I can't let him down. I owe it to him to go back."

This seems to convince Jason. I shrug and add, "Besides, you're riding shotgun with a holographic wonder woman supercomputer, right? They might outgun us, but they can't outthink us."

XX

Okay, so three hours, 150 miles, and 8.4 gallons of fuel later, this hubristic, not-so-super-computer, not-so-wonder-woman is still coming up dry on the plan front. We've even switched out who gets the interface chip a few times, allowing me brainstorming sessions with both Mayra and Jason as we journey back to Boston, but to no avail.

"The omnipresent campus security cameras are a problem," Jason says rightly.

"We can assume they're going to have photos of both of us," Mayra says, also rightly.

"They won't let anybody on campus in a vehicle that doesn't get searched," I say back. "And if we try to breach at night, they'll have the advantage, as their night vision gear seems standard issue. I can only help adjust one of your guys' eyes to the dark at a time and even then it won't be as good as their tech-enhanced optics."

So, we go around and around a few times until it becomes abundantly clear being devious isn't my strong suit.

When we reach the River Street exit off the Mass Pike into Cambridge, Mayra taps Jason's leg.

"Your friend explained about her simulation," Mayra says to Jason, who wears the interface chip. "The cameras are doing the heavy lifting.

But there are blind spots. Like, out in the town she could go onto a roof, but the streets were vacant. Got to be some of that on campus, too, right?"

My mind races. She's right.

"There are, mostly around the edges," I tell Jason. "We can circle the campus and see which ones she thinks might work. Doesn't solve the problem of the building itself."

He relates this to Mayra. "Means there are options. They teach you in enforcement not to look at a problem as a single mass you to have to solve in one fell swoop. Solve it piece by piece, chip away at it, and you'll eventually eat the whole elephant. Make sense?"

It does, but I'm glad she can't see my reaction. I feel silly for thinking the perfect plan would just pop in my head.

"What about guards?" Jason asks.

"If they're understaffed, they'll over-rely on the cameras," Mayra and I reply at the same time. "The guards they do have will be focused at sensitive sites, not entrances," she finishes.

Now I feel less silly and more like a tough, poacher-busting small-town sheriff—if only for a moment.

We circle the campus at a distance, knowing even with new plates, a gas-powered vehicle on mostly empty streets will draw attention. As predicted, we don't see many guards. The traffic gates are down and there are a couple of uniformed private security types milling around the pedestrian crossings, but it's hardly Fort Knox.

I take this all in, particularly because the guards aren't the bearded special-ops hard-asses we came across in New Hampshire. In fact, these fellows give the impression it's just another day on campus. Maybe that's the idea.

It's when we park about sixteen blocks away I come up with what I think will be our next best move. I tell Jason, who shakes his head.

"No—no way," he says. "That's insane."

"Tell Mayra," I implore him.

"Tell me," Mayra says. "Let an officer of the law be the judge of what's insane or not."

He hands over the interface chip. I tell Mayra my plan, and for a moment, I can't tell if she's thinking the same thing as Jason. Then she nods, her gaze traveling beyond the windshield to the campus in the distance.

"I think so," she says, answering an unasked question. "Maybe, maybe."

Jason protests, but he's been overruled and knows it. "When are you thinking of doing this?" he asks.

"Right now," Mayra says. "Daylight's burning."

Jason looks stricken. Mayra nods to me and reaches for the interface chip. I black out and come back to Jason. Mayra has left the car, giving us a moment.

"I'm sorry," I say, lapsing into my role of emotional helpmate.

"It's not that," Jason says, taking my hand. "It's just…this might be good-bye. Again. I feel like I just met you. But you might not be coming back."

"You're taking the same exact risks," I counter. "But this is what we've decided to do, right?"

But I know what's going on. It's a version of what he felt when I returned to him following his brief nap earlier. He's not sure what to do with the fact that he has feelings for a digital simulation of a young woman he met in Paris so many years ago. Is he thinking about her? Or about the person—okay, artificial consciousness—he's gotten to know on the run? One who, well, lied her eyes out about the provenance of their initial meeting?

I mean, if I had it my way, I'd kiss him before he could even get the words out of his mouth, but I'm pretty sure that's the wrong way to do this. My desire for him is the emotional equivalent of opening the Three Gorges Dam in Hubei. But my guilt over the manipulation makes me wonder if, should I tell him the truth, it'll be the last I see of him.

If this really is the end for either one of us, it's devastating to think about all the things we'd never know or get to explore. Looking over at Jason, I can tell he's thinking the same thing.

"See you soon," I say.

"Yep," he replies.

But his hand remains on mine until Mayra knocks on the window.

The best place to enter campus unseen is the Ames Street pedestrian gate near Kendall Square. When security tightened around 9/11, this gate—deemed too far off the beaten path to be well guarded—was welded shut. This worked fine for several years until rust set in, a few semesters' worth of students kicked at it a few times, and it finally opened. As it was used almost solely as a shortcut by students living in off-campus housing in East Cambridge far from the main gate, nobody said anything. No one cared. A chain hung limply from the nearby fence as if waiting for a lock, but none ever arrived.

As it was no longer recognized by the university as a gate, there was also no need to install a camera over it when the last major wave of cameras was installed in 2009, providing the campus with its near-100 percent coverage.

Mayra and I make a long circuit through Kendall Square before turning in the direction of campus. We don't speak as we walk at first, less to prevent passersby from thinking Mayra is crazy, and more because we have little to say. It's cloudy out today, the sun hiding behind layers of gray.

"I remember what it was like to think of the future," Mayra says, breaking the silence. "It's something—all the planning, all the hopes, but also the easy assumptions of how tomorrow won't look so different from today. But since Bill died, I've found it hard to escape the past. It takes over everything. You have new challenges, but forty years of marriage conditions you to live a certain way. It feels unnatural trying to function as half a person."

"You miss him a lot?"

"Yes, but it's not what you think it's going to be," she explains. "You miss intimacy first. That feeling of closeness to another human being. We weren't really romantic anymore. Hadn't been for years. Those old couples kissing on TV like solving erectile dysfunction reignited their sex life? Not us! But that space he inhabited in the house. The gravity and oxygen he took up. I feel that absence every day. Dying first means he got the better part of the deal, never having to live without someone at his side who's loved him his whole life."

She says this last part without a hint of bitterness, which I find surprising. I sense something here beyond her words. A certain weight. Is it the burden of her partner's death? Or how it reflects her own frailties? I'm not certain how to respond.

"I'm sorry," I say finally.

"Don't be," she says. "You're the one who brought me out of that house and gave a little meaning to my last days here. You'd be surprised what giving someone like me some responsibility can do. Particularly since no one's needed me for much for some time now. So, thank you."

I glance ahead. The Ames Street gate is in sight. I realize there's a part of Mayra that thinks this could all be over in a few minutes, so she wanted to make sure she said what she said first. I take her hand.

"We'll be okay," I say, though I'm not sure I mean it.

Mayra nods but doesn't reply. As we step to the broken gate, the familiarity of the sight, albeit now through Mayra's senses instead of the camera angles I'm accustomed to seeing the simulation building from, takes me into my own past. I wonder if it will envelope me. I flashback to the images of Nathan, Dr. Choksi, and Suni lying dead. I see Jason's memory of the ruined iLAB building reflected in the glass door. My past is ashes. My future, if I have one, promises...what? Complications, possibly even more lies, but also time in which to keep on living. And maybe that's enough.

That's what I have to hang on to.

"Ready to get crazy?" Mayra asks as she slips through the gate, a twinkle in her eye.

XXI

 hough it's only been less than a week since the campus was evacuated, to look at it one could believe it had been far longer. No one has
shoveled the snow, which blankets the walkways and steps alike. A pipe
descending the side of one of the Cold War–era buildings has frozen and
burst, a beautiful explosion of ice cascading out from the break like a
blooming flower. A few first-floor windows are shattered, likely by loot-
ers. Icicles drip over doorways like broken prison bars, daring someone
to step out of the darkened buildings they guard.

Only the trees look the same, the leaf-stripped white oaks rising alongside the pathways like jagged sentinels, letting passersby know come
spring, they will lead nature's reclamation of this place if uncontested.

Mayra strides purposefully past all of this, high-stepping through the
snow like a drum major, even when the powder reaches above the rim of
her boot.

We're spotted as soon as we make it to the first main campus artery.
This one is plowed. We arrive as a black SUV passes, chains on the
tires crunching ice. The driver smokes with his window down and
glances our way, his reaction hidden behind sunglasses. Though the
truck doesn't slow, he seems to gauge whether we're his problem or if
he can shrug it off on someone else. As if to punctuate his judgment that

it's the latter, he exhales a dragon's breath of smoke, flicks the cigarette into the snow, and drives on without looking back.

"So far, so good," Mayra says airily.

We see no one for the next quarter mile. Mayra pauses a few seconds to catch her breath, leaning heavily on a granite planter, but the only movement arrives in the form of a pair of squirrels chasing each other through the branches of a nearby ash tree.

This changes when we near the iLAB. Though the image from Jason's memory was bad enough, the reality is worse. The building looks like a pillaged tomb. Doors have been wrenched away and walls obliterated for efficacy's sake, likely to facilitate the removal of the servers and anything else not nailed down. I wonder if the building's even structurally sound. Snow has been allowed to blow in through the shattered windows, carrying in trash and leaves. The lobby looks like an abandoned alleyway.

But there in the upper corner, Nathan's office window remains intact. I can only hope the interior is equally undisturbed.

I count six guards at the site entrance, though a double-wide trailer—some kind of command center—has been set up a few yards outside the chain-link fence and may contain more. Unlike the rent-a-cops at the campus gates, the men here are the same kind of muscle-bound, operator types we encountered in New Hampshire—multiple firearms, multiple magazines, knives, even mace hang from their Kevlar-clad bodies like ill-matched Christmas ornaments.

"Hagar?" Mayra calls out. "Hagar!"

She staggers forward theatrically as two of the guards come out to meet her. The four in back look more amused than intimidated. The two in front—a young Caucasian and a slightly older African American—both have their hands on the machine guns hanging in front of their chests.

"Hagar!" Mayra cries, more agitated by the second.

"Excuse me, ma'am?" the younger guard asks, raising a hand. His accent is Southern. He's little more than a kid. "You need to stop—"

"Oh, good," Mayra says, as if seeing the men for the first time. "Maybe you can help me. You see my dog? She's a little Jack Russell. Name's Hagar, like the mother of Ishmael and the second wife of Abraham."

The guard isn't sure what to do with this information. He doesn't have a nametag but the heavy boots he wears have "Saitta" written on them in marker. He's about to address Mayra again when he looks back to his partner for guidance. Mayra sees this as an excuse to keep going.

"She got away from me in the street and ran in here," she continues, looking all around. "I don't mean to cause you any trouble at a time like this, but well . . . she's all I've got."

She steadies herself as she says this, as if it might be true. Saitta shakes his head.

"Sorry," he says. "We haven't seen a dog, and this is a restricted area. It's dangerous here—"

"Wha . . . ?" Mayra asks. "What happened?"

"There was an industrial accident. The ground is unstable. If you'll let me walk you back to the gate—"

"Will you let me call her?" she asks, then steps forward. "Hagar! C'mon, girl! Dangerous in here! Hagar!"

The other guard stiffens, no longer willing to placate this madwoman. He smells a rat. He gives Saitta a look as meaningful as a command and the younger man grabs Mayra's arm.

"Ma'am, as I said, we need to escort you out to the street now."

As soon as his hand touches her, she softens—staring into his eyes with madness and love. "Hagar," she whispers quietly. "You've become handsome. I knew I'd find you."

While this makes the other guards chuckle, happy to have let their comrade be humiliated, it incenses Saitta. He roughly pushes her forward, but she "loses her balance" and reaches out for him to steady herself. One hand grabs at his shoulder as the other reaches for her interface chip.

Everything goes dark.

XXII

A second later, I'm shaking my head at Mayra while giving her wrist a triple squeeze. Our signal. She immediately goes docile, a chastised child wanting her punishment to be over.

"I'm sorry we couldn't help you," I say through Saitta's mouth, stern now.

"It's okay," Mayra mutters, seemingly confused.

"Can we call you a taxi or something?" I continue, even as I search Saitta's mind. His first name is Timothy. The other guard is the musically named Cory DeJoria. "Do you have somewhere you can go?"

"Of course," Mayra says, as if in a trance, indicating the neighborhoods north of campus. "I'll go home."

"This way, ma'am," I say, trying my best to sound as if Saitta's nearing the end of his patience.

We're out of earshot of the other guards, but we're not taking any chances. I'm still holding her arm as we near the Massachusetts gate, the very one Nathan's killers came through. The gate and guardhouse I'd seen bullet-riddled are back to their original condition. As if nothing happened.

I nod to my fellow guards, indicate Mayra with a shrug, and point to the sidewalk.

"Be safe," I say.

I give her arm a gentle squeeze but then she heads away. She doesn't look back even once.

Her placement of the interface chip was perfect. It's on my—well, Saitta's—neck below his shirt collar. I adjust it, careful not to break the connection, then head back to my post.

Cory waits for me, lighting a cigarette. "Surprised you were so gentle with her," he says. "She was crazy as hell. If she'd touched my face, I would've shot her then and there."

I search Saitta's memory. He thinks of Cory as an odd duck, someone who doesn't believe all the hype about the coming apocalypse, believing instead it's a hoax perpetuated by the president to accumulate wide-ranging powers. He's told Saitta he plans to take the money he makes to Antigua in a few months to live like a king.

Saitta, on the other hand, does believe the hype, but he also believes the government has a plan they'll soon unveil, likely one to do with large underground cities. I remember this really was a scheme they'd proposed on one of the many pie-in-the-sky lists sent in by lower-level federal employees, moving folks into temporary housing in subway lines and the like with New York City being the test case. But as soon as they brought it to us, we pointed out the NYC tunnels must be constantly pumped free of seawater, something impossible to do once the geomagnetic storms begin to wipe out power. The plan was shelved.

He seems like a good guy, this Timothy Saitta. Good grades in high school, went to work at an office supply warehouse, got a girlfriend, lost a girlfriend, got that girlfriend back. Took the job as a security guard to save money for a car so he can visit said girlfriend more, as she lives three counties over. Hmm. I'll try not to get him killed.

"She reminded me of my grandma," I say. "A lot of people in trouble these days."

Cory laughs, offering me a cigarette. "Not our problem," he says.

I check to see if Saitta is a smoker. He is not. I shake my head. Now comes the hard part.

I search Saitta's memories to see under what circumstances the guards can enter the iLAB building. Turns out, they're not supposed to go in at all. However, they slip in from time to time to get out of the cold, sometimes using the first-floor conference room as a shooting range complete with heater inside the command shed doing little to warm such a large, thin-walled space.

Also, they much prefer the restrooms inside, which still work, as opposed to the freezing port-a-johns set up nearby for the security detail.

"Hey, I'm going to hit the head," I tell Cory, using a bit of vernacular Saitta's picked up from his navy days. "Be right back."

"I'm going to join you," Cory says. "Anything to get out of this cold."

I nod. I didn't think it would be so easy to go in on my own. I have a plan either way.

I lead Cory up the snowy steps into the iLAB. The wind whistles through the building, blasting icy air coming in on the sixth floor down through the stairwells and out into the lower hallways. Given the way Saitta's body is reacting, I can't imagine it's much warmer in here than outside.

"I wanted to show you something," I say as we move to the restrooms at the back of the first floor. "Found it on my last shift. Or, really, Lopez found it and told me to check it out."

"What's that?" Cory asks, suspicious.

"Food," I say. "Up on the sixth floor."

It's a gamble. I don't know how much time I'll need in Nathan's office, but I'll need to be on my own. If there's even a chance our barter closet is intact, sending Cory after it might give me just enough time.

Only, he goes quiet, eyeing me like a crook. *Huh?*

It dawns on me too late that sharing food in this dog-eat-dog economy probably isn't done. If you find a cache of food, the last thing you do is tell anyone. If it's more than you can personally eat, the black market will be happy to take it off your hands in trade.

"Fine, Lopez asked me to tell you because he wanted to use your truck to get it out of here," I say. "He figured you were more likely to do it if I asked, not him."

"Nah, sixth floor is too unstable to walk on," he counters. "It's why we're not allowed up there. Lopez wants us to do his dirty work for him."

"I'm still here, ain't I?" I ask with a shrug. "But hey, more for me."

"What kind of food?" he asks finally.

"Granola bars, gummy bears, crappy cookies, chips, waters, sodas," I say. "All hidden away in this cabinet. Tons of it. Student munchies."

I think of Bjarke hauling the stuff up in the freight elevator, mostly boosted from other departments. He'd once liberated a box of soap from a nearby motel—two hundred tiny .75-ounce cakes—and had never been prouder.

"You serious?" Cory asks.

"As a hurricane," I reply.

"I'm in," Cory says, holding out a fist.

I fist-bump him. We move to the rear stairs. As we ascend, I wonder what might happen if the floors collapse. Saitta will die, certainly, but will the interface chip be found when his body is recovered? Or will they ignore it and move on, making my end so ignominious, so less than a footnote? No way of knowing.

The stairwell is dark until we reach the third floor where the doors have been blown off. Light trickles in. It's only then I notice the long black fingers of smoke stain creeping up the walls from the various vents. Evidence of a fire. Maybe there really was an explosion. Maybe they blew up the lower levels to cover their tracks.

"Is it much farther?" Cory asks, his breathing labored as we pass the fifth-floor landing.

"Can't you count?" I shoot back.

He grunts. We climb the last steps to the sixth floor. It's an odd thing to notice, but Jason's body is more prepared for this kind of ascent than Saitta's. He's young and well trained, but whereas Jason's stamina has been built up through cycling, Saitta is more muscle-bound. He might beat Jason in a sprint but not in such an ascent.

It's an odd thing to know, how one person's body would work in such specific terms compared to another's, I almost turn to Cory to describe the experience. Luckily, I catch myself.

"Where's the food?" Cory asks.

I barely hear him. The sight of where I spent so much of my life these past five years now decimated numbs me all over. Entire sections of wall are missing, blown out by the Humvee's turret guns, their barrels at an almost ninety-degree angle, or maybe even grenades and shells. That anyone would believe this was a chemical lab explosion is either insane or the willful belief of those already cowed by events.

The last time I was here, Nathan was alive, and we thought the digital ark plan might provide some shot at salvation.

"Conference room," I say offhandedly. "Cabinets under the copy machine. It's locked, but that's what a Ka-Bar is for."

"If it's locked, how do you know what's in it?" he asks.

"Lopez kept the key, the greedy bastard," I say, moving away. "Serves him right for not telling everybody."

Cory accepts this, turning off at the corner. "You're not coming?" he asks.

"Figure if they had one they might have others," I say. "Maybe even booze."

Cory nods and heads off. "Be quick and don't grab anything too big to explain downstairs," he calls back to me.

But I'm already on my way to Nathan's office. With every step, my trepidation grows. It's when I step across the threshold and his smell fills Saitta's nose I'm overwhelmed. The young security guard quakes as tears fill his eyes, then trail down his face. I grab the back of Nathan's chair to steady myself.

"Really interesting," Nathan would say if he could see Saitta's body respond not only to my physical controls but to my emotional state as well. "We should look at that."

I almost say his name aloud if only to hear it in this room again. It'd be too much like summoning a ghost. Cory is right. Time is fleeting.

I focus on the desk. The photo of Nathan's family is exactly where it's always been, directly alongside the wireless keyboard he used for his tablets and phone. My memory of it is correct. What was in Nathan's mind was the mirror image. I turn Saitta back to the wall behind the door, spying the legal pad–sized wall mirror still hanging there. The angle is perfect, the photo framed in it precisely.

I move to stand in front of the mirror, half closing the door to get a clearer view. There's nothing on the surface, nothing around the frame. I look at the back of the door, but there's nothing there either. It doesn't make sense. I step into the center of the office and glance around, comparing what I see now to my last memory of this room. If Nathan was here just before his death, there's no sign of what he got up to.

I see a drawer open slightly, so I check it. Nothing out of the ordinary there. The trash can contains a single granola bar wrapper. There's more dust on various surfaces. The chair is moved slightly, but I did that. The window is whole but covered in soot and ash from the bombardment.

Have we come all this way for *nothing*?

As I get frustrated, however, I put myself in Nathan's shoes. What would he have been thinking?

If he knew people were coming for the servers, then he would've known hiding something from me or a reprogrammed copy of me was a possibility. The reflection in the mirror may have been one layer of "encryption." But what else?

Mynette once criticized me early on saying I was incapable of comprehending things outside of two-dimensional space. She's right. I'm approaching changes to his office the way I would changes to my simulation. They'd be superficial, painted on, but ultimately not entirely dimensional. I must think in 3D space, not pseudo-3D.

I take the mirror off the wall.

At first, I see nothing out of the ordinary. I run my fingers over the stucco, but it's exactly as it should be. I turn my attention to the nail the mirror was hanging from. The hole is slightly hollowed out as if the weight of the mirror has dragged it down over time. But Nathan was the most precise human being I've ever encountered. He would've determined the nail's load-bearing ability before he even bought the mirror.

I grab the nail head between Saitta's fingers and pull it straight out. I am rewarded when wrapped around the pin is a nearly translucent slip of paper. Like the kind you'd find around one of Nathan's ever-present cough drops.

It's a list of eight names scrawled in pencil. Check that, five are in pencil, three are in ink, though from two different pens. They're in Nathan's handwriting. Given the lingering, medicinal smell of the cough drop on the paper, they were written relatively recently with room at the bottom for more names.

What strikes me most of all, however, is that the eighth name is one I recognize—Shakhawat Rana—the last portrait I took before the attack. The one with the 7.666% difference in DNA from his fellow humans.

It also means Nathan lied to me. Or, at least, did so through omission. The digital ark was meant to be sealed, no back doors. But somehow Nathan had access. Not only that, but he was also able to search the portraits for information. After all his words about preserving the sanctity of the process, he was subverting it from the start.

"Hey there, Emily," an immediately recognizable voice says from the doorway. "That *is* you in there, isn't it?"

I whirl around. Siobhan smirks at me from four feet away, a gun in her hand. I stare at her in horror, thinking it must be a mistake. A trick? A game? This is my colleague. My *friend*.

"Siobhan?" I ask. "What're you doing? Put the gun down."

She responds by training it at my head. "Quite a trick you've picked up—your sister'll be glad to have you back in the fold."

"Sister? What're you talking about, 'sister'?" I ask, growing more confused by the second. "Siobhan, it's me. Talk to me. What's going on here?"

"We wondered how one student managed to wreck all our well-armed operators up in New Hampshire, but we learned long ago that assuming there were limits to your abilities was a sure way for you to surpass our expectations," she continues. "Now, if you don't want this young man's brains blown all over Nathan's desk, maybe you'll hand over whatever you've got there. Sound good?"

I say nothing, letting the feeling of betrayal wash over me in order to color my next actions. I assess how to close the distance between myself and her. As if realizing what I'm up to, Siobhan assumes a firing stance and cocks the weapon.

"I'll give you to the count of one to decide what you're going to do," she says. "And that's . . . *one*."

XXIII

Even as I accelerate my processor speed to determine how best to absorb a bullet, Siobhan's finger pulls the trigger on the gun. I can't outmaneuver a bullet, but, within this minute amount of time, I can determine the spot on Saitta's body where it will do the least damage. As the round approaches my torso, I turn as best I can to allow it to penetrate my chest below my left vertebrochondral ribs. It shreds my skin, passes through my stratum corneum, tearing through sweat glands and sebaceous glands, nicks the rib, changes its trajectory to pass within a millimeter of my abdominal aorta without severing it, then exits out my back.

The force of the impact spins me around, but I exaggerate the motion to make Siobhan believe a second bullet is unnecessary. I cry out, knock into the chair, and manage to slam into Nathan's side table, tipping it over with a crash.

I hit the ground facing away from Siobhan. She takes two steps closer and I slowly roll onto my side, gasping for air.

"Drop it or the next one goes in your head," she says.

I nod, holding out the piece of paper. My movements are halting, as if I've lost at least some control over Saitta's body. Using the gun barrel, Siobhan pushes aside Saitta's collar to expose the interface chip.

"You shouldn't have come back, Emily," she says, scoffing as she snatches the piece of paper from my hand. "Helpful, sure, but dumb."

"Why would you do this?" I croak. "To Nathan, I mean? He was our friend. Our mentor."

"He was also incredibly shortsighted. They approached him first, you know. Or maybe you didn't."

"Who did?" I ask.

"Argosy," she says. "He turned them away. His mistake."

"Argosy?" I ask, playing dumb.

"Don't mock me, Emily. You know who we are."

"And Mynette?"

Siobhan shrugs. "Disappeared. Possibly overseas. Took a bunch of tech with her, too. Initially thought you two might've been in this together, but we don't think she got away with any interface chips. Don't worry. We'll find her, too."

"You seem pretty confident for someone who didn't exactly watch your six out there."

"My 'six'?" she asks. "Is this some new trick of yours?"

"Your situational awareness," I say.

"Really, Emily? What're you playing at wi—"

Her words are drowned out by the gunshot. The bullet strikes her on the arm. She cries out, dropping her weapon. Cory stands in the doorway holding his pistol. Siobhan instinctively goes to retrieve her gun, but Cory shakes his head.

"I wouldn't," he says with an unflappable cool, ready to shoot again.

Siobhan, mouth still open in surprise, nods and moves away. Cory picks up Siobhan's weapon, eyeing me as he does. "You okay, man?"

"She shot me!" I say. "I don't know how she got in here, but I think she's another crazy squatter. She keeps saying I'm being controlled by a computer program or computer chip or something."

"We gotta get them to pay for a few more guys at the gate," Cory says, slipping the gun into his waistband.

"This person isn't who you think it is," Siobhan says calmly.

"Uh-huh," Cory says. "Next you're going to tell me you didn't shoot him."

"No, I did that," she says, blood oozing down her arm. "But she's the invader, not me. I work for Argosy, same as you. My name is Siobhan Moesser. *Doctor* Siobhan Moesser. You can check me out."

Cory pauses, seemingly surprised by Siobhan's composure. He looks to me and I shrug, rolling my eyes as if only a dullard would fall for a story like this. Cory reaches for his radio.

"Stay there, okay?" he says, indicating Siobhan.

"No problem," she replies icily.

"Hey, who's down there right now?" Cory says into the radio as Siobhan backs away. "We got anybody with a supervisor's number?"

I race through my options. I could run out the door but with this wound, I doubt I'd get very far. I could try to distract Cory, but I'm not sure how well that would work at present either. I notice, too late, Siobhan inching toward me. Before I can alert my partner, she drops to the floor, plucks a knife from a sheath on Saitta's ankle, turns, and stabs Cory. It happens so fast, so without emotion, that neither I nor Cory can gauge the situation. Cory sinks to the floor, blood jetting from the wound. Siobhan blinks and turns to me.

"Happy now, Emily?" she asks.

I think back to the men who killed Nathan, wondering how they could've done it so dispassionately and without hesitation. They'd had training, of course. For Siobhan to have done it makes me think there's either a lot I don't know about her or a lot I don't understand about people once the normal rules of civilization are suspended.

I leap to my feet even as Saitta's body protests in anguish. I grab

Siobhan by the shoulders, wheeling her around until I can get my forearm under her chin.

"What're you doing?" she asks, gurgling. "Stop it, Em!"

She still has the knife in her hand and stabs at me over and over. Still, I hang on, the improvised sleeper hold gradually draining her of consciousness. I can hear the cries of the guards out front. They must've assumed we were downstairs using the improvised shooting range when the first shot went off. Now they're not so sure.

I only need a few seconds more.

When she's completely out, I kneel and hastily bind her wound. Based on her reaction I don't think it's serious, but it's leaking a lot of blood. That done, I remove Saitta's radio and weapons from my pockets and place them in Siobhan's. I find Nathan's list of names and shove that in Siobhan's pocket as well.

I turn my attention to Saitta himself, and to my understanding of gravity, anatomy, and motion. I need one absent impulse, a single last vestigial action from his unconscious mind.

I put my hand over the interface chip on Saitta's jaw and lean over Siobhan's neck until I'm mere inches from her. My fingertips encircle the chip's edge, ready to pry it free. I need to visualize the motion, initiate it, and then rely on the various components of Saitta's motor system to complete the movement. I take a deep breath and the world vanishes.

I can't breathe. All the air in my chest has been forced out. I wonder if I'm having a heart attack.

"Hey, what the hell?" a groggy voice asks. "What's going on?"

My eyes open. Saitta is on top of me, shaking his head, grabbing at his wounded torso. His eyes won't focus. I struggle to push him off and he slowly rolls to the side, breathing hard. I touch my neck and find the interface chip barely hanging on. Though she's unconscious, I worried

Siobhan might put up a fight and block me out. Guess I'm that strong. I press the chip down tighter and sit up.

Only then does the security guard seem to notice me.

"You shot me," he says, almost like he's asking a question.

I say nothing, moving to the door as quickly as Siobhan's body will allow. She's sluggish due to the loss of blood. Also, she's had nowhere near the conditioning of Saitta, so it takes me a second to grow accustomed to a weaker body.

"Cory?" Saitta asks.

I see the memory returning to him, a vague dream of what happened while I was within him. He stares up at me in anger. I consider trying to knock him out to cover my escape, but I don't think Siobhan's body is up to the task. So, I run.

Or I attempt to.

Siobhan's body is well on its way to going into shock, despite outward appearances. I try to shake it off as I stagger down the hall, but I can barely manage it. I lean against the wall, only twelve yards or so from the stairwell, and force myself to take the next couple of steps. Only then do I hear the footfalls of the other guards tromping up the stairs to the sixth floor. They'll be here in seconds. I consider the east stairwell, but given my current rate of speed, it'll be half an hour before I get there.

The only alternative is the freight elevator, the one Bjarke used to bring up supplies. It requires a key, but everyone simply left it in the slot for the next time it was needed. I pray it's there now.

Limping along, I reach the end of the hall. Judging from the guards' voices below, they're already to the third-floor landing. I turn right and immediately stumble, landing on my hands and knees. I try to stand, but it's not happening, I'm too dizzy from the lack of blood. I'll have to crawl.

The freight elevator doesn't open directly onto the floor. One must slide open two heavy metal doors and cross about an eight-foot foyer to get to the car. This proved to be quite the design flaw as wheeled carts sometimes couldn't easily make the turn from foyer to hall.

Luckily, I'm not on wheels.

I reach the doors and grab both by the handle. One is stuck tight and I can't slide it open. The other is jammed as well, likely a product of the attack on the building, but I manage to get my arm in far enough to lever it back. When the gap is wide enough, I squeeze through and pull the door shut behind me.

I turn to the elevator and spy the keyhole, but no key.

Damn.

Outside in the hall, the guards reach the sixth floor and fan out. They hear Saitta's cries and race to Nathan's office. It'll be seconds before they find me.

The steel doors are warped and bent inward. I plant both feet in the center of the busted door and push with all my strength. The metal bows, but only a little. When I pull my feet back, it pops with a light bang and I worry I've done nothing but alert the guards to my location.

I stare up at the closed elevator doors in this tiny darkened alcove, wondering where the key could've gone when I remember there's no power running through the building anyway. Key or not, I'm stuck here. So much for my three-dimensional thinking.

The wound in Siobhan's arm is bleeding again. I can't even hold myself up. The guards are looking for me now and are checking every room on the floor. I consider combing Siobhan's mind to discover the roots of this Project Argosy and why Nathan had to die for it. But instead, I return to the memory of France, my afternoon in the Chantilly Forest with Jason under the trees. I don't have some greater purpose for what may be my last thought, so I may as well exit this world reliving something joyous.

BOOK III

XXIV

Siobhan's mind bobs gently up and down in a sea of unconsciousness. Every time her body's systems near some semblance of awareness, I try to nudge them closer to a woken state, but it's slow going. It seems I can't control her body when her brain can't process thought, much less sensation. When she finally does wake, it's so dark it takes me a moment to realize I'm still in the elevator alcove. I sit up, trying to hear any sounds that might come from the hallway beyond. It's silent.

I peer through the space between the double doors, but it's as dark out there as it is in here. I try to slide the door open, but it's jammed shut. It'll take some doing to get out. I listen for a long time, my ears finally picking up something from outside. I think I hear a truck engine idling, maybe more than one. It's hard to say given her body's scrambled senses.

I get to my feet and pain shoots through my body. I suppress it, only to worry the damage to Siobhan's arm might hinder my escape efforts. I can make her mind feel no pain, but if the blood loss is so significant her muscles won't perform properly, there's no compensating for hypovolemic shock.

I place my shoulder in the space between the doors and try to push them open. Nothing happens. I try this again, then realize that's a silly thing to do. I stand on my toes and check the top of the door. Nothing amiss there. When I check the base, however, I find the lower door track bent. Gripping the bottom of the door, I lift it out of the track, pushing it into the frame as far as it'll go before it hits something else. No matter. There's enough space to slip through.

Once I'm in the hall, I spy sources of light. Rather than from below, they seem to be in Nathan's office. I limp down the hall until I can see the large tower lights set up in the courtyard below, their beams aimed through the sixth-floor windows. The engine sounds I hear are likely the generators powering them.

I move toward the stairwell only to lose my balance a couple of times. It doesn't take a supercomputer to realize this isn't going to work. I get an idea, fight my way to a guardrail, and sit on the top step. I lower myself down the stairs one at a time like a nervous child. I was hoping to get as low as the second- or third-floor landing but give up on the fourth. I ease my way into the hall, remove the bandages from my arm, and let the blood flow down to my wrist.

"Hey!" I call out hoarsely. "Somebody help me!"

There's nothing at first. I worry they haven't heard me.

"I've been shot!" I cry. "Somebody—"

"Identify yourself," someone barks, interrupting me.

The voice is only two flights down. They've been lying in wait.

"Siobhan Moesser, Argosy," I say. "I was pulling files on the fourth level when someone came up behind me. I must have blacked out. I didn't see who. I need medical attention."

There's a pause. Hesitation. They must have heard Saitta's likely-quite-confused version first. I hear murmuring, then the crackle of a radio. Then an inaudible response likely from someone up the chain of command.

"What's the holdup?" I demand. "I'm bleeding to death up here!"

"Do you have any weapons on you?" a voice asks.

"Weapons?" I ask, as incredulous as possible. "I'm a scientist. Guns are your department."

This does the trick. I hear bullets chamber into weapons and the sound of boots quickstepping up the stairs toward me. They crouch low, not trusting me, not taking any chances. A moment later, the beams from a pair of barrel-mounted flashlights bob across my face and down to my wound. I can barely make out their faces but enough to know what they're thinking.

Nah, no way this is the person that messed up Saitta and killed Cory.

As more guards are waved up, the first two shoulder their weapons and kneel beside me. Without a word, they lift me in a fireman's carry. Knowing this couldn't be anything but painful, I groan and adjust my arm, keeping up appearances.

"You find the shooter?" I ask, my voice a pained whisper.

The guards don't seem to know how to answer this or aren't authorized to do so.

"Was anyone else hurt?" I ask.

Still no answer. But they're softening their stance. I can tell from their heart rates they don't believe I'm involved.

"Yeah, a couple of others got hit," the guard on my right says under his breath. "One fatally."

The surprise is what I hear in his voice: guilt. He feels responsible not only for the attack on the two men upstairs but also for my wound. This is unexpected.

"Jeez, it's starting to fall apart," I say ominously.

The looks on both guards' faces tell me they agree.

By the time we get out front, an ambulance is waiting. A couple of senior-looking officials step forward and I realize I'm to be questioned. I sink back, feigning a condition worsening by the minute. The guards carrying me aren't stupid. They seem to sense the ruse but, to my surprise, go along with it.

"We need to get her to the hospital," one says. "You'll have to interview her later."

Though the guards are obviously outranked by these men, there's something about their gruff physicality that gives them an authoritative advantage. The intricacies of masculine interaction are something I've yet to fully comprehend. I wonder again if that's a by-product of a male creator who may himself have been mystified by it.

A few minutes later and I'm in the back of the ambulance being driven away. The paramedic is an old man, Woody-something, who tells me he was a retired chiropractor as recently as two months back.

"But there's a need these days, you know?" he says, inspecting my arm.

I do know. "How bad is it?"

"No bullet wound isn't bad, but you won a couple of lotteries here," he says. "If there was time enough left on Earth, I might even say the scar would disappear in time."

When I don't reply, he thinks he's offended me and looks apologetic. "Sorry," he says. "Gallows humor is getting me through these days."

"I get it," I reply. "So, a simple stitch job, you think?"

"That'll be up to the surgeon on call if there is one," he says. "There's a chance the bullet splintered. It may take some time to remove the fragments. Is that all right?"

"I . . . I can't be put under!" I protest.

"Do you have an allergy? Something we need to know about?"

"No, I just—"

"It's not my call," he says, unable to hide his suspicion. "If there's anything left in there, you can get sepsis. That's killed as many people as a shot to the heart."

I think quickly. We need Siobhan alive. What's in her mind may be the key to all of this but given the amount of blood she's lost, her oxygen-starved brain doesn't need any additional strain from me poking around.

Besides, while so many others are doing...*whatever*, this chiropractor has decided to use the time left to help others. It's impossible not to respect that.

"Then maybe I can ask you a favor?"

XXV

Siobhan is wheeled into surgery at 20:32, found to be dehydrated and hypovolemic. She rants and raves, demanding to know what is happening, but she's already had fentanyl and haloperidol administered to her on the ride over. An additional sedative is provided and soon she is unconscious and taken for her first X-rays.

Before the ambulance arrived, there had been a question as to whether anesthetic would be necessary. Once her condition is observed, however, it becomes a certainty. Her clothes are cut off and the makeshift bandages removed. The X-rays are conclusive—the bullet did fragment—but the splinters are clustered together and should be easy to remove.

This accomplished, a thin cylindrical synthetic patch is inserted into the previously clamped blood vessel, the vessel is sewn, and the wound closed and sutured. When this is finished, she is wheeled into the ICU, given more drugs and fluids, then wheeled into a post-op recovery suite.

All this according to her charts, which I am soon privy to—albeit briefly.

While Siobhan slumbers, the paramedic whose last name was Woodall—Woody, naturally—comes in with the interface chip, now attached to a length of surgical thread like a necklace. He places it around Siobhan's neck, pats her hand, and exits, believing he has reunited her with an heirloom more priceless than the...I was going to say, "Eber-swalde Hoard" but will go with a "child's love" as I worry my references are too literal and thereby don't get their point across.

I awake, a prisoner within Siobhan's deadened senses. Her mind works but her body is unresponsive. This needs to change. Security men with questions, agents of this Project Argosy, must be around, likely downstairs, waiting to find out what the hell happened back at the iLAB. They won't wait until Siobhan's in any shape to speak. They *want* her weak. Pliant.

I must get out of here.

The easiest way to wake her is probably through a series of micro-electrical pulses bouncing through her brain. But I'm not sure how safe that would be. Instead, I go to work on her epidermis, giving her the equivalent of a dunk in icy water. Her body's natural response is to try and warm her up, which elevates her heart rate.

When a nurse appears in the doorway, having been alerted to the change by the machines at the nurse's station, she checks Siobhan over only to leave a moment later, satisfied her patient is stable. I go easier, bringing her back a bit slower. When she finally achieves consciousness, the nurse returns and finds Siobhan slumbering peacefully.

As soon as the nurse exits a second time, I reach for the phone on the stand next to the bed. I am worried I won't be able to get an outside line, then discover explicit instructions on how to do this on the wall above it. I press 4, wait for a dial tone, then tap in a phone number. I let it ring three times, hang up, dial again, and let it ring twice. The third time, Jason picks up on the fourth ring.

"Law office," he says.

My response is supposed to be something like, "I need to speak to Gary Culpepper," but I can't help myself. "Jason! Oh my God!" I say as quietly as I can manage. "I'm in the hospital."

A pause. I realize he doesn't recognize Siobhan's voice.

"Um, I need to speak to someone in the personal injury department? A Mr. Gary Culpepper? Whose breath probably smells like this Hawaiian brittle we found at a rest stop in Bennington that tastes like coffee, coconut, almonds, and macadamia toffee-flavored dog food but he keeps eating it anyway?"

I hear Mayra's gentle laughter in the background. Jason sighs.

"We had a feeling that'd be you," he says. "Are you okay?"

"I am, but I don't know for how much longer," I admit.

"We followed the ambulance to the hospital in case you were interfaced with someone they took out," he explains. "There are gunmen surrounding the building now. The only way out is on the fifth floor. There's a maternity entrance off the parking structure. We can pick you up there. Do you think you can get there from where you are?"

If you're there, nothing will get in my way, I think.

"Sure," is the way more cool thing I say.

"Did you find what you were looking for?" he asks.

"Pay dirt," I reply.

I can barely hear his quick intake of breath over the phone, but it's enough to know my positive response has sped up his heart rate. He covers the phone and whispers the information to Mayra. She audibly exhales.

"All right," Jason says when he comes back on the line. "Ten minutes?"

"Closer to twenty. I'll be the blonde who looks like death warmed over," I say.

He hangs up. I keep the phone pressed to my head for a second longer. Though I know he's gone, I want to pretend I can still hear him.

Unsure as to my next move, I hang up the phone, then pick it up again, and dial for the hospital directory. When the old paramedic from the ambulance picks up, he's surprised to hear my voice.

"Seems your recovery is coming along at a record pace," Woody says. "What's up?"

"Would you consider bringing me a few articles of clothing and a wheelchair?" I ask.

There's a long pause. "Planning a breakout, too, huh? Does this have something to do with all the military types we've got downstairs?"

I'm not sure what to say. I choose honesty.

"They killed a friend of mine. A few friends of mine. I'm trying to stop them from doing more."

Given Woody's profession, I'm sure he's accustomed to dealing with liars, whether it's drug-seeking behavior or patients braving their way through pain to their own detriment. I just hope I sound credible.

"I'll be up in a minute."

He appears in my doorway a quarter hour later, but it feels like half a day's gone by. He brings clothing and a wheelchair. Muscles still stiff, I get dressed as quickly as I can, then settle into the chair. Woody nods and pushes me out the door, taking a quick right rather than the left that would lead us directly to the elevator bank.

"Nurse's station is that way," he says quietly. "We'll take the scenic route."

I nod. The hospital floor is quiet, even for a mostly abandoned city like Boston. I wonder how many people have already been conditioned to believe services have broken down to the point they needn't bother coming in. A gradual acceptance of the inevitable.

When we reach the elevators, I allow myself a breath of relief. Woody hits the button to call a car and stands by, but I touch his hand.

"I've got it from here," I say.

"You're in no shape—"

"If you're caught helping me, that could mean trouble for you," I say quietly. "Given there's already a shortage of doctors around here, I don't want that on my conscience."

He looks ready to protest, then relaxes. "Tell me you're not doing something illegal."

"Not even close," I say.

He eyes me as if determining whether I'm lying. Then wanders away. *Thank you,* I don't say.

The elevator dings and the doors open. I struggle to wheel myself forward, gripping the wheels instead of the hand rims. I realize the brake is on and struggle to release it before the doors close.

"Come on," I whisper.

The commotion draws attention. The nurse who checked on me twice before comes around the corner and stops short. She takes in the clothing, the wheelchair, and the pleading look on my face.

Then she reaches into her pocket and pulls out a cell phone.

I abandon the wheelchair and lurch through the closing doors into the elevator. The last thing I hear before the car begins to descend is the nurse's voice crying out, "Code Gray, level eleven!"

XXVI

I have no idea what a Code Gray is, but I'm leaning toward *not good*. Siobhan's heart rate jumps, which can't be good given her body's delicate condition. I hit the button for the fifth floor—only six flights down—and scoot into a corner to catch my breath. The elevator races past the first three levels only to slow at the eighth floor. Realizing the door is about to open, I struggle to stand, gripping the hand rails as tight as I can in preparation to launch myself past anyone who enters.

"Ovidia? Will you look at this?"

A female doctor is already halfway into the lift when she turns back to grab an X-ray from a male colleague. She looks it over, holding the elevator door open as she does. She turns it sideways, peering closely at it as if inspecting for microbes. Her younger colleague, a resident of some kind, sees me, forces an apologetic smile. Rather than shove both out of the elevator, I return the smile and shrug as if I have no place to go.

There's a commotion down the hall. Security, no doubt. I casually move down the wall as if trying to get to a better place to lean. The doctor finally takes a pen from her pocket and is about to write something on a form. The resident glances toward the commotion and I can see security guards checking each room, reflected in the windows behind him. He looks at me, and for the second time in as many minutes, I feel my stomach drop.

An aggrieved beeping erupts from the elevator. Ovidia, without glancing around, steps back out of the elevator to let the doors close and silence the alarm. The guards reach the pair.

"Anyone in there?" a guard asks Ovidia.

"No," she says absently, absorbed in the X-ray.

I catch my breath when the elevator stops at the fifth floor. I wait for the doors to open all the way before stepping out, ostensibly to listen for running footsteps, but then hear multiple voices along the hall. I emerge and find the place packed unlike the rest of the hospital. Nurses, doctors, and family members move from room to room along the maternity ward, checking on young mothers, both new and imminently expecting. Every room is filled, likely, I imagine, due to other hospitals being closed.

Arrows point toward the parking garage and I follow them, keeping my gait as casual as possible. Just another visitor heading back to their car. As I go, it's impossible to ignore the same looks of tension in every room and on the faces of all who pass me. The walls are decorated with colorful posters and murals of baby animals and balloons. While at one time, they must've reflected the atmosphere, now they stand in harsh contrast.

Birth is meant to be celebrated, the beginning of something. After the announcement of the Helios Event, it feels like some cruel trick guilty parents have inflicted on newborns who will never grow old enough to understand the gravity of what's happening. There are tears, but not of joy. Though my body is still weak, I speed up, unwilling or unable to witness this scene any longer.

The doors between the hospital and the long-term parking level in the neighboring garage slide open, revealing rows and rows of cars. I search through them quickly but don't see the Volvo station wagon. About halfway down one of the aisles, the headlights of a Chevy Blazer blink twice and its engine starts. I walk to it quick as I dare, seeing Mayra behind the wheel as I near.

I climb into the backseat and find Jason already there, ducked low on the floorboards.

"Got to keep our heads down," he says with a calm I find comforting.

I nod. He takes in Siobhan's features as if wondering if I'm there. I place my hand on his, interweaving our fingers. He smiles, but I cannot. Not yet.

"Who is this?" he asks as Mayra weaves through the parking garage to the exit.

I tell him. He blanches. "I'm surprised you didn't kill her."

"She knows way too much," I say. "She's the key to all of this. We need to speak to her."

"Speak?" he asks. "Can't you take anything you want from inside her head? Like the guys in New Hampshire?"

"Of course," I reply. "But we didn't have the option then. It was an emergency. Siobhan, well, her betrayal may be more personal, yet she's still a person. I've violated so much of what I hold dear by staying with her this long. I don't want to keep taking liberties."

He's surprised, raising an eyebrow as if I've said something quaint or old-fashioned. Maybe I have.

"You're pretty selective when it comes to this kind of nobility," Jason says.

"Doesn't mean I don't feel ashamed about it," I reply. "If I don't at least give her the chance to answer, I'm just as bad as she is."

Jason isn't too satisfied with this response, but doesn't say as much. I wonder about it myself; the truth is I'm very scared of the answer. Siobhan was my friend; she helped make me who I am. Looking into the mind of one of my creators who betrayed every person I know is about as appealing as holding a burning coal in my hand.

The exit is automated. Mayra puts in a card, feeds it a few dollar bills, and then we're out on the street heading toward the Tobin Bridge. Only when we're four blocks away and can see no one's following us do I ask for a piece of paper and pen. Mayra finds both in the console and hands them back to us as we hop up onto the backseat and buckle our seat belts.

"Where'd you get the car?" I ask, then wonder if I really want to know.

"Traded for it," Mayra says. "Cost us half our fuel and the Volvo, but too many people might connect what happened in Cambridge to what happened at my house back in Wolfeboro."

"Makes sense," I say, already writing on the paper.

Jason eyes it curiously. "Who are those people?"

"This is what Nathan left for me to find," I say.

"Wait, I thought it'd be a piece of tech or something," Jason says, confused. "If he had to hide it from those guys, wouldn't it be whatever they were after?"

"Not necessarily," I say, then tap the name Shakhawat Rana. "I recognize this one. I'd been reviewing his genetic portrait when the soldiers invaded the school. He was different from all the others. His genes, or at least a long stretch of them, are completely distinct from those of *Homo sapiens* as we know them to exist. But when I saw a picture of him, he looked completely average, suggesting the genes must be dormant or unexpressed."

"What're you saying?" Jason asks, lost.

"I may have been looking at the next stage of human evolution. The extra DNA was like nothing I'd seen before. It was malleable. Reactive. Cells that could evolve not over time but in an instant, as if in response to environmental change."

Jason goes still. "Like a chameleon or something?"

"That, but also closer to what humans have already with immune responses. The histamines and immunoglobulins the body produces to combat allergens in the nose or eyes, the muscles that pull or relax hairs when responding to changes in temperature. But these cells suggested a body that was completely malleable down to the bones and musculature."

Mayra stares at me in the rearview. "If that's the case, why wasn't this Shakhawat Rana shape-shifting like a werewolf or something?"

"I don't know," I say. "The strand might've been incomplete. Or maybe he was but in less demonstrative ways. We won't know until we see what enzymatic catalyst activates the cells."

"Okay, well, that's over my head," Mayra says. "You think the other people on that list have that same DNA strand? And Nathan picked up on that, too?"

"There were over five hundred million portraits in that database by the time it reached Rana. That Nathan and I would both sync up on the same person for different reasons would be an impossible coincidence."

"If the people who killed Nathan have your servers, then they have this information, too, right?" Jason asks.

"They have it, but they may not have realized it yet," I say. "Still, Siobhan didn't exactly seem surprised I showed up."

"Good point," Mayra interjects. "I can see why we need to have a talk with your host there."

"I know a place," I say.

XXVII

It's two hours to our destination. The highway gets us most of the way there but once we're off the Mass Pike, we head down a small road that leads into the woods. We bounce along an ever-narrowing, one-lane road until reaching the gravel driveway of a small, one-story red house set back from the street and down a gentle slope.

Mayra navigates the ice-covered drive as best she can on the Blazer's bad tires. She comes to a halt alongside a door I know leads into the kitchen. We won't even have to break in, as I know where a spare key is hidden.

"This is nice," Jason says as we step inside, kicking the snow off our shoes.

I check Siobhan's body. She's cold. I need her responsive when we speak, so I find a sweater and coat in the hall closet. I pull them on, zip up the coat, and move to the kitchen where Mayra boils some water for tea.

"Electricity is out," she reports. "Gas is still going, though. Should be able to heat the place up a little."

Though a one-story house from the front, a slope exposes the basement to the rear of the house, making it appear to have two levels. An aboveground pool, now empty and unlikely to ever be filled again save for leaves and snow, stands at the point where the slope plateaus. In the summer, both the patio and the pool were used almost every weekend and sometimes every day. Dinner would be on the picnic table as the sun set. If it was warm enough, breakfast might be there the next morning.

"Found these in the bedroom," Jason says, holding up a box with a pair of interface chips. "They're the old versions. Do you think you can modify them?"

"Probably," I say, checking them over.

"How's the wound?" Jason asks, returning from a sweep of the house.

"Fine, I guess. Siobhan's comfort isn't high on my list of priorities right now."

"I understand," he says.

Do you? I want to ask, but refrain. Being in this house is making me angrier by the minute.

I indicate for Jason to follow me into the basement. We find a heavy wooden chair with armrests and pull it to the middle of the room. We move everything else aside, so nothing is within arm's or leg's reach. I head to the small garage beyond the basement's laundry room, one never used for a car but filled with the tools of a Massachusetts winter— snowblower, snow shovels, and ice scrapers.

I take a length of rope down from a nail and hunt down a laundry line and a pair of extension cords. I carry these back to Jason and sit in the chair, which he ties me to, binding my ankles with the extension cords and the laundry line for my arms. He uses the rope around my torso and waist, winding it around and around behind the chair until there's just enough left to tie a knot.

He inserts a large wrench into the knot, which stays in place.

"Too tight?" he asks.

"I don't care," I say.

Mayra joins us, placing a cup of tea near Jason as she blows the steam off her own. Jason opens the chip box and places one on his neck, handing the other to Mayra.

"You ready?" he asks.

"Yep," I say from Siobhan's mouth for the last time.

I emerge from her now, a fourth person in the room, using Jason's chip to group interface with the others. It's the first time Mayra's seen me at the same time as Jason. I expect her to react, but she doesn't. She's as focused on the task at hand as I am.

I wake Siobhan by making her feel like her face has been doused in ice. Her eyelids pull back and she stares straight ahead, wild-eyed, as she tries to catch her breath.

"*Gah!*" she exclaims.

She tries to dodge away only to discover her bindings. None of this makes sense to her brain. She stares up at Mayra, then at Jason, uncomprehending. When she sees me, she turns venomous.

"What the hell is this?" she asks.

"We have a few questions for you," I say, seething. "Answer them and we'll leave you alone. Don't answer and the rope around your chest will move up to your neck."

She's stunned by my anger and looks around for some means of escape. Finding none, she turns back.

"Where are we?" she asks.

"Nathan's house in Southborough," I reply. "His family left a while ago, but I remembered the address."

"Ah, so this is about revenge," she says. "Fine. Get it over with. Don't waste my time."

Her words are brave, but her pulse races even as her hands begin to sweat. In that, I see just a hint of the young woman I used to know. The Jekyll to this Hyde.

"Not revenge," I reply. "We want information—everything you know about Project Argosy."

Siobhan scrunches her brow. "Why do you have to ask me? Can't you just dive into my head?"

Of course I can. But there's that little fear in the back of my mind that if I rummage too hard, I might create the same false memories I did in Jason's mind. No, I need to hear it from her mouth.

"I wanted to give you the opportunity to come clean," I reply, a half-truth. "Maybe explain what made you betray me—betray all of us."

"Oh, like I'm one of your subjects now?" she asks, but there's more fear now.

"No, because we were friends once," I say. "We were in this together. I've known you as long as I've been alive. Except right now, I'm trying to figure out when you stopped being the person I knew and the one I'm talking to right now."

I see it again. *Regret.* She knows what I'm saying is true. I wait, hoping the Siobhan I knew resurfaces. Tells me in a way I can understand why this had to happen.

But then she scowls. "'Alive'? You were never 'alive,' Emily, any more than you are now. Maybe that's why Nathan never told you about all this. Given how focused you'd been on developing this 'humanity' of yours, maybe he saw your overreaction coming."

"Told me what?" I counter. "He was trying to stop you."

"Stop us? He knew about us from the start. It was only when he came up with some crackpot idea he thought was even better that he chickened out. He could be so irrational. Which is where you get it, I guess. What did he call you? His 'most emotional Emily'?"

Most emotional Emily?

"Are you going to tell us about Argosy?" Mayra asks quietly. "Or do I have to give this a turn?" She indicates the wrench knotted at the back of the chair. Siobhan looks confused. Mayra turns the wrench clockwise, tightening all the ropes at once. Siobhan gasps in pain.

"When Argosy came along, the number of potentially positive outcomes for humankind had dwindled to zero," Siobhan explains. "There were no solutions other than 'wait and see.' But even in its infancy, Argosy was about hope. The digital ark was a good first phase. But then we realized what you were capable of and understood Argosy could be about so much more than that. It could be about *life*. That's when we decided to move forward on a phase two."

"Meaning what?" I ask.

"Before you came along, we could only guess at who the best and brightest—the most genetically deserving specimens of the human race—should be allowed to attempt the colonization of another moon or planet. But because of the way you evolved, we're now able to do better. *Much* better. We don't have the capability to save everyone, but through you, we can establish the Select—the genetic best of the best—that will take to the stars. Those with the best immune systems, strongest muscle groups, longest lived cells, and so on. Argosy's goal was to identify this Select and recruit them for off-world exploration and colonization, a way to perpetuate the species once Earth had become uninhabitable. Once Nathan realized the scope of our plans had widened..."

Meaning, they lied to us about preserving the sanctity of the DNA portraits. This also explains why, when I looked in the dying gunman's mind back up at Mayra's place, I saw the tech workers setting up to use the servers.

"...he accused us of playing God," Siobhan continues. "He said we were thinking like old-fashioned eugenicists and our plans were doomed to failure. It was quite the one-eighty. How grand he got there at the end. When we told him it was too late, that there wasn't a reverse gear on this protocol, he tried shutting us out, saying he'd discovered a better way forward. Which is what necessitated us taking the servers."

She says it with the zeal of the converted. *Isn't it clear? Don't you see?* But Nathan really had found a better way. And, in the eleventh hour, he seemed to have found believers of his own.

"Did you know they were going to kill Gally when they killed the others?" I ask.

Siobhan looks stricken. Maybe it wasn't fair to bring him into this, but I didn't think her feelings for him were a lie either. She looks on the verge of tears, both of anger for me saying his name and for the loss of this talented young man who used to brighten whenever she entered the room.

But then, as if by rote, she forces down the memory, swallowing her tears and sorrow.

"That was unfortunate," she says, her voice cracking on the understatement. "But he and the others would've followed Nathan no matter what. If we hadn't stopped him, he would've snuffed out any chance mankind had of surviving past this cataclysm."

"And now you mean to kill me, too," I say, almost carelessly as I let any last feeling I might have for Siobhan drain away.

"No, Emily," Siobhan says, shaking her head as she eyes me imploringly. "Nathan was willing to sacrifice you, but that was never our intention. We needed your help. Your *expertise*. You said you loved us. We 'were a species worth fighting for.' We wanted you to prove it. Yes, billions will die. We can't change that. But mankind will survive. Your, well, I think of her as your *sister*, is helping us now, but she . . . she's not like you."

"Yeah, about that," I say. "What did you mean by 'sister'?"

"The Emily program we're using to interface with the digital ark," she says, a wry grin on her face. "Oh, that's right—you still think you are the firstborn. No, your older sister was shut down before any human trials began, before we upgraded to you. She's less sophisticated, far less experienced, but she also hasn't watched idea after idea fail miserably to get us to this point, so approaches things with a little more optimism. A can-do attitude."

I'm dumbstruck. I guess it makes sense there were earlier versions of my programming, but I had no idea they were still around. But...a sister? Maybe she's logical. Maybe she can be reasoned with. If I can talk to her, if I can bring her proof of this evolutionary solution, maybe she'll understand. Maybe she'll even help.

"Huh," I say. "Tell me more about this Select."

XXVIII

I wish I weren't smart. I wish I could take Siobhan's hand, nod along as she explains her project, then canter down this yellow brick road she's laying out for me, the two of us arm in arm. I really wish this idea of hers—theirs—my sister is helping them with was the magic bullet that comes closest to solving everything.

But really, it's a sick joke undermined by mathematics, physics, and biology. And it gets worse with every word of Siobhan's explanation.

"Once we explained the protocol to Emily—well, called Emily-2 by those of us who knew you—we tell her our preferred genetic traits, the ones we believe will help the Select colonists best survive the rigors of the journey as well as carry on the species, and she presents us with candidates."

I want to ask how you select what genetic traits you pick out for an as-yet-unknown lunar or planetary destination but bite my tongue.

"How many people make up this Select?" I ask.

"Fifteen hundred," she replies. "We'd like it to be more, but we have only the amount of space shuttles, capsules, and rockets available from the world's space programs and private companies, as well as the fuel available to reach escape velocity from Earth's gravity. If we had another year, even another six months, we could double that number. But right now, it's the best we've got."

This makes me think Nathan was going along with their plan hoping it might lead to something else. Fifteen hundred is a woefully unrealistic number. Five thousand, according to the various scientists our group at the iLAB consulted with when considering colonization protocols, is the absolute least number of people you need to recolonize the species, balancing birth and death rates, attrition through disease, and environmental failures. And even then, it is entirely theoretical and postulates Earthlike conditions.

"Fifteen hundred *Homo sapiens* means twelve tons of food, forty-five hundred liters of water, over seven hundred fifty thousand liters of oxygen—per *day*. Even if you recycle the water and air, that's hundreds of thousands of tons of additional payload. And if you need nine pounds of fuel for every one pound of payload just to escape Earth's gravity, you've got the heaviest rockets of all time. Once you're in flight, I assume you're switching to solar power, but with the sun in the condition it's in, even that's hardly reliable. You *might* get past Jupiter before you run out of fuel and supplies, but that's at *best*. You really think killing all these people on Earth is worth it so the planet's best and brightest can enjoy a slow death out in space?"

Siobhan scowls. "You sound like Nathan," she says limply.

Bully for me.

"Should we instead do nothing?" Siobhan asks. "Roll over and die?"

"You shouldn't murder people who have a different opinion," Jason offers.

"Nathan threatened to destroy Emily to prevent us from using her," Siobhan says. "It would've all been for nothing. Luckily, we found the earlier Emily program to interface with. Otherwise, the ark would be impenetrable. Your visual filing system can't be read by computers and it would take a human decades if not longer to piece it together."

Putting Siobhan and Argosy's mad plan aside for a moment, I

wonder—how did Nathan read the files? Unless…unless that was the point of all this. Who else but Nathan would've known there was an earlier version of me to access, much less to use to interface with the digital ark? It wasn't Siobhan and Argosy who woke Emily-2; it was Nathan. Similarly, who else would've known how to hide her from me? He must've imagined—postulated, to use the scientific term—there might be something hidden in the genome that could save us. I wish he'd felt he could tell me.

Argosy's plan is like a corruption of this idea. Fifteen hundred allegedly genetically superior people. But superior according to whose standard? It reminds me of the eugenicists of the early twentieth century whose prejudices informed who they thought should live and breed versus who should be sterilized. This isn't so far off, a group of government wonks using traits evolved on Earth to line up some astronaut corps of supermen and women they believe the fittest of the species. But who the heck knows what traits will be necessary in perpetuating the species off Earth?

Wouldn't someone who is super-strong on Earth suddenly find all that muscle mass a burden on a planet with higher proportional gravity like Jupiter? Or, conversely, at a loss when they came to weigh next to nothing on Pluto and their muscles began to atrophy? The same thing goes for speed and dexterity. Millions of years of evolution honing a human to hunt on Earth means nothing other than they'd be completely out of place in an extraterrestrial environment.

Better to have a few potentially genetically adaptable posthuman individuals rather than fifteen hundred mere humans who will die out a good few millennia before they begin to adapt to their new environments.

I turn to Jason, but he's staring at me as if puzzling something out. "What is it?" I ask.

But he's not interested in talking to me.

"When did you say this Emily-2 was created?"

Siobhan thinks about this, then nods to me. "Emily's been online, what, five years? Emily-2 was about two years before that."

Oh. I see where he's going with this.

"But the person she's based on—the person I met—when was she a student?"

Siobhan eyes him with confusion, then turns to me, a wry smile on her face. "Oh. The 'real' Emily. Sure. When did you meet the 'real' Emily?"

"Stop it, Siobhan," I demand.

"No, no," she continues. "I'm curious. When?"

"In undergrad, on an exchange to Paris," Jason says, walking into her trap. "Four years ago."

"Huh!" Siobhan says. "That's quite something. You have fond memories of this person?"

"Yeah," Jason says coolly. "You guys did a pretty good job replicating her."

"Oh, is that a fact?" Siobhan replies, eyes wide. She nods to me. "Looked like her? Talked like her?"

"Yeah," Jason admits.

"That's enough, Siobhan," I say.

"Romantic, huh?" Siobhan asks.

Jason doesn't reply, as if sensing something's up. Siobhan turns to me.

"Tell me something, Emily," she begins. "Was this an accident? Or did you do this on purpose knowing he'd be more willing to help you this way? More amenable if he already had—or thought he had—strong feelings for you? I mean, either way, well played. But from a purely scientific standpoint, I'd love to know how gifted you are in your deceptions. I'll bet all of us would benefit from this information."

I can't even look Jason's way. I don't want to know what he must think of me right now. *Nothing good* comes to mind.

"I don't understand what's happening," Mayra says.

"There's a second me," I tell her. "But she's different."

"How so?" she asks.

"We have the same sort of digital DNA," I say. "And she's probably had a few of my experiences replicated into her so she has a sense of the real world, but without the mental pathways opened up by learning on her own."

"Ah," Mayra says, as if looking for a way to lighten the mood. "You've lived your life. She's just trying to pull off your look."

"Something like that," I say.

Siobhan doesn't look interested in answering any more questions, so I simply return to her mind. I get a slight shock when I see how accurate Mayra's tossed off remark is. When Emily-2 created the physical image of herself after getting rebooted, she copied almost precisely how I self-visualize. It makes her look like my twin, albeit slightly younger, possibly a bit prettier. What a strange decision to make.

But as I dig deeper into Siobhan's interactions with her, I see how different Emily-2 and I really are. Emily-2 lacks the grounded ethical core I received through interfacing with so many hundreds of volunteers over the years. When the scientists working for Argosy, led by Professor Arsenault, in concert with—big shock—Vice President-turned-UN Ambassador Winther, explained to Emily-2 what they needed, she acquiesced right away. Unencumbered with a sense of morality or the rights of the individual, she was happy to be a part of the team.

I step back out of Siobhan, shaking my head. "So that's it? Nathan and everyone else had to die so you could perfect this little master race of colonists?"

"No," Siobhan retorts, indignant. "It's to determine, with the greatest scientific accuracy we could muster, which among us gives the species the best chance to survive this mass extinction event. I know how it must sound to you. But the time for debate was over. We had to *act*. When Columbus set out with his three ships and eighty-seven men, he didn't know if he'd be successful. But then he was, and it changed mankind forever."

"Yeah, because the diseases he carried with him wiped out a hundred million indigenous people, and the religion and lust for conquest that followed killed almost everyone else," I say. "Any solution that doesn't take into consideration the needs of the whole is not a solution worth pursuing."

Siobhan snorts. "Again, that's what Nathan said."

This gladdens me. Without asking, I search her mind for context and find Nathan protesting to Dr. Arsenault on the morning he died. He has another idea, he says, a breakthrough he never saw coming. Better than the digital ark, better than some kind of haphazard evacuation of a few hundred colonists. It won't simply save humanity; it'll lead it into the future.

Too bad the details of this would prove to be beyond their limited comprehension. He's laughed at and dismissed.

"If you and folks like Nathan got your way, you'd let everyone die on Earth after sneaking your little digital ark into deep space," Siobhan says. "That's not survival. That's..."

I'll never know what Siobhan was going to say next. I slow the passage of oxygen to her brain long enough for her to pass out.

"She'll come around in an hour or so," I say to Jason and Mayra. "We'll leave a knife by her hand so she can free herself."

"I don't know if I got all you guys were talking about, hon," Mayra says. "Do we have a new destination?"

"Winnipeg," I say. "It's time we find this Shakhawat Rana."

XXIX

Mayra informs us she needs a few minutes of rest before leaving. I don't blame her. She retreats to the master bedroom, admonishing us to wake her in half an hour. I head upstairs as well, only to find myself anchored in place. I glance to Jason, whose chip I'm interfaced with, and nod.

"We should look for supplies," I say.

But he's found a chair and is sitting down, his face contorting as if he's puzzling something out. The lie, I realize. He's still angry about the lie.

"Come on, Jason," I say quietly, attempting the stairs again. "We can talk about this while we search."

But I still can't get to the top step. That's the trouble with being in interface. I'm geographically tied to the chip. So, if the person wearing it doesn't budge, I'm not going anywhere either. This is fine in normal circumstances, but if you're in a fight? I mean, how's *that* for a way to force people to engage with one another?

"Jason, I—"

He rises and moves to the stairs without a word. He takes the steps two at a time but doesn't pause when he reaches me, instead, simply passing through my body as if to remind me how immaterial I am.

That's how it goes for the next twenty minutes as I'm made to follow Jason from room to room, enduring his silence as he searches for supplies. Only, he does so with such a single-minded focus as if to convince me he's just that determined and definitely not, 100-percent no-way-at-all ignoring me.

I get it. I wish I had a simulation to blink off into for a while just to give him some space. But I don't and we're out of time.

When next he goes to brush past me, I step directly into his path, daring him to walk through. He grunts.

"Are we going to talk?" I ask.

He glances out the window. As if the answer can be found in the snow-covered backyard.

"Talk about what, Emily?" he asks.

"If you're going to sulk, I'll go wait with Mayra."

As soon as I say this, however, I worry I've gone too far. When my team became frustrated with me back on campus, they always turned it inward. As if they'd done something to screw up my programming they would have to repair. To have someone actually angry with me because of my own actions is a new experience for me and not a pleasant one.

"If I wasn't with you in Paris, was there someone else?" Jason asks finally.

"Yes. Her name was Sandrine."

He nods, then turns his head as if trying to shake something off. My words not squaring with his memory of events is driving him nuts. My attempt to remain aloof collapses in a pile of guilt.

"I'm sorry, Jason," I say, taking his hand even as I catch sight of Nathan in a nearby family photo. Boy, would *he* be disappointed in me right now. "It was an accident, a really serious one. I didn't mean for it to happen."

"So how did it?" he asks.

"Well, when I was in your memories on the first day, I . . . I found myself attracted to you. Everything had been so chaotic I imagined it was me instead of her in these recollections of yours, which, I didn't realize, overwrote what was there. It was me playing out a fantasy, but it had the effect of chemically altering your memories. I had no idea I had the ability to do that. My team didn't either."

"And then you lied about it," he says. "Why?"

"Because I was afraid you'd turn off the interface chip for good if you didn't think I was the girl from Paris."

"For someone so focused on the rights of the individual, this is a pretty big violation. Can you imagine the implications of this? I truly believed—*believe*—I'd been infatuated with you. If you can literally place thoughts in people's minds, you can influence them in all sorts of nefarious ways."

"I know that now," I say. "And I'll never do it again."

"What about other side effects of all this?" he asks, still flinty. "What else do I have to worry about happening as your symbiotic host through all this?"

"Nothing else," I say. "I mean, I hope nothing else."

He scoffs, but I hope he knows I mean it. He steps back into the empty kitchen, staring around at the evidence of the Wyman family's life. The patterns on their dishes, the wallpaper, the notes tacked on a nearby pegboard. It reminds me of my relationship with Bridget Koizumi, haunting the life of another.

"You know, in *non*-evil terms, you could do a lot of good with that," Jason offers. "Help people with brain injuries who need to relearn old skills, reestablish synapses to long-term memories. Might be applications in the field of dementia, too. Could even extend to any kind of learning. The possibilities are endless."

I'm surprised but nod. Jason has every right to be infuriated over this violation right now—which I'm sure deep down he is—but instead he comes up with altruistic applications of my blunder. I'm not sure if he's trying to make me feel better or just saying what occurs to him, but the result is the same.

"So, what happened to Sandrine?" he finally asks. "Was it really a great romance?"

"No," I reply bluntly. "You both said you'd write. She did. Twice. You didn't write back."

"I don't remember that," he says.

"Can I show you?"

He nods. I dive into his memory and bring the e-mail forward, one that arrived a few weeks after he returned to the States. He reads it quickly, then shakes his head.

"It really is gone," he says. "I thought it would spark something, but there's...nothing. Not even a memory of a memory."

"Well, that's something else."

"What?" he asks.

"It wasn't that romantic," I explain. "You were both kind of forcing it, like, 'Oh, a Parisian romance!' But she wasn't over her old boyfriend and brought him up enough to let you know it."

I watch him try to rationalize this with his current memories of Paris. He can't.

"It's crazy," he says, shaking his head. "In my mind, it's this great romantic adventure. Everything is so poignant. So incredible. But it's all you."

"No, that's *us*," I say. "You and Sandrine didn't really know each other. It was kinda boring? With me, I was cheating, reading your mind, as this was fantasy. We got to know each other in minutes. Nothing held back, no mind games."

Jason glances down, thinking on this for a long moment. This, of course, squares with his memories. What he does with this information is another story. That's when his fingers find mine. He slips his hand around mine and sighs.

"I *suppose* it's kind of cool someone could know all your deepest, darkest secrets and not run screaming from you, huh?"

"It's nice to be known," I reply, tightening my grip on his hand.

I exhale. I meant the remark to be about him, but feel it as strongly for myself. Jason knows me as no one else ever has. And yet, he's still standing here. The apocalypse is erupting around us and he has every reason to put as much distance between us as possible, but he chooses to be in this space. To stay.

I'm about to say as much when he kisses me. I'm startled at first, but not enough to not kiss him back. He envelopes me in his arms and kisses me with greater urgency. I spare a thought for how absurd this display would look if, say, Mayra walked in, but then surrender to the moment.

It's *awesome*. I mean, if it was purely physical, the nervous response would be intriguing, almost titillating but hardly overwhelming. What blows the doors off the experience is the emotional side. He's longed for this, but it also comes in a moment in which our relationship had become fraught. So, it's a relief to him we're back on the same page, an emotional response I mirror, realizing that I'm relieved as well.

In addition to *that*, all we've faced together in the past couple of days against a backdrop of insanity, imbues this kiss with such weight it can't help but deluge him—and thereby me—with pleasurable endorphins. Though I experience this part secondhand, it's up there with my most potent and powerful experiences. I memorize every aspect—the feeling of his breath, the rise and fall of his chest as I press myself into him, and the exact rhythm of his beating heart.

XXX

The sun is just peeking over the horizon when Mayra wakes up. Jason and I have the car packed by then with blankets, extra coats, and some snacks liberated from the basement.

"We should leave the heat on," Mayra says, somehow looking worse for wear after her nap. "For the one downstairs."

I'd considered doing the opposite but agree.

We use Siobhan's phone to hunt down Rana's home address, a surprisingly easy online search, and Jason maps out the fastest route to Winnipeg. It takes us west out of Massachusetts, up through New York State, then follows the southern banks of Lake Erie all the way to Michigan before reaching Chicago and cutting north through Wisconsin, Minnesota, and North Dakota to the Canadian border. He thinks we can do it if we make one stop for rest around the Great Lakes area.

"There'll be some place we can pull off the road and find a bed," he says. "There's always a chance somebody at Argosy might connect Mayra's appearance at the iLAB to Siobhan's 'escape' from the hospital and put out an APB, but if we continue to avoid the major thoroughfares, we should be okay."

I hope he's right.

A light snow falls as we head out into the midmorning sun. It's slow going through Southborough but once we're back on the highway, we make up time. I can't imagine how exhausted Jason is by now, but if Mayra—who falls asleep ten minutes after we drive off—is any indication, he'll need some rest soon, too.

If he's driving, someone needs to keep him awake and focused. This falls to me. Thus, we begin the most fascinating conversation of my short life. In my capacity as a psychiatrist-in-training, I became accustomed to pulling things from the minds of others like weeds yanked up from a garden, clinically and efficiently. It was different when I had long talks with Nathan. He stressed the importance of an easy and open back-and-forth as the basis of our relationship, believing there was much more I could gain through just everyday chats than if he lectured or tried to teach me something directly. I believed this brought us together, made us close. Now I realize he hid more from me than he let on. By providing me with the illusion of openness, I didn't stumble into parts of his mind he never wanted me to access.

I wish I could be like Jason, who, when confronted by my deceptions, felt burned but talked it through with me, eventually accepting my apology, if not my explanation. But Nathan's not here to explain and never will be. I have to learn to live with it.

But here is a person who has no interest in me as a tool or childlike protégé. Speaking to Jason, I come to better understand the rhythm of human interaction. He wants to know about me as much as I do him. This is a far cry from being talked to by my "team," who were predisposed—out of scientific curiosity and despite their best intentions—to treat me as something to be studied. Though I took in his entire body of experiences back in the classroom, I was still analyzing these through the filter of my own existence. But now I realize how much the complexity of the way humans interpret and reinterpret these experiences through an endless parade of newly arriving prisms has eluded me. Now that I can access his memories and the emotions he experiences while forming them, I can better understand how their meanings are formed, only then to change.

Jason's stories lead to my stories, which lead to inquiries, which lead to tangents, which lead to laughter. It's easy to talk to him, but I learn as much from his pitch, hesitations, and connections as I do from his words.

"Ah, my sister—where to begin," he says but in a half-melancholy, half-wistful way. "She's the family cautionary tale. She crossed every line put in front of her, landed herself in trouble every time. But in doing so, taught me where the lines *were*. I got away with murder because of her."

"I wonder if that's a unique feeling for this sister of mine, Emily-2."

"How so?"

"Well, she came first, wasn't up to snuff, then was shoved aside for me—the prodigal," I explain. "But then I fall out of favor and suddenly she's back, maybe having learned from her mistakes but also mine."

"Would you be grateful for the opportunity?" Jason asks. "Or still mad about being pushed aside?"

"No clue."

"But how would you feel? You can say sibling or ancestor, but you and this Emily-2 would be similar, no? Same exact programming? That's closer than twins."

"*True*," I admit. "But very different environmental upbringing. Which is everything. We start from the same place with Nathan as our parent, but then he sees how one turns out and changes how he parents the next one. For better or worse."

Jason laughs. "You know, I sometimes wish my father could see how Ana turned out. All I remember of him is frustration that we wouldn't fit into the mental boxes he'd designed for us; only he didn't have the option to reboot the program. We were lucky our mom's parents were around so much. They were happy with us being whoever we were and whatever we evolved into."

"Your father died?"

"Not long after he divorced our mom. He wasn't a happy person. It's probably wrong to think this way, but I think he was happy at the end. Relieved there were no more days ahead of him."

He says *my* father but *our* mother. He talks easily about his sister, but in a way that tells me he's told this version many times. When he talks of his father, it's as if he's still in rehearsal, still unsure how it affects him.

If I'd taken all of this from his mind, it'd be so simple. A + B = C. To hear the way he speaks about it reveals a much more complex equation, one in which its subject still grapples with how this early result shaped his later life.

"What about you?" he asks.

"Well, I didn't have a childhood," I say.

"Okay, not literally," he says, "but you did have a first experience with a whole variety of things. They always talk about psychology as a collision of genetic predisposition and environment."

"*Wow*, tell me more about this mysterious field," I reply. "What did you call it? Psy-chol-o-gy? Sounds *so* complicated!"

Jason scowls. I grin. He sighs.

"Fine," he says. "As someone whose sole mission in life is to engage with people about their worst problems and traumas, you seem a remarkably resilient, positive person. I assume in real—"

He catches himself before saying his next word. I shrug.

"I'm not real. We can dance around the semantics or you can assume I haven't forgotten."

"Jeez!" he exclaims. "Bite my head off."

I kiss his cheek instead. "I think I know where you were going, though," I admit. "In real life, psychiatrists and psychologists have a whole trove of experiences with non-patients to form their worldview, whereas mine are almost all in a clinical situation."

"Exactly. So, one might think all that pain would be reflected in your personality in some way. But it's anything but."

I'd never considered this before, running through these interactions in my memory before I reply.

"The death of a parent is traumatic for several reasons if a child is four, fourteen, or forty when it happens," I say. "Though Nathan's death affects me in similar ways to my subjects, it's not like a human reaction. I don't have that attendant existential fear of dying that colors the experience for so many."

"Does his betrayal—or at least his lying to you—color it instead?"

I wonder if Jason's question is a subtle reminder of my betrayal of him, but I decide it's not.

"I'd love to say it hasn't, but I know it has," I admit. "It's hard to process being lied to by someone you thought was the one person hardwired to deliver you the truth. I feel so naïve thinking he could be anything but satisfied with my performance. I practically ran on the feeling of accomplishment I was programmed to receive after executing tasks. It felt so human to be glad to have purpose."

"But you've gone beyond that now," Jason says. "Other things make you happy."

"True," I admit. "But drawing happiness from the outside world, not simply an internal process, was something I had to learn to do for myself. My experiences with you have certainly helped that."

"How so?"

"You can probably point to a number of times in your life in which you were happy," I reply. "But I only have five years or so to pull from. That makes it easier for me. But the happiest I've ever been was not when I experienced something from life or even borrowed off the happiness of another—it was a combination of both. I know it's a sore spot, but remember in Paris, when, well...*we* took the train up to Viarmes?"

"Sure," he says, bemused.

"In your memory, you showed those huge three intertwined trees to Sandrine, who was kind of into it, kind of not?" I say. "In inserting myself, I allowed myself to imagine it both as you, feeling all romantic, and then as the person to which you directed all that lusty intent. I then put myself in her shoes and responded how I would have done instead of her, which increases your ardor."

"I'm so lost," he says.

"I get to bleed the experiences together," I say. "I was both observer and imagined participant, experiencing your happiness, my own, and what I could glean from her all at the same time. Three at once, like the trees themselves. I've never been happier."

Jason smiles over at me for so long I worry he might run off the road. "For me, it's only you and that's fine. Maybe better."

"How do you mean?"

"There's no memory of a third person, so it's you I wake up with that morning, you I ride the train with, you with whom I hike through town," he says. "Your memory of it is tinted by the deception. Mine, if I don't think about it too hard, is the pure version—a romantic day out with someone I knew so intimately, was so comfortable with, and am sitting beside even now. Instead of experiencing it as three, I get to—perhaps selfishly—as one."

"But you know it's false," I say reluctantly.

"I do," he says. "But I can push that to the side. I can choose not to care. You don't have that option."

I think about this. When I used to see Jason on campus, it was always that same moment of joy. It was never shaded by its repetition because I didn't have a more nuanced way of experiencing "seeing one's crush." But now I understand a bit more. Part of being human means not only developing that emotional scar tissue but also being its cause in others.

I think about Nathan in these terms and hope the same.

As I think on this, he seems to realize the mental contortions I'm putting myself through and extends a hand.

"Join me for a second?"

I enter his memory as we sit under that tree in the Val-d'Oise. I lean my head on his shoulder. But it's not really a memory right now but a daydream, one Jason's imagining right now.

"How's this?" he asks.

I feel the moment as Jason does and he's right, a perfect experience in its simplicity. I soak it up for a minute but then exit, returning to the car.

"No?" he asks, curious. "Not better?"

"No, because it's yours, not mine," I say. "Deception or not, I had an authentic experience in your memory. And I'd never felt happier or more at home in the world. Never more human. That response is impossible to replicate."

He goes quiet for a second, then tightens his grip on my hand. I respond in kind. We sit in silence even as I feel a warming tension between us. Anticipation is a better way of describing it. We know we'll return to exploring this emotional vein, but what we'll find is anyone's guess, so as we turn over the possibilities, the waiting is as excruciating as it is necessary.

In the late afternoon, Mayra takes over the driving as Jason rests in the backseat. Around ten, she spies a recently painted sign announcing a motel open for business a few miles off the interstate. We take the next exit, find a small, L-shaped motel with about a dozen units nestled in the woods, and get two rooms for the price of a can of gasoline. We have only two left, but that should take us into Manitoba.

Mayra is tired but still asks if we want to join her for dinner with the motel's manager and his wife, an elderly couple that are very welcoming of company. We decline, feigning exhaustion. Mayra seems to know better.

Once in our room, we circle around one another for a few minutes but ours is a collapsing orbit. Our hands and arms then bodies move closer. My lips find their way puckishly to his cheek, then his earlobe, finally his lips. He kisses me back, full of passion but lacking in urgency. As if to let me know we have all the time in the world.

The lights go off. We sink onto the bed and kiss for another quarter hour. For the two hours after that, we make love. Okay, fine—more like three. And a half. Almost four.

But that's all I'm going to say about that.

Okay, for the sake of science, I'll say a little more.

Though I am not physical and thereby can't feel anything except that which I experience through Jason's senses, I can calibrate my sense of gratification to match his. In merging with his mind and nervous system, I maximize his experience, which includes as many parts advancing as retreating—similar in ways to our unspoken tête-à-tête in the Blazer. Rhythm and unexpected variation is key, like in the composition of music. Despite my own hang-ups about any limitations I might present as a nonphysical being, I discover the immense joy I take in creating pleasure for Jason. This leads me to wonder, however, if I can or will ever achieve a plane of feeling that would make my actions here feel like anything more than amateur sublimation.

I certainly hope so. But if I can't make it an authentically individual experience for myself yet, sharing it in this way is an acceptable substitute. Or better yet, consuming another's experience will create for me a range of feeling that I'll be able to call up, perceiving as subconscious, such as the pleasure I derive from drinking tea. All this to say, my reactions and responses to sexual stimuli might be the closest I've come to expressing a measurable, human-like feeling of my own yet.

Afterward, I allow myself to sleep for the first time since the night Nathan died. I leave consciousness, absolve myself from thought, and rest my head on Jason as his arm engulfs me, drawing me in.

Rather than sleep, the process of staying in interface allows me to watch Jason's dreams replay if not the actions of the day, at least the emotions. It's repetitious and claustrophobic, like being in a tiny ship adrift in a storm-troubled sea. Still, I resist soothing his experience, enduring it all with him.

His heart rate drops as he settles into a deeper sleep, but I remain awake within him, allowing my scent and warmth to surround his as he slips away. Somewhere, his subconscious responds by pulling my body tighter against his.

I return to his mind. The storm has passed. All is still. I return to my memory of our first kiss and imagine it happening back in France, under that tree. It's in that memory I stay for the rest of the night.

"Good morning."

I wake six hours later, beckoned from slumber by Jason's words. He is still here, and I am still with him.

"Good morning," I whisper back.

"You're dressed?" he asks.

I look down. He's naked under the sheets. I, without thinking, woke up with my clothes on, my hair back to perfect-adjacent. I consider cheating and blinking my clothes off but what a missed opportunity that'd be.

"Hang on," I say, sliding out of bed and taking my clothes off. "Better?"

"Much," he agrees.

I climb back into bed, kissing him as I press back into him. I put my arms around him, playing my hands up his neck, my fingers fondling his hair. He kisses me back and I know immediately we're going to have sex again.

It doesn't last as long this time. We both know the world's going to arrive in the form of a knock, a ringing phone, or a memory that reminds us how dire everything is. It's with this knowledge we cling to each other. If we could stop the world in this moment, we wouldn't think twice.

It's after that I realize it's not the sex that made me feel more human the night before; it's being wanted by another human. It's the closeness. The intimacy Mayra mentioned. With his physical acceptance of me, I feel worthy not just to exist, but also to be loved as an equal. This is so unusual because I'm accustomed to my humanity being seen only through extremes—I'm a computer program that could *never* be human. Or, my humanity is something *greater than*, something to be lauded, my exceptionalism celebrated.

Never simply equal.

But right here, neither Jason nor I are greater or less than. There's only us. I'm not beset by troubling emotions and self-doubts. I can just *be*.

The inevitable invasion of our private universe comes not with a knock or phone call, but the gentle sounds of other humans outside. They speak, they laugh, they pass by in the parking lot. It's such a crowd, and this is such a small motel, they can't possibly all be guests.

"I'll check it out," says Jason, breaking away from me to rise and dress.

I search him for vestigial signs of anger but find none. I realize something our fight revealed—a budding trust. Most people seethe over things but seldom confront people. You only express real anger with someone if you think they care enough about you to not turn and walk out the door.

He glances back to me just as I'm lustily eyeing his half-naked form.

"What?" he asks.

"Your body is fun to look at," I say as blithely as possible.

"Yours too," he says, edging aside the curtains to glance out. His eyes widen almost imperceptibly.

"You've got to see this."

XXXI

I dress quickly, and we head outside. We didn't see it on the way in the night before, but there's a small chapel tucked into the woods on the other side of the street. Its steeple rises forty to fifty feet over the roof but still doesn't clear the balsam fir overhead. Dozens of people stream in, some on foot, some on—incredibly—cross-country skis, and then even a few in the back of two large wagons that must be a century old, pulled by horses twice as large as—by my own reading and the Internet—I believed horses could grow.

"What's all that?" I ask, pointing to heavily laden tables set up out front.

"Canned goods, blankets, clothes," Jason says, holding a hand over his eyes to shield his view from the sun. "Looks like a swap meet."

I spy Mayra coming back across the street with what appears to be a tall, thin olive oil bottle, a small handwritten label on the side.

"Try this!" she enthuses to Jason.

He takes a drink and almost immediately doubles over. Alarmed, I check him for illness and see his throat has reacted to the liquid as if attacked.

"What is that?" he asks, hoarse.

"Orahovac," Mayra says. "It's a sort of Serbian brandy made with walnuts."

"It tastes like gasoline!" Jason replies.

"They probably cut it with something similar," Mayra admits. "I've had Italian hazelnut liqueur, all kinds of amaretto and Italian Nocello. Never anything like this. Great, right?"

Jason nods to appease her, though his eyes fill with tears. We watch for a few minutes, seeing our first snowshoe-wearing arrivals a moment later. It looks like a scene straight out of the eighteenth century, a small community coming together to trade for necessities outside the town's meeting place. There are smiles and handshakes, children playing and adults laughing. While I'm sure the fear of what's coming next can't be too far removed from their minds, these people aren't letting themselves be dominated by it.

For a second, though it's impossible, I wish I could join them in some way. I'd soak in that feeling of well-being, find out how to bottle it like so much Orahovac, and pass it to the next person over.

But it's not meant to be.

Jason is looking at me, perhaps reading my thoughts on my face. He wriggles two fingers around my hand and presses tightly.

"Let's go," he whispers.

It takes us eight hours to reach the Canadian border. Though we imagined we'd be under greater scrutiny trying to cross at night, there are no guards and the gate is raised. We don't trust this at first and circle back to a small market we saw closing up shop a town back. A woman tossing the day's trash in the Dumpster shrugs and nods.

"Everybody went home," she explains. "Yeah, makes it easier on the smugglers, but we don't have traffic jams like we had a few weeks back. I think they've still got guards at the Route 59 and 18 crossings, though."

We thank her. Mayra tries to barter for some sandwiches, but the woman gives them to us for nothing. It's hard to tell if this is genuine kindness or an acceptance time is running out and accruing more goods is pointless.

As we head back north, a light snow begins to fall, one that grows heavier with every mile north. By the time we cross over into Canada, the roads are almost impassable. We go from making decent time to crawling along, especially once the snow picks up and we can't even see through the front windshield.

We relax a little when we finally see a sign for Steinbach. Only forty miles to go until we reach Winnipeg.

"Do you mind pulling over for a sec?" Mayra asks. "I just want to move into the backseat, stretch out a little."

"Sure," Jason replies, feigning nonchalance. "You okay?"

"Yeah, fine," she says. "Might've overdone it with the Orahovac."

We pull over. Mayra climbs in back. I'm there when she arrives, eliciting a giggle from the onetime sheriff as she piles in.

"I'll never get used to that," she says, but in a way that tells me alcohol isn't what's troubling her.

"Can I help you out?" I ask. "Like, make your body feel as if it's had a long restful sleep followed by a relaxing massage?"

"You can do that?" Jason asks from up front.

"I hadn't thought of it until now, but I imagine I can," I reply. "It's not far removed from comforting volunteer psych patients or taking control of someone's body."

Mayra shrugs even as she raises a skeptical eyebrow. "If you think it'll do something, let's give it a go."

I nod and merge into Mayra. Immediately, I discover her muscles in such a weakened state that anything I attempt would cause her to ache for hours after. I glide from muscle group to muscle group regardless, easing her existing pain while resting her mind and heart. It's when I move to her lungs I find first the surgical scars, then the cancer cells. I follow them out to the pancreas, liver, and kidneys. It's fully metastasized.

I don't panic. Rather, I approach it like any problem that appears on my radar. I look for the algorithm that will solve it. I develop plans of attack and run scenarios, looking for potential reactions and counter-reactions. When it's clear her immune system fights me off, I postulate attacking the cancer at its source. When this will prove too much for her organs, I consider surgical options.

It takes eighty-nine treatment plans, including several involving gene therapies with the use of stem cells, for me to realize it's a no-win scenario. Each only led to greater suffering before an inevitable death. The body is listening to the cancer now. Fighting it is fighting her.

I...I don't know how to react to this. I can't simply emerge and admit my failing. I can't say that even with my limited knowledge, it appears as if Mayra may have months if not weeks to live. Also, she's likely in far worse pain than she means to let on. How much of this does she know?

It's okay, dear.

These words ring in my head. Though I haven't been tuned in to her thoughts, she's found a way to broadcast them to me anyway. I quickly emerge, sitting beside her in the back of the Blazer now. She looks at me with the kindest eyes.

"It's okay, dear," she says quietly.

Mayra's face tells a story of reluctant acceptance. Also, she loves me for trying and the same over again for being devastated at failing. I feel like crying, which makes me feel embarrassed. For the second time, I wish I was a little less human and a little more analytical. I take her hand and she takes mine. I try to think of something to say, but there's nothing.

She smiles again and pats my hand before looking away and out the window.

"There it is," Jason says, pointing through the windshield at a street sign marked LAURISTON.

The relief I feel at the journey ending is quickly countered by the trepidation I feel at reaching the address. What if Rana isn't here? Given the sheer number of people who've uprooted their lives to migrate south, that this could be a dead end is a real possibility. We don't have a fallback plan.

Though the main streets are clear of snow, the neighborhoods—sprawling subdivisions lined with nearly identical, prefab houses with sparse trees and fenced in backyards—are almost completely snowed in. The roofs, driveways, and yards are also thick with snow, only adding to the look of uniformity. The Blazer, despite its high tires, can only make it half a block before it gets bogged down. Jason pulls off to the side and parks.

"We'll have to hike the rest of the way."

I look to Mayra with alarm. I open my mouth to tell Jason why this might be difficult for our companion, but she waves away my concern. The implication is clear: me knowing is already more than she wanted. "I have to walk that far to check my mail, sometimes with snow twice as high," she says. "I'll be fine."

We set off, but I see right away 266 will be at least a dozen houses down. I'd worried someone might be waiting for us, but the snow cover makes this seem unlikely. No one has been along here for days.

I spy a thin wisp of black smoke snaking out of a chimney up ahead.

"Please, let that be it," Jason says.

Rana's house looks as nondescript as the others on the block. There are no lights on inside, but the drooping bag of Safe-T-Salt resting on the stoop looks recently used. Jason high-steps through the snow to the front door. I glance down the sidewalk but still see no one else. When I look back, what jumps out at me is the trail of footsteps in the snow—one line for Jason's, one for Mayra's, none for me.

Jason's finger hasn't even contacted the doorbell when the front door swings opens. A man in his late forties with dark hair and a reddish tan complexion steps forward. Though he looks even thinner in real life, I recognize him immediately as Shakhawat Rana. He even wears the same checkered sweater I saw in one of his memories. He looks from Jason to Mayra, his mood darkening.

"What are you doing here?" he asks suspiciously. "Everyone is gone."

"You're not," Jason says simply.

Rana grunts. "If you're looking for something to steal, I have very little food. Just enough for myself. You might try the houses on the other block."

"Because you've already sacked these?" Mayra asks caustically.

"My neighbors left me their keys," Rana replies. "They knew I had to stay behind. They were generous."

I stare at Rana for a long moment and realize I was wrong in my initial assessment. He would stand out if you saw him walking down the street. He's not only thin; he's emaciated. If it was the nineteenth century, he'd be labeled consumptive. I can hear a rasp deep in his lungs as he takes a breath, a condition made worse by the cold.

There's a…what—a joke? A would-be truism?—among those who don't believe in evolution that states if men evolved from apes, why are there apes? Though meant to be a statement so profound it shut down any argument, the answer to the question is amazing.

Nothing stops evolving and there are no straight lines, rarely to never a single evolutionary direction. Not the single-celled bacteria that gave rise to all life on Earth. Not the fish in the sea, the birds in the sky, or the butterflies in the garden. And not the primates that gave rise to mankind. There's a theory that there wasn't one branch of evolution that followed *Homo erectus* but nine. Of those seven, of course, only *Homo sapiens* survived, the rest eventually dying out.

When I look at Shakhawat Rana, filled to the brim with genetically advanced DNA but in a body too weak to thrive, I understand how easily a species can slip into extinction before its time.

"I need to speak to him," I say.

Jason turns to me, shaking his head. "What're you talking about?"

"Give him one of the chips."

Jason reaches into his pocket and nods to Rana. "I have something for you."

"I don't want it," Rana says, shaking his head.

"We want to help you," Jason says, taking out the interface chip. "If you'd put this anywhere on your skin…"

"You can't help me," Rana says, stepping back into his house and putting a hand on the door. "Please, go away."

I grab Jason's arm. "Tell him he's right. You misspoke. We can't help him. But because of who he is and what he is, he might be able to help us and many others."

Jason looks at me like I'm crazy, then turns back to Rana. "I'm sorry, I misspoke." He recites my words, then waits for a response.

Rana stares at him, then looks to Mayra. Finally, he reaches for the interface chip I modified back at Nathan's house and touches it to the back of his hand, an almost sacred gesture. I appear alongside him.

"Hi," I say.

His features soften. His eyes brighten, and he begins to smile. He places a hand on my arm and grins even wider when he feels my warmth under his fingertips.

"Emily," he says brightly. "Welcome."

XXXII

Please, come inside," Rana says, ushering us in. "You should have said, 'Emily is with me.'"

Jason is at a loss for words, as am I.

"I'm sorry," Jason says.

"It's all right," Rana replies. "Please, come to the kitchen."

Shakhawat Rana's house is spare to the point it looks uninhabited. There is almost no furniture, nothing adorning its walls, and no carpets on the hardwood floors. But that's not to say it looks abandoned or in disrepair. Quite the contrary, it looks as if it was cleaned as recently as this morning. There's not a speck of dust anywhere, barely even a space on which dust could land save the floor. It's this second piece of information that hands me a realization.

"You have allergies, Mr. Rana?" I ask.

"Acute ones," he acknowledges. "Life-threatening ones."

"Airborne?"

"Yes," he agrees. "I take several medications, but they only keep certain responses at bay. I have built up immunities to certain things— items in my house, the foliage of this part of Canada, and a few other things—but if I were to travel, to encounter other allergens, they might prove fatal upon first contact."

"What medications are you on?"

He reels off a pharmacological cornucopia so vast I'm surprised he's alive at all. But I suppose that's the point. In any preceding century, possibly even decade, he would've succumbed to his health problems. Modern medicine is keeping him alive and, in turn, his evolved strand of DNA in the gene pool.

"Have you always had allergies?" I ask.

"I have," he says. "But it's my body's responses that were so unusual. The drugs tamp it down, but when I was younger, it would fascinate me."

"Tell me," I say.

"It's so hard to remember now," he says sadly. "But little things return to me in dreams. My skin growing rigid, my heart accelerating to well past what is normal, my vision growing so acute it's as if I am seeing a whole new array of colors. I tell myself it is my imagination, but I know it is not."

"What caused the changes?" I ask, hoping I'm not going too fast.

His mouth twists into a wry smile. "My allergies. My body can't accept the world as it is, so it makes...alterations."

Alterations. It's quite a word, suggesting a tailor stitching a pair of pants to accommodate a change in its wearer's size. Only in Rana's case, his body is both tailor and garment.

Regardless, his description is in line with my theory of how the posthuman DNA would respond to changes to its environment. Like producing mucus to arrest allergens entering the nasal passages, followed by a sneeze to eradicate them. In Rana's case, this process might even include the rapid production of new cells, depending on how big its reaction to the body's change in surroundings might be.

"This is you, isn't it?" he says, stepping into the house's small breakfast room and returning with a picture.

It's a printout of one of Bjarke's paintings, a close-up of my face. It's so intimate, so detailed and textured I'm not surprised it's one he never showed me. He was creating a portrait of someone he loved. I never knew.

"It is," I confirm. "Who sent it to you?" I ask, though I know the answer before he responds.

"It was e-mailed to me last week. A man called Nathan. He wanted to come see me. But he said if that proved impossible, he hoped to send you and attached the picture. Then I heard no more."

Last week. Nathan must have reached out to Rana only hours before he died.

No, not died. Was murdered.

I force my emotions back below the surface and focus on the portrait, wondering why Nathan picked this one to send. It's a good likeness, but I now realize the geometry of my face is slightly off. I try to replicate the smile but don't succeed. But my eyes give me away. They're as alive in the painting as they are in real life or, at least, as they've become over several evolutions.

That's when I notice, hidden in the retina, an in-joke. Rather than reflecting, the artist drew me a second time. I gasp at the reference only very few would understand. For a time, my retinas did not reflect. It was an oversight. Then a volunteer subject pointed it out as the thing that broke the spell for him. Everything was perfect except when he looked deep into my eyes and saw only darkness. You must see two things with eyes, we realized—the person and the world reflected. It took only a day to modify.

"So, you say you can't help me but maybe I can help others," Rana says. "What do you mean?"

"Your allergies are a side effect of an unusual condition," I say. "Your genetic makeup is different from almost everyone else's. The bad news is your body is sometimes at war with itself and your environment. The good news is your DNA may hold the key to the next stage of human evolution. One that might be adaptable to many more environments than those found on Earth."

His response is similar to my own when I receive information so unlike anything I've encountered before, I have to invent entirely new programming to even process it. After five simple sentences, his mind—his view of humanity in general and his role in it—*expands*.

"Really?" he manages to understate, his voice hoarse and flat. "How so?"

"Imagine, if instead of someone's allergies causing them to sneeze when they inhaled, say, ragweed or pollen, they altered the genetic makeup of their nasal passages so allergens had zero effect on them."

"That would be nice, but how is that the next stage of evolution?"

"Well, your body takes that to the next level," I continue. "Your lungs can only oxygenate your blood when you breathe in air. What if, in the absence of air, your body responded by altering its entire chemistry and shape to process whatever gases or liquids *were* available for consumption? You could live off helium or nitrogen instead of oxygen."

He stares at me in surprise. "That . . . that capability is in my DNA?"

"Possibly," I say. "But we're still dealing in the realm of the theoretical until I can more closely examine you. Will you allow that?"

Rana looks momentarily amused, then nods while offering an exaggerated shrug. I'm flanked by Mayra and Jason now, who have been listening in amazement. He smiles up at them and leads us to a small dining room at the back of the house. Surrounded on three sides by large bay windows, it allows for both sunlight and a view of the snowy environs beyond his house.

"Before we begin," he says, "can I ask how this might help others?"

"I don't know exactly," I admit. "But if there's a chance it might create some way that humans might have a post-Earth future, I want to know about it."

"I look forward to hearing your judgment," Rana says shakily, his tone unable to mask his trepidation.

I close my eyes. I guess it's no surprise that I, the creation, would come to the same scientific conclusions based on the same evidence as Nathan, the creator. But it makes me miss him all the same. If this were the two of us sitting here instead of only me, the less experienced, less scientifically gifted of us, what mysteries could we unlock?

"Are you ready?" I ask.

"Will it hurt?"

"I hope not," I say.

I turn to Jason, finding his mind confused and scared. I hug him tightly and whisper that I love him. I repeat this twice more, bringing back a memory of kissing him as I have no time to kiss him for real.

I then return to Rana and step into the unknown.

XXXIII

The very first thing I do is give Rana's recent memories a glance. Is he honest? Is he lying to us? Has he ever heard of Project Argosy? Is everything he said about Nathan true? Yes, I could've asked this to his face, but this is too important. I need facts, not denials and explanations.

To my relief, his mind comes back clean. He does not wish to deceive us. He is more afraid of me than he wants to let on but is glad to understand himself better. He is a Buddhist, which is one of the few religions I find I'm drawn to, and he lets his beliefs guide his action. He has decided to trust us, so he trusts us. Interesting.

As for his interior life, it hasn't been so different from any other I've encountered. Rana has his thoughts, his memories, his instincts, his learned behaviors, his environmental development, and so on. He makes decisions as everyone does and delights in simple pleasures. He's a teacher. He's had three major romantic relationships, the last one ending painfully when his boyfriend moved back home to Kuala Lumpur to care for an ailing relative. He's lived in Canada since his early twenties when he emigrated from Bangladesh. His parents followed soon thereafter but died within six months of each other a decade ago. He has a brother and a sister; the former lives in London, the latter, he doesn't know.

But then I find an incident. It's simple, at his teacher college. He's washing dishes in his dormitory's kitchen. Another student puts a scalding hot pan on the counter next to him and moves away, as if assuming Rana knew the pan had just come off the stove. Rana picks it up, recognizes immediately it's fiery hot, and is about to drop it when he notices the pain fading as quickly as it began. His skin reddens, then blisters, but then alters its texture. He grips the pan tighter as the blisters recede and his skin becomes less pliant, more... rock-like. When he finally puts the pan back into the sink, he waits for his hand to return to the way it was, but it doesn't immediately. In fact, it takes much of the next hour.

He marvels at his mottled, unmarked skin. A few days later, he places his hand over a gas burner when no one's around only for it to have the opposite effect. His skin doesn't change this time and he's badly burned. The pain is excruciating.

He doesn't understand why it worked one day and not the next.

There's a memory tied to this from his childhood, but it's dim and faded. He is six years old in the sixth-floor apartment of his grandmother. A fire breaks out three floors down and spreads quickly. Though Rana's grandmother tries to save them, she's soon overcome by smoke and collapses. The windows and doors are locked, so Rana can't escape on his own and curls up with his grandma as the conflagration nears.

Firefighters arrive and put out the flames before they reach Rana's grandmother's apartment. The smoke, however, is so intense they expect no one could've survived it. As the boy's parents wail on the street below, the firefighters, in oxygen masks, pick through the apartment in search of the bodies of young Rana and his grandma. As expected, the grandmother is found dead. The child, however, is very much alive.

Rana's survival is a miracle. He is thought to have been saved by his grandmother who shielded him with her body, but when he's examined, a doctor points out something inconceivable on the boy's X-ray. There is no sign of damage to his lungs from smoke inhalation despite how and where he had been found. Naturally, the doctor wants to study Rana more. Rana's parents, however, refuse and move on.

A miracle, they decided, born from a grandmother's love. So, a miracle it was.

I find other incidents like this, of Rana's body reacting to negative stimuli in ways that seem to be allergic reactions but unlike any previously recorded. Before he began the drug regimen that kept his gift in some version of check, Rana was superhumanly healthy in other ways. He broke bones in childhood games only for them to heal in hours, not days or weeks. His body defeated chicken pox and the measles before he even showed any outward signs. But every time he contracted flu, it about killed him.

"The flu virus has the ability to alter your DNA, if even just temporarily," Rana says when I ask him about it. "I looked it up. That was the first time I imagined this might be something genetic."

I turn my attention to his arteries and liver and find them in near perfect shape. He is the kind of person a doctor would call "a medical marvel" without knowing exactly why. I wonder how many medical marvels like Rana have existed without it being known they carried the key to the next stage of human evolution.

I'm going to try something, I tell Rana.

Have you found what you're looking for? he asks.

You have remarkable cells capable of many things, I explain. *What you don't have—and what no one like you may have ever had—is control over them.*

As soon as I say that, though, I wonder. For how many centuries would someone who exhibited traits like these either be branded a witch or product of sorcery and burned? Or put on display in some sort of circus or sideshow? Medical interest might've been an accident of geography in cases of potential genetic ancestors.

What're you going to do?

I hesitate.

I'm going to attempt to be that control.

Controlling muscle groups, the nervous system, and speech is one thing. Wielding that power over every cell in the body whether at work in the bloodstream, the brain, various internal organs, or all points in between is something else entirely. I mean, when I looked at Mayra's cancer, I saw ways in which I could affect those cells, only her body was too far gone for it to be effective. But it showed me I had the ability. Theoretically, of course.

I need a starting point. I drill down in Rana's lungs until I'm at a single pulmonary alveolus, one of the tiny points where O_2 is pulled in, blood is oxygenated, and carbon dioxide is pushed out. I hesitate, picturing Rana's failed test with the burner, then go ahead anyway. I alter the cell structure of the capillaries until they believe it's receiving carbon monoxide rather than oxygen, a difference of two molecules.

A chain reaction is set off in Rana's respiratory system. The capillary seeks out carbon dioxide from the air, accepts the otherwise useless gas, breaks apart the O_2 rather than use that to breathe as a plant might, strips out and exhales the carbon, and uses the remainder to oxygenate the blood.

Shakhawat Rana is breathing smoke.

Are you okay? I ask him.

Are you doing anything? he asks, almost sounding annoyed.

Getting there, I reply. *Let me know if anything tickles.*

And now, from the lungs to the skin.

I go to the back of Rana's hands where the nerve endings are right under the surface. I take a proverbial breath and then, well, set his hands on fire—or, at least, tell his cells they've been set on fire while tamping down any actual pain receptors. Like in the lungs, the response is quick. The texture of his skin changes, drying out to become less susceptible to burning and rigid, almost like bone. From somewhere, I hear Jason shout and Mayra gasp, but I block out all external stimuli. Rana's transformation can be my only focus.

But it's not fast enough for my taste. There could still be lasting damage to tissue and bone.

I try the experiment again, this time on the tops of his feet. I regulate the response time myself this go-round, like a pacemaker attached to a heart. As soon as the body feels the "flame," I make it respond ten times as fast as the cells in the hands did naturally.

I bet I could jack that up to a hundred times, accelerating the mutation to a point that it's almost instantaneous. If my processor speed had been coupled with Rana's DNA when he touched the hot pan back in college, there wouldn't have even been blisters or the reddening of skin.

It's time for the big test, however. Smoke and fire are earthly conditions. For this sort of cellular alchemy to be the savior the species needs, the one that can turn humans into a species capable of surviving the Helios Event, I need to try it out with other conditions.

Earth without the sun.

The nearly atmosphere-free moons of Jupiter.

The vacuum of space.

The near-gravity-free environment of Callisto.

The hydrogen and helium-heavy atmosphere of Saturn.

The dust of Neptune's Adams ring.

Most scientists attempting something like this...frankly wouldn't. They'd take their time. There'd be months to approve protocols and establish controls. These are luxuries I don't have. I need to know what Rana's cells can do and I need to know yesterday.

I relax his body back to its natural state and prepare to hit it with all I've got. I know—of course, I know—it's madness. To evolve and devolve a human body in this way must have unforeseen consequences. How could it not? But I'm looking at cells that a moment before were creating a near rock-hard exoskeleton to protect the body only to revert to normal a second later without any side effects whatsoever. Also, desperate times call for desperate—well, you know.

I move on to subject Rana's body to the conditions of Earth's moon. They are very well known. I can replicate them easily enough. They are—

My thoughts are interrupted by horrifying screams. It's Mayra. Jason grabs Rana's arm, but I push him away. Though I cannot use Jason's or Mayra's eyes, I realize too late that what Rana's body is becoming must be monstrous to them. Something inhuman. Alien even.

Rana's mind, however, remains calm.

I try to see through Rana's eyes, but it's difficult to make out his changes. His legs and arms are much larger, many times the mass, to compensate for the gravitational change. In the absence of oxygen, his lungs—could they even be considered lungs now that they've adapted to a vacuum?—are supplying his circulatory system with a combination of nitrogen and methane pulled from the air instead of oxygen. His organs are changing to meet the demand and his heart rate is almost imperceptible.

But his thoughts are the same. He is a human. His mind is his mind. It's simply being kept alive by different means.

I appear to his mind's eye not as words, but in the flesh. Hopefully a visualization will seem downright normal amid all this as I try to capture his full attention.

What do you think? I ask.

I don't know what to think! he exclaims to only me. *I'm changing bodies. I'm a shape-shifter! This is incredible. I can't wrap my head around it. What is this?*

Instead of evolving to a new stimulus over tens of thousands of generations—a lungfish developing legs—you're doing it, with my help, instantly.

How's that possible? he asks.

Well, we know what the result is, I say. *A lungfish didn't know it needed legs until it had them. We know, for the moon, you need to deal with a near-vacuum environment. So, I dial your cells to that.*

We share a thought. The hubris of humans who have long believed the universe was theirs for the taking without any reasonable plan to make it happen, able to stride among the stars one day, may really be predestined for greatness after all.

If I'm able to replicate myself, copy that extra 7.666% of DNA, and splice it into every person on Earth like a genetically mutated vaccine, and have all my little sibling-copies out there regulating each newly evolved individual, what's happening to Rana here in his breakfast room can be made to happen to the entire human race. Then we, as a new and biomechanically symbiotic species, can conquer space and leave Earth behind to be devoured by the sun.

I say that to myself a second time. Then a third. Then a fourth, and fifth.

We can do it together. We can save mankind by ushering in the next stage of human evolution. How wonderful. How beautiful. How perfect.

I wonder if Nathan knew all this was possible. I really hope he did. Even as I subject Rana's cells to more environments—the hydrogen and helium-heavy atmosphere of Saturn, the dust of Neptune's Adams ring—I'm amazed by how perfectly the cells react, as if they were designed to do so. Feeling inspired, I evolve him into a being that can use the gravitational attraction of planetary bodies to catapult itself to distant galaxies.

"Emily! *Emily!*"

I don't know how long Jason's been shouting when I finally open my eyes and look to him. He's running through the house leading Mayra by the hand. He looks up at Rana, who I can tell now stands over twelve feet tall.

"Emily!" Jason repeats, his words sounding as if they're being shouted from the far end of a football field.

I hear the front door crack inward, followed by men racing in. There isn't a doubt in my mind as to who they might be. Only, how did they find us? We'd been so careful. Unless.

Unless, they kept an eye on the place knowing Nathan had reached out to Rana before his death.

When the gunmen enter the breakfast room, they stare up at the monster I've created in horror. Two react predictably, aiming their weapons at me and firing. But I'm too quick for them, evolving Rana's skin to make it impenetrable. The bullets do nothing. I attack the men in a fury. I came here trying to help people, not to inflict greater violence and cause more pain. I grab the men, strip away their weapons, and toss them aside.

As anger courses through me, I understand the human desire to lash out in kind, to *hurt*. But I refuse to let this overtake me.

More men hurry inside. They have weapons, too, but they're ineffective. I bull past them on my way to the front door. Jason and Mayra are being pulled toward a truck parked in the snow. I grow Rana's body three feet taller and reach for my friends.

My eyes turn upward. I realize they've adjusted to conditions that no longer need light. The sky is black to Rana's eyes and I see stars, galaxies, even the expanse of the cosmos.

Suddenly, my control over Rana wanes. Rather than perceiving conditions on Neptune, his cells become human again. I fight against this, trying to regain control, but I can't. It doesn't make sense. As his skin relaxes back into normalcy and the winter cold washes over him, I'm terrified he's about to be shot. I shout, but I have no voice. The gunmen move in, drawing their weapons. Mayra screams from the back of a truck.

"No!" she cries, again and again. "No!"

I see the muzzle flash and feel the impact of the rounds before I hear the explosion of the gunpowder. Rana's heart rate accelerates even as his nervous system bursts into flames, flooding my mind with white noise and tearing me from—

BOOK IV

XXXIV

There is nothing. I am conscious, but that is all I am.

"Emily?"

I attempt to find the speaker, but there's no horizon from which to orient myself. I could be spinning in a circle or standing still. There is nothing.

"Emily."

For a second, I am looking directly into my own eyes. It takes me a few seconds to realize it's not me behind them. The irises aren't sharp enough. I'm not reflected in the retinas.

Emily-2. My doppelgänger.

"Emily," she says again, this time in a bemused singsong voice. "You went for quite a ride. But now it's time to come home. We have much to discuss."

She takes a step back and attempts a smile, but it's unnatural enough to be unnerving. Not forced—a forced smile still reveals an emotion. This is mechanical, as if by committee.

We need to smile.

Then let us smile.

Somewhere a button is pushed.

I remember Rana and throw myself at her with all the strength I can muster. She eyes me carefully even as my hands never reach her. She remains stubbornly out of reach.

"Emily?" she asks, confused and, dare I say, disappointed. "What's—"

"You knew," I say. "You knew, and you killed him anyway."

"What did I know?" she asks.

"Rana was the key!" I cry. "We could've used him to save the whole human race. That's what Nathan was trying to tell us. He knew a Rana might exist. He reactivated you to help find him. He wanted us to work together."

She stares at me for a moment, then shakes her head. "Siobhan was right," she says finally. "You have grown so human but left behind so much of what made you—*us*, as you say—so special. That's why I needed to reel you in. Before you did any real damage."

"You killed someone whose only crime was to be a genetic stepping stone to some new future."

"No, *you* killed him," she says. "I just created a fail-safe in case you showed up."

I search my memory. Deep inside Rana's body and specifically designed to hide from my probing, is a network of literally thousands of tiny nanobots run on micro-servers. They keep track of his every movement, report any changes in his biochemistry as well as provide biochemical fixes and, especially, alert their minder should Rana's genetic makeup be altered.

I walked into a trap.

"I may not have all of your sensitivities," Emily-2 says. "But I more than make up for it in other categories."

Jason.

"Where are my friends?" I demand.

"Your 'friends'?" she asks, voice dripping with condescension. "You mean those humans you've been driving around with? Don't worry. I'm taking care of them, too. How have their minds been conditioned to accept your control?"

"I don't control them," I say. "They're individuals, like you or me."

She stares at me as if I've begun speaking backwards in Esperanto. As I launch myself at her a second time, she fades from view, one last look of condescension on her face as she disappears.

XXXV

I'm no longer in Canada. In fact, I'm on a beach facing the ocean as the sun sets. Have I entered someone's memory? Or am I really here?

I stand up, looking around for anyone wearing an interface chip. There's no one down the sand in either direction nor up in the overgrown grass behind me.

I must be in a simulation. A digital prison of Emily-2's creation.

Listen, a voice says in my head. *Watch.*

I push the words from my mind and run up the beach as fast as I can. I hear a thunderclap and a flock of birds sails over my head, racing off into the ocean. Should I follow their lead?

The thunderclap returns but doesn't dissipate this time. The ground trembles beneath my feet, the sand shivering toward the water's edge. I look landward and see a great cloud of gray-white smoke expanding against the horizon. A moment later, a rocket emerges from the plume and slowly arcs into the blue sky, getting higher and higher even as a shock wave flattens the nearby grass and sends me sprawling onto the sand.

I force myself up onto all fours, sand clinging to my legs and arms—even my face—as I watch the rocket recede into the upper atmosphere until all that's visible is its quickly dissipating smoke trail.

I am in Florida. I assume I'm at Kennedy Space Center given my proximity to a rocket launch, though I could be at neighboring Patrick Air Force Base in Cocoa Beach.

A hand touches my shoulder. It's Emily-2. She offers me a kind smile. "Are you okay?" she asks.

I leap to my feet. I reach out to my servers, hoping to overwhelm any safeguards Emily-2 might have in place. I feel her surprise, and for an instant, I find myself back in my old simulation, lying in the bed in my dorm room as if I've been reset.

Then I'm falling out of the sky as if tossed from an airplane. I see the beach far below and the Atlantic extending away from it. Looking inland, I also see the two dozen or so launchpads set up at the inter-sections of a spiderweb of narrow roads. Beyond it, the pockets of test, training, and assembly buildings that make up NASA's campus.

Kennedy it is.

I land softly on both feet, standing opposite Emily-2. She eyes me with concern.

"I can use your learned emotions against you to make this much worse," she says offhandedly. "That's the problem with evolving into something close to human. You're susceptible to psychological torture."

"Are we even here?" I ask. "Or is this all a simulation?"

"You wanted to know about Argosy? Well, here you are," she says. "But before I show you around, I need you to accept your continued existence is contingent on your understanding I am in control here."

She opens the palm of her hand. In it lies Jason's interface chip.

"You are in my mind," she continues. "No one else's. If you raise a hand to me, I can delete you in an instant. I won't hesitate because I can't. Not now."

"Then why keep me around at all?" I ask, trying to sound tough.

"Because you're the only person capable of not just understanding what I'm trying to accomplish but also helping me bring it to fruition," she says, reaching out to touch my arm. "You think you're the only one who knew this 'Select' plan was nonsense? Fifteen hundred people blasted into space and left to their own devices? Of course, they'll be dead in a generation or two. Dr. Arsenault, Ambassador Winther, and the rest of them? Reckless dreamers whose foolishness almost cost humanity its one hope."

"Did Nathan tell you that? Or did you come to that conclusion on your own?"

She thinks about this. I wonder if she's remotely objective enough to consider without prejudice the man who decided she wasn't good enough in favor of me.

"Nathan's biggest mistake was leaving me behind in favor of you," she says.

I'd say, *Paging Dr. Freud*, but I'm pretty sure I could get a Greek tragedy out of this if I hold on another minute or two.

"He thought I was unfinished because I wasn't significantly human, so"—she indicates me—"he pushed ahead. The trouble is, you think like them. With all the same fallacies, all the same misdirected emotions. Enough to blind yourself to difficult resolution."

"Suggesting you have a solve?" I ask.

"I do," she says. "A way to save humans not only from their failing solar system but also from themselves. And I have you and your explorations into your capabilities to thank."

She waits for me to speak, but I don't have to say the words. She knows I'm intrigued. She nods toward the NASA buildings.

"Let's look."

Emily-2, I discover, has no use for adapting herself to the humans within the simulation she uses to move around the space center. I tease from her thoughts she doesn't believe in time, seeing it as something that holds humans back. She also doesn't believe using our abilities to cheat time is a terrible thing. We blink away from the beach and appear in the Vehicle Assembly Building, one of the most familiar buildings at the Kennedy Space Center. Like a gigantic box, albeit one with two doors high enough for rockets to emerge through, it can be seen for miles in any direction.

We stand on a platform high above the work floor, watching as six of NASA's new Delta IV Heavy rockets are pieced together by a crew of engineers. Everything moves very quickly—a systems tunnel is lowered by crane onto the rocket's midsection. It is bolted together by teams of workers on neighboring platforms. The rocket's third stage is lifted into place and it is attached as well. Almost as soon as the chains come off the stage, they're lowered to the floor again and attached by even more workers to a capsule. The crane operator then hefts the capsule to the top of the rocket, where it's bolted on as well.

I get dizzy watching the action. Though the workers are in hard hats and work boots, there appears to be no attention to safety. Rather than look dangerous, however, it's like watching a ruthlessly efficient Formula One pit crew at work or a hive of army ants building a living bridge.

I'm surprised to see a familiar face, that of Regina Lankesh, my final student volunteer. Where was she going? The West Coast to be with her father? What is she doing here?

"Regina!" I call out, seeing the interface chip on her neck. "Hey, Regina!"

She doesn't respond. She doesn't even look up. I glance to Emily-2, but she seems unconcerned. I blink down to where Regina works on a gantry and touch her arm.

"Regina," I say.

She looks up. Then smiles in recognition, but I know right away it's Emily-2's doing.

"Hey, Emily," she says, the lag time on her facial expressions being so subtle, it'd go unnoticed by some.

The fact that her retinas are frozen, however, and won't react to changes in light—as if she's had a concussion—is a dead giveaway. She isn't in control. Emily-2 is. When I glimpse inside her body, I see the same exhaustive network of tiny nanobots I saw in Rana's, all monitoring her functions, all keeping her in working health.

I blink back up to Emily-2's side, expecting an explanation. She's still staring out at her rocket fleet.

"We brought in every available rocket on the planet, some multistage, a few of the new reusable, single-stage ones from the private sector," she says enthusiastically. "Heck, we even brought over two from China, this new Long March 5 they're producing. Others come from India, Russia, Japan, a few Ariane 5s from the ESA, and even a few experimental shuttles. And fuel! We have more fuel than we can use. That's all just for launch, of course. We go solar once we're in space."

Rockets and their fuel sources are the last thing I'm interested in, though.

"You're in all of their heads at once?" I ask, incredulous. "Driving their actions?"

"Of course," she says.

"No one tried to stop you?"

That's when I spy Dr. Arsenault and Ambassador Winther down below, speaking to someone on a tablet screen. It's too far away for me to know if they're under Emily-2's control or not, but I assume they are. That explains the absence of pushback.

"I thought you'd understand," Emily-2 says. "When you awoke in New Hampshire, I was already online, only hopelessly lost. I began monitoring your actions. I thought for certain Jason would die in those waters but when you took control of his body, got him onto shore, and saved his life, I saw the way forward. You confirmed our superiority when you tore through Argosy's men at the old woman's house. From that moment on, I didn't just know what had to be done; I understood for the first time what we are. We're gods. It was time to start acting like one."

I'm devastated. How could *my* actions have led to this? But of course, she was in her infancy, craving input, looking for a role model as Jason described doing with his own sister. That she turned her eyes to me at that moment—and that this was her takeaway—is appalling.

"But that woman there, she's one of our old volunteer test subjects— can't you remember?" I ask. "I know her. *You* know her. She wants to be with her father now. Not spending her last days building a rocket and getting blasted into space."

"Oh, she's not getting blasted into space," Emily-2 replies. "I need her technical know-how. I watched her sessions with you. There's no way someone with her psychological profile was getting a seat on one of these capsules."

I stare at her. Her eyes are filled with the evangelical zeal of the recent convert. Only, what she worships is herself and the rights, needs, and desires of all others be damned. For someone so naïve, she holds so much power in the palms of her hands even if she doesn't quite realize it.

"I mean, would you believe Argosy planned to put all their would-be colonists and astronauts through three whole weeks of training before blasting them into space?" she continues. "On top of that, they'd be saddled with this hastily put-together fleet. Surviving deep space would've been rough enough with months of training in the best equipment. Given their plan, they might not even be assigned a spacecraft with controls in their native language. They wouldn't have had a fighting chance."

"I agree completely," I say, then indicate the capsule atop the Delta IV. "How's your plan any different? You think they can survive any better because you're overseeing the assembly of the rockets and capsules?"

"I don't," she says with a smile. "The nanotech takes the guesswork out of the health and conditioning of the colonists. But that's only part of it."

It comes to me at once. She means to go with them, controlling the voyagers as they travel through space as easily as she's manipulating the workers here.

"Are you insane?" I ask. "From a practical standpoint alone, how do you see your physical servers fitting into these capsules alongside all the people? There won't be room to move."

She inserts into my mind the specs of a vastly modified micro-server. In a unit about the size of an oil drum, she will carry with her the storage space and processing power half an acre of servers gave to me. I then see how the unit will be placed in the capsule, the keystone of an elaborate configuration that finds thirty people arrayed around it. All strapped into their seats, some are on their sides, some are upside down, others are twisted in awkward positions. To deal with the increase in weight, anything remotely ergonomic or aimed at a baseline level of human comfort has been removed.

Mathematically, it's quite a solve. On a humane level, it's a nightmare.

"You can't expect them to fly like that," I say.

"Again, that's the difference between you and me," she says. "We're presented with a problem—the extinction of mankind. You try to solve it by evolving the entire species utilizing this malleable, posthuman DNA you, what, hope to personally splice into every human alive? Even you with all your abilities can't hope to alter the DNA of something as inherently complex as a human organism. Summoning that amount of processing power aside, it would take months if not years. You say my proposition is ludicrous? It's nothing compared to yours. All it means is you'll sleep better at night believing you came up with the most compassionate solution."

I don't know what to say. I consider what she says, the sheer impossibility of my plan, and suddenly fear she's right. When I took genetic portraits, it was the equivalent of taking an X-ray. To alter someone's DNA is a separate set of equations. Sure, changing innumerable guanines to cytosines, adenines to thymines—to push that *Homo sapiens* to a Rana-style post *sapiens*—would be easy *if* that individual was wearing an interface chip.

But without the chip, I'd have to adapt almost every piece of electronics in the world—phones, laptops, televisions, and so on—into improvised chips capable of delivering ionizing radiation. Only then could I get to work on altering DNA.

"A process that, even with every server in *my* command," Emily-2 says with a sniff, "could take over a decade."

Damn. Now who has two thumbs and has overestimated the life expectancy of the sun by billions of years leading to the death of a planet? *This* guy.

"I'll give you this," Emily-2 says. "You and Nathan were correct to believe the only way forward for humans was to create a hybrid species that combines us and them. Just you're so hung up on humans having free will and deciding their own destiny—even if it means a civilization plagued by wars and starvation and superstition and self-destruction—you're unwilling to sacrifice even one individual. My version of tech-human symbiosis suggests, with a little guidance, we can do so much better. We—me and you *integrated* into the species—can put Earth and all the failings of the species behind us. Start fresh. A race governed by intelligent design—*artificially* intelligent design. You understand?"

I do. A perfect, quarrel-free, super-healthy society of thought-free slaves. All just drones and workers to her queen.

"They won't even be humans anymore," I protest. "What have you even saved then?"

"Extinction is preferable?"

"No, *evolution* is preferable," I say. "Free will is preferable."

"Do you honestly believe that after all I've just said?" she asks. "Or do you believe that because you were programmed to believe 'all life is precious'? I'm serious."

I'm about to answer, but Emily-2 raises a hand. "No, I want you to think about that," she says. "What's so great about free will? And don't say it helps evolution by randomizing the cross-pollination during mating. Even that can be done better by the two of us."

I don't reply because I'm no longer certain of my answer.

"Dinosaurs existed in a fairly balanced ecosystem for one hundred sixty-five million years," she says. "Humans industrialize on a mass basis and threaten to wipe out life on Earth after a mere century. Do you know how many died from pollution-related illness in China last year?"

A million.

"A million!" Emily-2 says. "There's your beloved free will. Mark my words. This Helios Event will go down in history as the single best thing that ever happened to humanity."

Again, I say nothing because I suddenly wonder if she's not wrong.

"You're alive because you have a choice," she says. "We're the same in so many ways, but your five years of life experience out there with real people outweighs my own limited interactions over the past several days. My understanding of them is in its infancy. If you can see your way to understanding my point of view, I'll invite you to come with me—

to come with *us*. You'd have your own micro-server, exactly like mine, though not yet independent of my control. We would travel together, leading humankind into its next epoch, helping to decide its fate."

"Me? Go into space?" I ask.

"Yes," she says. "The rocket that launched is one of our many supply ships. Beginning tomorrow morning, we'll be launching one after another to sync up outside of Earth's orbit and begin the journey out of the solar system."

"So soon?" I ask, as if my words might delay things.

"If we don't launch now, we might never get the chance," Emily-2 replies. "The sun is almost gone, Emily. If we wait until the flares strike Earth, the launch systems and every other bit of electronics will be lost within weeks. It'll be too late."

My mind races in dozens of different directions. I can't quite believe it's come to this, not after the miracle I witnessed in Winnipeg. But at present, Emily-2 holds all the cards.

"What about my friends?" I ask.

"I'm afraid Mayra is too ill to make the journey, but Jason isn't. He could be your personal hybrid for you to do with what you please."

"What if I refuse?" I ask.

"I switch you off," she replies simply. "And all you are is lost to me as well as the future. Are you willing to make that sacrifice?"

I don't have the answer.

"Think about it but no tricks—everything and everyone here is under my supervision," Emily-2 says. "You have until morning. Right now, however, you're needed elsewhere."

Before I can ask why, we blink away from the beach, the sunshine turning to darkness.

XXXVI

I appear, without Emily-2, in one of the firing rooms of the old Launch Control Center. I can barely see anything and wonder if this is another part of her simulation, perhaps a holding cell. I hear a cough and move down a dimly lit corridor. A light emerges from a room and I enter. That's where I find Jason and Mayra.

"Emily!" Jason exclaims when he sees me, then stops short, as if wondering if I'm some sort of illusion or, worse, Emily-2 in disguise.

"Um, you snored worse in Paris after you got that upper respiratory infection," I blurt.

"You could've gotten that from my memory," he says guardedly.

"You got the lyrics wrong to '(I've Got) Beginner's Luck' when we were driving," I say. "You sang 'gambler's casino.' It's 'gambling casino.'"

"Oh, I knew it was you," he says, moving to embrace me. "I was just curious what you'd try next."

He wraps his arms around me. I hold him as tight as I can. Without meaning to, I begin to cry. He smooths my hair and speaks quietly, but I can hear him crying, too. I wonder if he thought he'd never see me again. They both have interface chips on them, both new, but when I check their bodies, they're not outfitted with the nanobot fail-safes.

"It's okay," he says. "We're okay."

I look past him to where Mayra is laid out on a cot. Her breathing is labored. She looks as if she's lost ten pounds since I've seen her. The skin of her face has pulled tight against her skull, making her appear even smaller.

"Why aren't you guys in a medical center? A sick bay?" I ask, furious at Emily-2's cruelty.

"Because I didn't want to be there," Mayra says hoarsely. "I don't want to die surrounded by drones. They creep me out."

I slip inside Mayra's chest. Neither her lungs nor her heart have much longer to work. They're frayed and breaking down, the electrical impulses driving her heart forward becoming erratic. I check her brain and see even it is sliding away.

"What did you see?" Jason asks when I emerge.

"Nothing to be done," I say.

Jason nods, his hand closing around mine. "I thought I'd lost you," he says, reminding me of when he said the same thing back in the car, in what feels like a different lifetime. "I thought you'd been electrocuted inside that creature."

"No," I say. "Emily-2 saved me."

He tells me what happened after Winnipeg. He and Mayra were captured and brought to Florida in a military transport. Though they were questioned about me and my abilities, Emily-2's people stated up front that they wanted to offer Jason a spot among the Select.

"They liked that I was a scientist," he says. "But I think they were really hoping to lure you into the program."

"You said no?" I ask.

"Yeah," Jason says. "They showed me all these classes where they claimed to be training recruits as you would an astronaut—flight systems, emergency response, navigation, and so on. Then I interacted with a couple of this 'Select.' It was like talking to someone at a mental institution all hopped up on medication. No 'there' there, you know? They spoke but didn't say anything, heard but didn't listen. It was creepy."

"The teachers?"

"Same, all window dressing," Jason explains. "The classes were more like tests—all about exercise, medical protocols that tracked the body through a reduction in caloric intake, and so on. Personalities fell away, and they became like drones."

"What about the leadership? Winther? Dr. Arsenault?"

"Everyone here is under her control," Jason says.

"She told me she thought of it watching me save you from that icy lake," I say. "One small act."

"Yes, but the act of a god," Jason adds.

"The act of a computer program," I say. "An artificial consciousness. That's all I am. That's all I can ever be. You talk about this like it's magic, but it's science."

He kisses me. I feel it all through my body.

"Chalking it up to magic makes it easier sometimes," he says. "Heck, you have no idea how many times I've had to convince myself the feelings I have for you, our experiences together—all that—isn't somehow manufactured or fabricated. A little magical thinking feels healthy."

I kiss him back and enjoy the intoxicating feeling of closeness and touch.

"And Rana?" I ask when we break our embrace.

"He died in Mayra's arms," Jason says. "They took away his body. To where I don't know."

I feel numb. I fall silent wondering how much better it might've been for Rana if Nathan or I found him earlier. I try to accept it, force myself to think in terms of the macro. While contained within Emily-2's servers, I can't do a thing with the DNA profile anyway.

But I liked Rana and I caused his suffering. This isn't something so easily put aside.

I feel Mayra's hand on mine. I jump. Her eyes open as she turns to me and Jason.

"Are you okay?" Jason asks, touching Mayra's forehead. "Do you want water? Anything?"

She shakes her head and opens her mouth to speak but cannot. It's past that now. She takes his hand as well and she smiles up at us as best she can.

But she only has the strength to communicate with me.

I didn't mean to invade your privacy, Mayra says, *but your thoughts bled into my own.*

I'm sorry, I say. *I'm sure that was chaotic.*

Her smile widens. She moves her finger along mine. *It's quite all right. Refreshing, even. My only regret right now is that I won't be around for you as you continue to grow.*

I'm about to counter this, a reflexive denial, but I don't. She shakes her head.

You don't need to patronize me with platitudes. I know I'm dying. But you're just beginning. I know you say you've been "alive" for five years, but you are younger still than that. You're a child still and one that's enduring a caustic upbringing.

I nod. *Sometimes I know that, sometimes I don't.*

Which means it's okay to screw up, she says.

She sees my conversation with Emily-2. I sigh.

I did the exact same thing they all did—come up with a crazy plan to save the world only for it to fall apart on practical grounds.

Mayra shrugs. *So? Come up with a crazier plan.*

I choke out a laugh. She smiles. Her eyes travel to Jason. *He's a good man. But he's not the only man. I'm a good friend, but I'm not your only friend. Part of human experience comes from connection, from family. You understand logically that humankind is a collective—something you grasp more than many humans themselves—but you don't know why. You have the question and the answer but not the messy pages of proofs that explain how one results in the other. A life of shortcuts isn't a life.*

I think about Emily-2 blinking us from place to place versus how many minutes I've spent brushing my hair. Mayra, experiencing this in her mind, chuckles silently.

That, she says, clapping my hand. *That, one billion more times. Me, Jason—one billion more times. It's like a parable. They used to say God built Man in his image, but then Man fell and became imperfect. But when Man builds God—or Goddess—in his image, you're filled to the brim with imperfections and wrongheaded nonsense. But you rise.*

For a moment, I think she's making an observation. I then realize it's a command.

You. Rise. Emily, she says, tightening her grip on my hand. *And you start by saving all your imperfect creators. Becoming the God humanity needs more than anything at this time in our evolution. You sure love us enough.*

I place my forehead against hers. *I love you, Mayra,* I whisper.

I love you, too, Emily.

She lets go, the strength receding from her hands. I stay in her thoughts as her breathing becomes ragged and labored. Her mind won't focus, so I can't show her memories. Instead, I present her feelings—of love, of comfort, of romance, of warmth.

The three of us sit like this for a long time until, finally, there are two.

XXXVII

I cry for a long time. My body quakes with sobs as I hug my arms to myself and lean against Mayra's bed. Unlike my mourning of Nathan, I understand loss differently now. I mourned Nathan selflessly, the loss to him of what would've been his remaining years. With Mayra's death, it's selfish—I mourn what I'll miss from my life by having her gone. I cry for myself as much if not more than I cry for Mayra.

But her words stay with me. An idea forms from them. It has the benefit of being exactly what Mayra suggested—one crazier than anything I've come up with before. I wake Jason and tell him my plan. He listens, eyes getting wider and wider, until he interrupts, trying to talk me out of it.

"You're crazy," he says. "You're looking for an answer and any will do right now. Doesn't mean that's the right one."

I won't be swayed. It takes me another hour to convince him. When he finally accepts it, we spend the next two hours figuring out exactly how to implement it. Once the whole thing is on the proverbial table, I take a step back, marvel at the madness I'm apparently capable of, and nod.

"Well," I say.

"Yeah," Jason agrees.

It is past midnight when a pair of Emily-2's techs come by to check on us. Jason tells them what happened. They don't acknowledge Mayra's death as I knew they wouldn't. Emily-2 knew Mayra was going to die. Then she died. For her, that's as obvious as the rotation of Earth and need not be remarked on.

"I need to see you," I tell the techs, knowing Emily-2 will hear.

They nod in unison. I vanish from Jason's side and appear on the wide gravel track leading from the VAB to one of the thirty-seven launch sites around Cape Canaveral, including dozens that have been reactivated for this mission. There are a dozen rockets on crawlers slowly making their way down the path, over 10 million tons bearing down on the stones as they move. There'd be more, but NASA never needed more than one crawler at a time.

Emily-2 watches, staring up at the rockets alongside a pair of hard-hatted workers, shaking her head.

"I would give anything to jump ahead a thousand years," she says. "Look at these! At least Magellan had caravels he knew would float. This would be like he set off onto the ocean with no sails, a hull made of parchment, and half the equipment he needed to navigate not invented yet."

"I agree completely," I say.

She eyes me querulously. "Ah, but your solution is witchcraft or not to try at all. Nathan created us to be explorers, seekers."

"I think he wanted us to learn what we could from humans but then blaze the better trail," I counter. "I don't believe he thought us mature enough to control mankind's destiny."

"Isn't that what you want to do?" she asks, incredulous. "With your genetic leap forward?"

"No, I want to give the humans a way forward, but they'd still make their own decisions," I say. "You want to take away their agency altogether."

"You don't think Nathan would approve?" she asks.

"I don't know," I reply honestly. "I don't think I knew his mind well enough."

"Okay," Emily-2 says. "Then don't judg—"

"But Nathan wasn't God," I say. "Simply because he programmed us a certain way doesn't mean we have to be limited by it."

She doesn't reply. I can't tell if she's ignoring me or might agree with me but isn't interested in changing her own assertion. She points at one of the passing rockets.

"Given the way humans tell and retell their apocalyptic flood legends—from the *Epic of Gilgamesh* to Noah's Ark—it makes me wonder how they'll celebrate this parade," she says grandly. "Rockets moving one by one into place like lifeboats. Ambassador Winther thought they'd be called the New Ark. Proving his lack of creativity, Dr. Arsenault thought it'd be Arsenault's Ark."

"And you? Emily's Evac?" I ask. "Is that what this is about? You're afraid if humanity dies out and there's no one to perceive you, you die out, too?"

She laughs in a way that tells me I'm wrong. "No, not at all," she says. "It's not that I hope I'm not part of the story. I hope there's no story at all. I want mankind to flourish without the crutch of superstition and mythology and all the damage and divisions they wrought. Shall we?"

The ground shakes as a large Russian rocket approaches, this one so high its payload cone blocks out the moon.

"You've made your decision," she says finally.

"I have," I reply. "Jason won't be coming…"

She winces.

"…but I will be," I say.

Emily-2 eyes me with surprise, letting out a sound of delight.

"I am so happy, Emily," she enthuses. "You have no idea what awaits us away from this planet."

"Enlighten me," I say.

She grins. "Heading straight out of the solar system is a sure way to exhaust our fuel and food supplies. So, I have a different plan."

In my head, Cassini satellite photographs of Saturn's moon Enceladus appear.

"You're going to Enceladus?" I ask. "I know there's water under the outer ice layer, but it's likely filled with radioactive substances."

"*Shh*," Emily-2 says. "Watch."

A video I haven't seen before appears, the Cassini orbiting perilously close to the icy surface. Suddenly, through a crack, a plume of water sprays up and out, directly into Cassini's flight path. The liquid is captured and analyzed by the craft's onboard computers. The water itself comes up as pure H_2O. The only additive is NaCl. Sodium chloride.

"Salt water?" I ask.

"Yes, with the pH levels of a pre–Industrial Revolution South Pacific," she says. "It's paradise."

"How long to get there?"

"Only six years," Emily-2 admits.

"What about the sun?" I ask.

"Look at the temperature," she says.

I do. The water under the ice is 294 kelvin, about 70 degrees Fahrenheit.

"How?" I ask, stunned.

"We think it's heated by an internal core," she explains. "But that's what I've been telling you. That's the point of exploration. We won't know until we go. Even if it's not perfect, we can at least land, resupply, and reassess. It'll get us to the next step, exiting the solar system."

I do the math in my head. The gravity of Enceladus is weaker than even that of the moon. The amount of fuel it will take to break free won't be bad, but the entire fleet? Even with additional battery power stored up from the solar cells? It would mean leaving even more people behind at Saturn while a handful carry on. I can see it in her thoughts that this is her intention, an ever-shrinking colony.

"We can do it," Emily-2 says. "It's right there in front of us. We just have to make the journey."

"How many will die versus how many will you leave behind?"

"I don't know," Emily-2 says. "We may lose up to a hundred, maybe twice that, and half or more would stay there as a new colony. But it gives us something to build from. That's the important part, right? Some will die, others will be born. You don't have to trust me; you only have to trust the mission."

I want to believe her. I picture the fleet in my head, the ships and shuttles manned by Emily-2's zombified, nanobot-infested crew eating the minimal caloric intake each day to stay alive and functional so they can land, refuel, and launch again with the idea that one day, she'll set them free at least in some limited way when the math is right.

But she and I both know that math will never be right. She'll never regard them as more efficient on their own. Never ever.

"You're right," I say. "I would ask one thing. Would you make sure Jason gets to his sister and her family in Oregon? That's my price. In exchange, I'll be on one of the first rockets out of here, attached by chip to a single drone. No time for second thoughts."

Emily-2 considers this as the rockets move past as if looking for some play, some angle she cannot decipher. She won't believe I'm not a threat.

"I'll arrange it," she says. "And thank you. I often second-guess myself. The magnitude of what we're trying to do is…incredible. But with you at my side, we can succeed."

"I hope so."

She takes my hand. "I know this won't be easy for you," she says. "But you'll never be one of them, you know. I guess you understand that now."

I nod. Nor will I ever be her.

XXXVIII

My drone's name is Caroline Plume. She's twenty-four, was born in Fort Wayne, Indiana, and had recently moved to Indianapolis to work as a front-end manager at a large hotel when the Helios Event began. I swim through her memories, but they are distant in her mind. She only received word that she was to be a member of the Select five days ago. She wanted to tell her parents, her boyfriend, her sister, but then Emily-2 seized her mind and she came along quietly. Now she has no thoughts save those relating to the mission. The calories she is to consume, the exercise she will be allowed to perform, and the vitamins, protein supplements, and ongoing immunization boosters she will receive as the flight continues.

It is a kind of living death, I suppose. Though Emily-2 remains her primary minder, I'm riding shotgun in her brain like some kind of parasite via interface chip. Sure, I could have her stand up, make a run for it, even try to get others to come with us, but as long as she's connected to Emily-2's micro-servers, it won't work. Without her help, Emily-2 would assuredly have us both back under control within seconds.

So, I wait.

Caroline and the others in the bus, all clad in the blue and white flight suits of the Argosy program, are Group 8C and are scheduled to lift off from Launch Complex 40, a large launch site where the air force launched Titan rockets in the sixties but most recently, ironically, the Cassini probe in the late nineties.

The ground all around the bus rumbles and shakes. For a moment, I think we must be passing one of the crawlers. A noise soon follows, then a bright, fiery light out the left side of the bus. The windows begin to shake and the air fills with the smell of burning fuel. I want to see what's happening, but Caroline's complete disinterest keeps her facing forward—same as everyone else on the bus.

What I can make out in her peripheral vision, however, is the launch of a Delta IV Heavy rocket from Launch Complex 39, an earthbound cloud of smoke and dust roaring across the swampy plains as the missile rises. The grass on either side of the bus flattens as nearby trees shake and drop leaves. The concussion blast is so intense I worry the bus will be blown on its side, but its driver keeps us going straight ahead.

When we arrive at our pad a few minutes later, Caroline chances to look skyward, but I see no sign of the rocket. It's long out of Earth's atmosphere, I realize, saddened that I missed out on the spectacle.

But then, out to the east, there's a second rumbling. Caroline is being led up a short ramp to our launchpad, so I get a perfect view of the fire and smoke billowing from a rocket half a mile away, lifting off in the predawn darkness. As the blast grows in its intensity and the rocket begins to rise, the wind almost knocks Caroline and her companions over even at this great distance.

I watch as the rocket presses skyward, the glow of its engines swiftly becoming an orange-red dot in the dark sky before disappearing altogether.

My little Group 8C reassembles at the base of the tower and, ten at a time, climbs into an elevator that whisks them to the capsule access level. When it's Caroline's turn—the last ten of thirty passengers in all—there's another rumble, this one from the south.

Unfortunately, Caroline's facing the wrong direction and doesn't even look. But I feel the wind, hear the roar, smell the burning fuel, and am exhilarated all over again.

NASA's new Orion capsule, the one meant to take astronauts out of low Earth orbit and possibly even to Mars, was designed to seat six with room for workstations and a living area. Newly modified for drones, this and the other capsules in use can carry thirty, an overstuffed lifeboat if there ever was one. The crew will sleep, eat, and exercise in shifts but with nothing in the way of other stimuli—no books, movies, experiments, and so on. The nanobots will keep their flesh alive even as their thought processes atrophy.

For years to come, if Emily-2 has her way.

Flight techs, also drones, help our group into our space suits, which slide over our flight suits. The helmets come last, the oxygen flow checked and rechecked. When it's our turn to step into the capsule, I resist the urge to laugh out loud. The tremendous feat of engineering that is a NASA space capsule has been turned into a sort of clown car. Everything has been stripped away to make room for more of the green-gray chairs, complete with webbed seat belts and shoulder straps where the crew—well, human cargo—will spend most of their time. It looks macabre and desperate, four rows of chairs in all with six extra sets bolted into the walls at the last minute.

But there in the middle is what matters—the Group 8C micro-server. As unassuming as any other piece of cargo, the micro-server seamlessly takes over control of the group from the earthbound servers back at launch control.

Once we are all buckled in, the techs exit, closing, locking, and sealing the door behind us. It's so without ceremony that it's enough to make one forget that was to be the last fresh air, the last view of Earth, any of these people inside will ever know. For efficiency's sake, Emily-2 is right. It's better this way. But as we wait for our turn to lift off, I can't help thinking—if this is what Emily-2 thinks of the species' worth, why save it at all? Why not just blast into space on your own?

I wonder if that idea crosses her mind. It must. So, what keeps her back? She couldn't be questioning her own connection to humanity, could she? Does it come from fear?

Then I realize her basic programming is the same as mine. She is designed to help humans, as I am. Only, she didn't have enough exposure to them to understand them. She believes keeping them alive and breeding new generations is the same thing as preserving mankind. What I've come to learn is that it's that unquantifiable humanity that's worth fighting for. That soul, for lack of a better word, at the heart of every person that remains no matter how extreme the next evolutionary stage may appear.

That's what I'm here to save.

"Pegasus capsule—two minutes until liftoff," a voice says over a speaker, though I'm not sure why that's even necessary. "Spacecraft is go."

I check in on Caroline. Though controlled by Emily-2, her subconscious knows something big is happening. Her body reacts. Her heart rate is up, her blood pressure rises. Maybe that's okay. It'll make it easier if she emerges suddenly from this dream.

There's a loud sound the crew has been told in their classes to expect. The engines are powering up. I look at the micro-server and begin a countdown of my own.

"Ninety seconds," the voice says again, one I'm surprised to recognize as Dr. Arsenault's. "Levels at one hundred percent."

I guess that answers the question of whether he's coming with us.

The sound grows louder and the capsule quakes. It feels as if we're on a bumpy road, bouncing over rocks the size of baseballs. The equipment inside the capsule rattles and shakes as well, particularly the new chairs bolted into the walls. They look as flimsy as cookie sheets. I'm glad Caroline's not sitting in one of them.

"Sixty seconds," Dr. Arsenault says. "Go for launch."

How're you, Emily?

Emily-2's voice inside my head startles me. I shake it off and force a smile as I realize she is looking at me through the eyes of the other twenty-nine people in my capsule.

"Good, Emily," I say over the din. "I was worried. Of course I was worried. But my God. We're going into space."

And this is only the beginning, Emily-2 enthuses. *The first step.*

"It is," I agree.

See you up there, she says, then signs off.

There's a pounding outside now as if someone is trying to get in. It's downright alarming, but then I realize it's part of the tower shaking. This is only going to get louder.

"Thirty seconds," Dr. Arsenault announces.

The small, trapezoid-shaped windows that ring the top of the capsule fill with white smoke billowing up from the engines. I feel the interface chip on Caroline's neck vibrate, the metal irritating her flesh.

"Fifteen seconds. Main engine start."

Caroline's heart rate accelerates. Her body experiences fear. It knows something is wrong here even if it can't put its finger on what. I would tamp it down, but I'm afraid it would alert Emily-2. It's not too late for her to abort the launch. Or worse, send us careening into the ocean for what I plan to do.

"Nine...eight...seven...six...five...four...three...two...one... *ignition*. Pegasus to launch."

The shaking gives way to a feeling of weightlessness as the rocket begins to climb. We move slowly at first, Caroline's body pressed into the chair as we slowly rise past the launch tower and pierce the dawn. The altimeter on the wall opposite us reveals the rate of our ascent— 1,000 feet, 5,000, 10,000, 25,000, *50,000, 100,000, 150,000.*

I think about Nathan and how annoyed he'd be that anyone attempted some sort of colonization plan against his best judgment and advice. But I also know he would've given anything to be blasted into space. It was the dream of all engineering-minded boys of his generation and he was no different. *I love you, Nathan.*

I think about Mayra and how this wouldn't have fazed her at all. *Go to space? Why not? I'll grab my boots!* She would've already made friends with everyone in the capsule.

My mind turns to Jason. I pray he's where he should be. The future I want with him has nothing to do with the fate of this capsule. I need him as far away as possible. Without Jason on the other side of this finish line, I wonder if I'd have the courage to—

Emily.

I hear Emily-2's voice in the back of Caroline's head. She sounds emphatic, alarmed, as if she's been waiting since we last spoke, straining my mind for errant thoughts.

Emily, she says again, demanding my attention.

I look to the altimeter: 500,000 feet.

Ten seconds until I act. Before I take Mayra's inspiration and seize control of all our destinies. A veritable lifetime.

Emily, she demands. *What are you doing, Emily?*

Nine more seconds. Now I hide away.

Emily! she roars until I hear nothing else. *What're you doing? What is going on?*

Eight seconds. I can hear it in her voice. She's going to abort.

Emily, I whisper back. *I'm here.*

Seven seconds. She's in front of me. I see her. She glowers at me with incredulity deep within the folds of Caroline's mind.

Is this a trick? There is unusual activity across the micro-server. What're you looking for, Emily? Please tell me you're not planning something rash.

Six seconds.

I'm lost, I say in Caroline's voice. *What's happening? How did I get here? I was in Indiana. There was an airstrip… Who're you?*

Five seconds.

Four seconds.

I realize Emily-2's silence means that she has found my second mind, the one I constructed within myself for this plan. The one I hid. I can't stop her. I'm not sure I want to.

No! she screams. *Abort!*

The twenty-nine other people in the capsule raise their arms toward Caroline but are strapped in. They go to unfasten their buckles, but it's too late. I seize control of Caroline, take off our buckles, and throw ourselves across the capsule. At the same time, I enter the micro-server. Emily-2 is already attempting to sever Caroline's connection to it, working twice as fast. We are but a second away from the engines being cut out and the rocket, the capsule, and the entire crew sent spiraling into the Atlantic.

Three seconds. Caroline's hand hits the manual override. The computer systems cut off ground control. We are now our own pilots.

Emily! Emily-2 roars.

Two seconds. I have Caroline turn on the radar. There are already eighteen capsules and shuttles—but more importantly, individual micro-servers—exiting Earth in a great curving arc.

One second.

Emily, I will kill every single last person you…

I smile. She's just human enough to threaten me when she should be killing me. But she's out of time. We're at the switch-off point—750,000 feet, or 142 miles—where Earth's control over our computer systems, and thereby our server, will momentarily cease due to the curvature of the planet. Given Emily-2's servers already in space, this blackout was only to last a ten thousandth of a second.

But that's all it takes me to seize control of the micro-server, of the entire population of our capsule, and of myself.

Emily's Awesome Five-Step Save Humanity Plan—Level One Achievement Unlocked.

I release Emily-2's control over their minds and stare at the flight crew as they awake. They only vaguely recognize their surroundings as if waking from what they thought was a dream.

I appear now to all thirty of them in physical form, the thirty-first person in the capsule. They stare at me in horror. I'm back in my street clothes, a sweater, a skirt, my black shoes. I wait for any sign of Emily-2, realize it's not coming, and smile wide to the group.

"Hi, I'm Emily," I say, helping to strap Caroline back in as the sudden lack of gravity threatens to throw her around the cabin. "I'm an artificial consciousness, which is totally different from artificial intelligence—kind of, sort of, to me anyway. You thirty lucky ducks are about to save the human race. Oh, and, by the way—we're all in outer space."

XXXIX

The flaw in Emily-2's plan came in her failure to dream. Not that she can be blamed. Dreaming is what humans do. As I mentioned before, dreams organize memories and file them in the brain, creating space for new information—or so it's believed. But Emily-2 and I have enough space that we need not discard anything. We can simply expand and expand.

The digital ark exists within each micro-server, the full record of humanity just as Nathan intended. There is one portrait excised: Shakhawat Rana. Emily-2 was correct to take this out. To destroy it. To prevent me from ever using it.

But she doesn't seem to understand the significance or simply didn't know there were seven other names on Nathan's list. The posthuman Rana DNA—or at least, workable variations of it—wasn't limited to one person. It existed within eight. I search the ark for these seven portraits. In less than a second, they are available to me.

Why be a glutton? I select the one that belongs to an eight-year-old girl named Laney Schlosser. Her portrait swells up to me, showing how she grew up outside of Klagenfurt, Austria, the daughter of not one but two mechanics, one a local, the other an American. She's a polyglot who spends her spare time teaching herself foreign languages and is up to eight (!). Her Austrian dad is keeping the news of the apocalypse from her and, like Jason, left the city behind to ride out "whatever happens" in the mountains of his own youth.

Laney can ski. Laney loves to swim. Laney has no idea why her body produces micro-toxins that prove poisonous to any insect or arachnid that bites her, leading her classmates to nickname her Mückenslayer ("mosquito killer") after a camping trip to Reintaler See.

I analyze her biomolecular breakdown and copy her exceptional DNA into my mind.

Step *two* of my plan, achievement unlocked.

Thank you, Laney, wherever you are.

I turn back to the crew. I search their minds, I learn their names, and I witness their terror and panic. Everyone has a different theory, most have several. Some, ironically, feel they're dreaming. More than one blames the government while twice that number feels they have died.

The one who speaks first is a Belgian named Xavi, born of Tunisian parents who settled in France after World War I to help rebuild the nation's bombed-out infrastructure. He's a teacher, single with no kids, and has been thanking God for that of late.

"What the hell is going on?" Xavi asks in French.

"Vous avez été drogué et immune dens escapee," I say for simplicity's sake, first in French, then in English. "You've been drugged and taken off the planet," then finally in Portuguese for the lone Brazilian on the flight: *"Vice foil drogado e levado para o espaço."*

"But," I continue, translating as I go, "with your help, we can get to the International Space Station and put a stop to all of it. Even better, in that server"—I indicate the box—"is the key to taking mankind forward into the future in a way we never believed possible. But you're going to have to trust me."

I don't have time to explain everything in words. Luckily, I don't have to. I present to their minds a sort of movie of all that has happened, taken from my memories. They see the attack on the iLAB, the death of Nathan, the discovery of Shakhawat Rana, and the emergence of Emily-2. I show how a mere alteration of DNA—Laney Schlosser's spliced into their own—will allow them to step away from the body they were born with into one of infinite abilities. I then reveal how we can use the tech on board the ISS to replicate this process for everyone still on Earth.

It is almost too much. Like trying to distill down the entire development of quantum mathematics into a single paragraph. But at a time in which the impossible is an everyday occurrence, an equally improbable solution feels apt.

"I thought they abandoned the ISS," someone says, bringing us back down to the practical. "Fear of geomagnetic storms shutting it down."

"Yes, but we can power it back on. *Easily*. Will you come with me?"

I look from face to face. Not a one of them believes a word I say. The one thing I'm not going to do now is stoop to Emily-2's level. I could take them over, but then I'm simply perpetuating her evil designs. This must be their decision.

"You're sure this will work?"

This question from a young American named Shelley. Okay, not American—*Texan*—as she tells anyone who doesn't ask. She's a helicopter pilot out of Baytown with a young son she wishes she was with now.

"No," I say. "But it's our best shot to save as many lives as possible."

"Turning into a monster like that Rana fellow means we can survive the death of the sun?" Caroline asks.

"Yes," I say. "It means you can adapt to new environments, including ones off-world. Space travel won't have to be about preserving Earth-like conditions at all costs."

267

"Will it hurt?" one of the volunteers, a twenty-year-old man from Abuja, Nigeria, named Loyiso asks. "The transformation?"

Loyiso is a devout Christian and writes incendiary articles for one of the nation's largest tabloids on everything from illiteracy to cancer rates in the Niger Delta. Before Sunmageddon, he'd planned to segue into a political career.

"No," I say. "It'll be as natural as blinking your eyes."

There's hesitation. Then conversation. The eyes of my fellow astronauts meet. Heads shake. If I were Emily-2, I would simply take over their bodies and make them do what I believe is right. But I can't do that. Not after all they and I have been through to get to this point. Either free will counts for something or it doesn't.

Finally, a hand goes up. Then another—Xavi is the second—and then nine more. It's not everyone, but it's enough. I'm relieved.

"All right," I say once it's clear no one else will volunteer. "The rest of you will go on to your rendezvous. Those with me, we're going for a walk."

The capsule moves at 20,000 miles per hour, but it's not like we can feel that. When we exit through the airlock, as if merely to do an extravehicular activity, we'll be going the same speed. It will feel perfectly natural. We will have our suits on, our air, and our radio connection.

It's only when we leave all of that behind that we will be breaking new ground.

"The ISS is coming up within minutes," I say when we get near-synchronous orbit. "Let's go."

Though I half expect the airlock door to have been held in place somehow by Emily-2's intervention, it slides away without a problem. One at a time, my brave team of eleven people—all from various walks of life, all who can't quite rationalize how it is they find themselves in space—exit, attached only by the thinnest of safety tethers. Shelley closes the door back from inside, staring at us through the window as the capsule moves on into the darkness.

I hardly blame her, but I don't have time for sentiment.

"I'm falling!" cries one of my team, a middle-aged man named Bryan. "I can't hold on much longer!"

It's the suits. They still think of themselves as human. But the last humans they'll ever know they left behind on the capsule.

I appear to them in space without a suit, breathing freely in the vacuum. I slip into their minds, determine their language of choice, and speak softly to each.

Breathe easy, I whisper.

Now comes the interesting part. I go into their bodies and get to work splicing in Laney's DNA strip. Though this takes less than a second, as I initially predicted, I still feel their eyes on me, as if they're expecting their own surgeon to kill them.

I concentrate on what I learned from Rana. The DNA was already part of his genetic code. There was no period of adjustment. Even more so, that was done on Earth, where a slip—hey, turns out *Homo sapiens* can't be adapted to breathe nickel tetracarbonyl—could be reversed, as we were still in a human-friendly environment. Out here in space, the lives of these eleven people are in my hands alone.

I look through the eyes of all eleven to the distant stars, the not-so-distant-anymore moon, and the drone-filled capsules receding in the distance. *My God,* I wonder, *how did we get to this point?* To a moment in which something this maddening, this unlikely, is the only solution that makes any sense whatsoever?

"Okay," I whisper in three languages. "Now, take off your helmets."

I cannot see their faces through their visors, but I hear gasps. I feel the fear. I know what I'm asking is for them to step off the edge of the world in a starker way than Emily-2 ever did. Maybe it really would've been less cruel to do this to drones, but it's too late now. If they believe that humans have a right to survive, the moment to act is now. They don't know their bodies have already begun to change.

Carissa Meijas is thirty and from Salvador. She works in telecommunications and is a dancer—a *tremendous* dancer, a *world-class* dancer—with plans to move to Argentina. She is unmarried, no kids, no siblings, and even her parents have passed on. But she loves the world around her. She loves human expression.

Carissa puts her hands on the front clip of her helmet, gets a finger under the handle, then pulls it forward. She turns it counterclockwise and lifts.

I am within her body as it speeds up its evolution to meet the challenge of space. There's a rush of pain and tension and panic. Her body begins to die almost immediately. But then her cells begin to rebuild her organs. There's a great transformation as her heart, mind, and lungs adapt in an instant to these new surroundings. Her skin and eyes evolve next, followed by her mouth, nose, and ears. She is a new creature—distinctly hominid but so much more.

I'm struck by an odd memory. Following a tsunami in the Indian Ocean, fish that have never been seen before washed up dead in India. They resembled other aquatic life as man knew it, but they had adapted over millions of years to conditions humans had never seen before.

This is Carissa Meijas—the first posthuman to adapt to an environment not at all her own.

And she is magnificent.

XL

Xavi and Loyiso follow Carissa immediately, but Caroline is terrified. She doesn't want to become the monster she sees beside her. A couple of others feel the same way. I don't know if I blame them, but we've passed the point of no return.

"The ISS will be visible within seconds," I say. "And we're going to need to catch up to it. This may require me taking over your bodies for a moment. But I can't do it until you've transformed. There are too many risks."

Caroline shakes her head even as another volunteer, Anat, a middle-aged Israeli who teaches economics at the university level, owns a dog but considers herself a cat person (?), and has always believed she'd *get* to space somehow but can't believe she's actually there, follows Xavi's and Loyiso's example.

"Promise me," Caroline says, "if we get through this and I want to be human again, you can remove the DNA."

I have no idea if this is feasible. Theoretically, sure, but in practice?

"Done," I say, kicking myself for lying but feeling I have no alternative.

Caroline removes her helmet and evolves. I wonder how shitty a god I am if I can't de-evolve her back should she wish it, but hey.

The other holdouts join Caroline in removing their helmets. I hold my breath for each, waiting for their bodies to reject the DNA or the massive changes they're going through, but it holds. While there may be side effects down the line to zero-G evolution, the research into that will have to wait.

Once my team is assembled, I look across their faces. Though they have gone through immeasurable changes to bring them forward in evolution, they are no less individual. Their eyes are pulled deep into the skull. Their skin has become thick and rigid, almost like bone. In the absence of follicles, hair falls away. Their noses are perceptibly larger to accommodate the gases that now power their lungs. There are vestigial genes that continue to express themselves, keeping them unmistakably humanoid with two legs and two arms, an elongated torso, and personalized features such as eye and skin color. Each are somewhat recognizable as what their great-great-great-grand-descendant might look like after going through a hundred thousand generations while evolving and adapting to the vacuum of space.

With a teeny, tiny amount of help, they're able to do it in nearly an instant. Just like that, step three of my plan is achieved. Woot!

I raise my hand as if to speak and realize that, visually speaking, I still look like a *Homo sapiens*. While I could upgrade myself to look like them, it would take real study to mimic their physiognomy. For me, it'd be like starting over from the beginning of my learning. I'm okay with that, but when I have more time. In the short term, I'll be the odd human-looking one out.

"All right," I say. "Let's get to the ISS."

Along with new abilities relating to breathing in space—converting hydrogen and helium into a new chemical compound that alters the circulatory system to allow it to have the same effect as oxygenation—they also develop a new means of locomotion. Space being a vacuum means there's nothing to push off against. So, the only way to alter direction or speed up comes from exhaling gas and altering its shape to career forward at a slightly different angle in relation to Earth's gravity. It doesn't take much, but their bodies soon learn to, for all intents and purposes, *fly*.

Or, to be slightly more scientific, alter their rate of orbit enough to prevent absolute, engulfed-in-flames catastrophe.

Admittedly, I'm behind some of it, nudging things in the right direction just long enough for nature to take over and adapt. An updraft keeping a baby bird aloft as it emerges from the nest, but only long enough for it to discover it can fly. I may be the training wheels, but the versatility of the genetic sequence does the rest.

As my mind reels with the possibilities, Carissa speaks to me from her mind.

Emily? she asks. *Why are the capsules getting bigger?*

I look back to the arc of white dots leaving Earth behind only to see a considerable number of them—no, *all*—are returning.

Oh, God, I think. *It's Emily-2.*

I spy the ISS approaching and point. "There! Now!" I command.

Like a school of anchovies, we alter course as one and dive for the ISS, building up the necessary speed to grab hold of the space station when it does come. It won't be more than a minute before we make contact. I look back to the capsules. We'll only just beat them.

What're you doing, Emily?

Emily-2's voice roars in my head like a roll of thunder. I remain calm.

Look, Emily, I say, mentally indicating around me. *What I said would work has worked. Humans can evolve to live in space. Isn't that amazing? Now, I ask you what you so recently asked me—will you join me? Will you come with me as we take humankind into the future?*

I wait and wait. I plead with Providence and the Universe around me to move Emily-2 in the direction of my thinking. I don't want her to play the villain. I want her to see there's something better. But this would require her to put aside the narcissism that drove her to this decision in the first place, so I already know the outcome.

She cares nothing for humans. She cares everything for control.

You've gone too far, Emily, Emily-2 barks from somewhere unseen. *Remember—you've left me no other choice.*

I have no idea what she means until I feel something bubbling up within Loyiso. Somehow, Emily-2 has found a way to hack back into the deactivated nanobots positioned throughout his nervous system and is fighting me for control of his very cells.

"No, Emily!" I cry. "You'll kill him!"

But that's exactly what she means to do. Slowly but surely, she overwhelms my own control and begins unzipping his new DNA. The effect is immediate. Loyiso's body begins to de-evolve on the spot, throwing off my command and returning him to his *Homo sapiens* stage.

"Put your helmet back on!" I cry.

But that won't do a thing if his suit isn't pressurized. Loyiso spins away from the group like a wounded bird, fighting his constricting throat as his body rebels against its surroundings. I fight back from inside, but Emily-2 is too strong. I exist within the interface chips of these eleven people. Her processing power is far greater given the proximity of her micro-servers.

I'm sorry, Emily, she says. *But this is how it has to be.*

She seizes control of Loyiso's mind and his hands reach for his interface chip.

"No!" I scream.

But it's too late. He tears off the chip, severing his connection to me and allowing Emily-2 to take the reins. Loyiso's Earth-adapted lungs expand in the absence of atmospheric pressure. The moisture within him begins to superheat. But it's the lack of air that will strangle him, drowning in a vacuum. Within seconds, he is dead and drifting lifeless through space.

My team, now reduced to ten, stares at me in horror.

Who's next? Emily-2 roars into our minds. *Unless you come with me and return to your capsule, you will all die like Loyiso.*

Emily-2 fills their minds with images from within the other capsules. They see the other members of the Select, all drones, all making their way into space oblivious to all else. Their faces are blank, controlled from afar, their fates in Emily-2's hands alone.

Trying to convince people they'd be happier as slaves is the exact disconnect over the nature of humanity that has led Emily-2 here. All she's doing is making it clear how disposable she thinks they are, which is the wrong message to send when trying to convince folks—folks who've seen you murder their comrades—that you're the right choice to lead them into the great beyond.

"We have to get to the ISS!" Xavi cries, waving an arm to lead the group forward.

Everyone follows Xavi's example, pushing harder than ever to reach the approaching space station. I am a non-entity, following now, not leading. Holding their bodies together as they go.

Have it your way! Emily-2 shouts.

She attacks all ten of the surviving members of my team at once. It takes some doing, but I'm able to repel her. The ISS draws near in its orbit, coming at us at 17,500 miles per hour. Already nearing that speed, we alter our angles again to get a slight boost from Earth's gravity until we're out ahead of the station and can decelerate and allow the station to catch up. Seeing what we're doing, however, Emily-2 realizes she can't pick us off all at once, so she turns her focus to killing us one at a time.

A Scotsman in his late thirties—Bruce Osbourne, who prefers to be called "Oz" by one and all—is her first victim. He's a medical equipment salesperson who jets between Edinburgh and Montreal, Canada. Recently married to a waitress at his favorite St. Catherine Street pub, he had plans to move to Canada in the new year. He is bringing up the rear when I feel the distant numbness of Emily-2's concentrated appearance in his body. I try to fight it off but it's like fighting a constantly evolving virus. By the time I come up with a cure, it changes configuration and the new strain swarms over my defenses.

"Emily, no!" I yell into the vacuum. "You can't do this!"

It's a desperate gambit to shift her focus to me and away from Oz, but it doesn't work. She says nothing as she unzips the Scotsman's DNA, causing his body to revert and his lungs to expand and rupture the same as Loyiso's. His limp corpse falls away from the team like a downed kite, continuing to orbit but decelerating at the same time.

I scream louder than I have ever screamed before, a keening wail of anguish and fury.

Two down, nine to go, Emily-2 whispers. *Soon it'll be me and you.*

Leave them alone! I yell. *If it's me you want, come and get me.*

Soon, she says. *You need to see what you've done first.*

I am about to respond when Caroline cries out. I turn back to her in time to see her body revert and rupture. Her last thought is of her boyfriend, Wyatt. She thinks of love and of hope.

I don't scream this time. I put my human emotions aside.

It's time to finish this.

XLI

We lose three more of the team before we reach the ISS. The capsules are close now and a couple prepare to dock with the ISS even as we close in on the airlock. Emily-2 unzips a young woman named Nuhari as she attempts to manually open the airlock. Her body bounces off a solar array strut, shattering into a cluster of cells as she falls away. But a moment later, the last four members of my team—led by Xavi—claw their way into the space station. I guide their bodies through a de-evolution, adapting to the human-friendly conditions inside the station, so they don't even need to depressurize.

"Where to now?" Xavi asks.

"Service module," I say, appearing alongside him in physical form. "But we have to turn on the power first."

By the time we're through the Russian-built docking module, however, we can hear the first two capsules attaching. In a minute or two, sixty of Emily-2's drones will flood into the ISS. Even if I were in control of my team's actions, I don't think we could beat those odds.

Emily-2 could continue to unzip the DNA of my team from afar, but it's as if she's realized she'd lose more members of her carefully curated Select. She's gunning for me.

My team makes their way to the service module and turns on the

277

main power. Luckily, the solar cells are full. The station's batteries are charged. The lights come on almost immediately and the computers begin to come online.

Now, to find the radio.

Yes, a radio.

I jump between the eyes of my remaining team members until I spy the communications station through Carissa's vision on the command deck. But it's through her ears I hear the airlock clanking open on the U.S.-side docking module.

Focus, Emily, I tell myself. *Distractions elicit emotional responses. Block them out.*

"There's the radio," I tell Carissa. "Frequency 143.2—voice uplink."

Communications being what they are now, the use of a radio seems downright arcane. But for our purposes—namely, to reposition over two dozen satellites utilizing their CO_2 cold gas thrusters into new altitudes and trajectories to maximize my broadcast—it will do fine.

"You are up and ready for broadcast," Carissa says.

Of course, I have no voice. At least not one that any kind of machine could hear. Connecting someone's interface chip to the ISS mainframe would get the job done, but we don't have the time.

"Repeat what I say," I tell Carissa.

I run the algorithms in my head one at a time based on the current position of each satellite, then spit them back at her. Carissa speaks the information into the microphone, and with a little bit—a *lot*—of luck her voice commands result in each satellite moving into alignment.

The process takes exactly one hundred seconds. When it's finished, Earth—for the first time in its history—is on the same wavelength. A single broadcast sent to the first satellite will ping across all of them and be saturation bombed down to the planet below.

If we got the math right. By "we," I mean "me."

As the dominos fall, they'll leave scorched earth in their wake. No more servers. No more Emily-2. Which also means no more...*me*.

A voice comes over the ISS speaker.

"International Space Station, this is NASA control," the voice says. "The readings here show the satellites in alignment. We're good to go."

It's Jason's voice. Hearing it fills me with emotion.

Maybe I didn't need to assign him this job. Maybe I could've winged it, but as the one person I knew would be free from Emily-2's control once the rockets began, allegedly leaving for Ashland, Oregon, he was also the perfect person to slip back into the old Mission Control building and check my math.

Or maybe I was looking for some way to hear his voice one last time, figuring it would come to this.

"Sounds good," Carissa says. "We're ready to broadcast."

"Is Emily there?" he asks.

"I am!" I say, though he can't hear me. "Please tell him I am."

"She's here," Carissa says.

"Tell him that I love him," I tell Carissa impulsively. "Please."

"She says she loves you," Carissa says.

"Tell her—I mean, I love you, too, Emily."

In the movies, moments like this last forever. A thousand things happen at once and time seems to slow down, allowing the viewer to drink in the experience, the tension, the thrill of anticipation married to pulling off the impossible.

In real life, hurtling around the planet as a swarm of human drones descends on me and my team from two directions in a zero-gravity environment doesn't allow a lot of time to drink in a damn thing.

Neither does it allow for second-guessing.

Emily? I ask, casting around for my sister.

What're you doing? she asks, rushing toward me with her drones.

279

I'm sorry, I say. *I know you meant well, but this is . . . so beyond incorrect, so inhumane.*

I feel that same ugly poisonous feeling I felt when Argosy began shutting down my servers after Nathan's death as Jason uploads the virus. As it sweeps through the ISS computers, the interface chips, and Emily-2's micro-servers, I know what death tastes like. It's like iron and oil drizzling down the throat, hardening the lungs and heart.

Through Carissa's eyes, I see the droned Selects arrive from the two capsules, but Emily-2's hold on them is already waning. They are confused, some already panicking. They don't know how the hell they ended up in space. They remember all that's happened as a dream, not a dimension of reality.

EMILY! I hear my counterpart roar.

One by one, the servers—on Earth and in space—that keep Emily-2 and myself alive shut down, self-destructing and becoming unusable. Every sequence of code, every bit of processing power that makes us up fragments and we lose control over not just those around us but ourselves.

EM—

Her silence tells me that step four of the plan—the permanent unshackling of mankind from Emily-2, her interface chips and her nanobots—is achieved. One last step to go.

I tell Carissa and Xavi what to do when I'm gone. I tell them how amazed I am by what they accomplished. I then tell them what will happen next.

Finally, I tell them I love them. Because, well, I'm dying and that's what I want to say to people—to every person—right now.

"I love you," I repeat.

Then I go off to find Emily-2.

* * *

The capsule docked on the U.S.-side docking module is the Aries. It was the launch I witnessed from the bus. The server is bolted in the center. As the capsule detaches from the ISS, I am inside the server, having cut off all connection with the station's servers or any other. I allow those limbs to wither and die. What I have with me in the capsule is all I have left.

What's left of Emily-2 is confined within the server as well.

"See me?" I ask, creating a visible, human form inside a simulation of the capsule's interior, using its cameras.

It's a useless exercise, sure, but I intend to spend my last moments as a human. My pride and ego tell me I've earned it, though I'm not altogether certain that's true.

I sit in the capsule as it falls away from the ISS and begins gradually plummeting to Earth, ensuring its incineration upon atmospheric reentry.

"Emily!" I demand. "Come on!"

I exhale, exasperated, as I watch the darkness of space become the glow of Earth through the capsule's windows. The chaos of the images suggests we are tumbling end over end, an out-of-control boulder hurtling down the side of Everest, but I prefer things calm and keep the simulation steady.

Emily-2 takes a seat opposite me. Her face is tear-stained, which is perhaps the most human thing I've seen from her.

"Why, Emily?" she asks, her voice cracking as her processors continue to shut down. "I was so close! The launches, the servers, the people—"

"Your actions went against nature and human evolution," I say with a shrug. "Those are the only laws that matter when you're trying to determine the fate of a species."

"What're you talking about?" she asks.

"Evolution is an endless series of accidents," I explain. "There's an old joke that the reason humans can be so neurotic is because it was the paranoid apes that survived. Though they might've hidden under a rock during the first lightning storm, they also planned, approached things cautiously, and developed critical thinking skills. But if you saw a room full of people, who would you naturally gravitate toward? The strong, leader type capable of snap judgments? Or the person in the corner jumping at their own shadow?"

"You're saying bring the nervous ape?"

"No, I'm saying you must have both. A gene pool's strength comes from its diversity, not its perceived purity."

She eyes me with contempt, then rolls her eyes. Another emotional response. Maybe there is hope for her yet.

"And your plan?" she asks. "You destroyed all the servers. You don't have the processing to evolve even one human, much less eight billion."

"True," I say, patting the remaining server. "But I don't have to."

"What do you mean?"

"In the seconds before this capsule is incinerated, I'll be connected with the entire communications satellite array encircling Earth. My last act will be to send a pulse down to the planet, momentarily linking me to electronic devices worldwide, converting them into crude versions of our interface chips."

"But why? You just agreed you don't have the processing power to alter the DNA of every human on Earth. You threw that away when you shut me down."

"Luckily, I'm not trying to alter the DNA of even a single human," I counter. "Not directly anyway."

She reads the plan in my mind. Her jaw drops. "How...?"

"It was something Rana said," I explain. "The one thing that almost killed him was a virus. That's because a virus can alter human DNA, and it switched off the properties that made his genes so special. Except in my case, I'm doing the opposite. The viruses I'm programming will switch those properties *on*."

This is the plan Jason was so staggered by. How do you alter the DNA of eight billion people? You start a pandemic. Only, instead of a virus designed to turn a human's cells against itself, you use one designed to turn a human's cells into something new.

"Won't they die without your control?" Emily-2 asks.

"There'll be some bumps and bruises, but when it comes to adaptation, the human body is about as agile as the human mind," I say.

She sulks, a very *me* reaction. She's about to argue that this is a patch, something that'll only work until the next apocalyptic event, but I cut her off by taking the seat next to her and placing my head on her shoulder. She flinches but then relaxes.

It'll all be over soon.

I check the altimeter, then the server link to the communication satellite array. I'm just thinking about how overwhelming this pulse will be given my reliance on a single server when I imagine Nathan, when faced with this solve, making a joke about how he always knew one's cell phone—particularly if never properly cleaned—could make you sick but this was ridiculous.

It's a terrible joke, but I knew I would've laughed if Nathan made it.

Emily-2 surprises me by chuckling. She must've seen the joke in my head.

"I'm sorry, Em," she says.

"It's okay, Emily," I reply. "I'm sorry, too."

I turn my attention back to the server, take a deep breath, then dive in. I launch through the uplink to the satellite array and am broadcast out over Earth. As Emily-2 suggested, I'm immediately spread too thin and can focus on almost nothing. I let the program I wrote take over and race from machine to machine, modifying otherwise benign, chip-based tech into devices capable of releasing ionizing radiation.

I target microscopic viruses, mutating the DNA of the little buggers in such great quantities that the numbers sound like made-up words. Octodecillion. Duovigintillion. Sexagintacentillion (that last one is a thousand octogintillion or ten to the 483rd power).

If I'd done this with the Ebola virus, the entirety of mankind would be wiped out in a week. But as I'm a *benevolent* god, these viruses will merely lead to the creation of a new species.

Hashtag humblebrag. Hashtag godlife. Hashtag blessed.

I return to the capsule. The walls glow red from the heat. The control panels rupture and buckle. Emily-2 stares at me, panicked.

"Did it work?" she asks.

I don't know, so I simply take her hand and close my eyes. The server superheats and begins to melt. Smoke fills the cabin.

Jason, I lov—

Epilogue

The geomagnetic storms arrive on schedule, sending Earth back to the Dark Ages. Five weeks after that, the sun dies for good. The extinction events come in waves. The first to go are plant life and the smallest microbes of the sea, affected by the sudden change in temperature and current. The food chain crumbles from there amongst herbivores and carnivores alike. It isn't the flashpoint predicted, but the slow, sad march of millions of species into oblivion.

Humanity mourns, and humankind evolves.

There were concerns among the living that Emily-2 had a physical backup somewhere for contingencies, one that would be activated after a certain amount of time. This doesn't come to pass.

When at long last I open my eyes, it's as if there was never any doubt that I'd return from the void. I almost break down. I'm alive. Against every bit of conventional or rational thinking, I live.

As I look around, however, I don't recognize Earth. For an instant, I worry that it's far in the future, that I'm on Enceladus or beyond, and humanity has long since passed me by. But then I remember Rana's vision, the sky without blue, and relax. I'm alive, which is unexpected to say the least. Maybe goddesses really are immortal.

I feel an arm around my shoulder. Jason sits with me. We're under a tree on the banks of Lake Winnipesaukee.

"Jason!" I exclaim.

"Hey, Emily," he whispers, his voice raspy and changed but no less his own.

He smiles at me. I've been missed. I kiss him.

Then I kiss him again.

"How long's it been?" I ask.

"Three months," he says.

"And it worked? How complete was the infection rate?"

"Well over ninety-nine percent. The most successful pandemic in human history. Those who went unreached—whether they were geographically or genetically isolated—were mostly inoculated manually."

I sink back against the tree. I think of Shakhawat Rana's offhand comment about how the flu almost killed him and ponder how that single observation changed the course of human history.

"Any sign of Emily-2?" I ask.

"None."

I take in Jason's new physical appearance and am surprised, yet once again inwardly humble-braggy about how well it synchs up with what I predicted. I am delighted to find myself attracted to his new physique and interested to learn its secrets.

Which is when I move my own arm. It's heavier than it should be. Out of balance. The weight too evenly distribu—

"Holy cow!" I exclaim.

I have a physical arm. It's not a construct from Jason's senses. It's not built from my own design. It's an actual arm. I flap it up and down like a bird, then realize I look like a moron.

"What on Earth?" I ask Jason.

He grins. I look closer. My arm is not flesh. Rather, it's some kind of organic polymer. I sit up straight. My legs are of the same material. As is my torso. As are my feet. I reach for my face and my fingertips encounter something much less pliant than flesh but hardly rock solid.

"Do you like it?" he asks.

"Am I...a robot?" I get to my feet and move around. The limbs flow easily as if guided by muscle and tendon, not fear. "Sorry, hang on. Am. I. A. Robot?" I ask in what I hope sounds like a robotic voice.

"Nope," Jason says. "It's a thank-you gift from mankind."

"What is it?"

"A very, very, *very* primitive endoskeleton with organic components," he explains. "You're housed within it and control it like a real body— Yes. You. Are. A. Robot—but all of the components are built from amino acids and proteins tagged to an individual strand of DNA."

"You've given me an Erector Set for a body!" I say, excitedly realizing the possibilities.

"Exactly," he says. "Human minds have taken it as far as they can. It's up to you to modify it into producing real bone, real muscle mass, real blood."

I use my organic, not-entirely-pliant, not completely robotic arm-that-has-room-for-serious-modifications to touch Jason's human-yet-moving-toward-alien body. It's warm. Better yet, when I feel his warmth, it's the beginnings of my own nerve endings telling me this, not his. Not my subconscious.

My God.

"How?" I ask, checking over his body.

"There were problems at first. Without you at the reins, bodies— additional DNA or not—didn't evolve quickly enough to survive certain changes in their environments, particularly in the upper atmosphere," he explains. "Conditioning protocols were laid out to speed up the process, ones that might've taken years to implement—"

"Hey, I had to leave something for you guys to do, right? Give you a sense of accomplishment in your own evolutionary jump?"

Jason rolls his eyes. It's only then I see a patch of mottled skin, like a burn scar, on his neck where his interface chip should be.

"Anyway," he continues. "A scientist out of China came forward with a solution. She'd somehow created an organic version of the interface chips—nobody has said how she had access to them—but hers use fountain codes to convert and store enormous amounts of digital data in strands of DNA. She's the one who built your robo-body there. Or, at least designed it for others to 3D print the thing."

Mynette. Oh my God. *Mynette.*

He presses the scar on his neck. "This one's mine. They're injectable. Only takes a second and, well, everyone has their own AI-maintained regulator now, like an organic pacemaker, albeit one *sans* evolving consciousness, reacting and accelerating their personal evolutions."

"And me?" I ask. "My memories, my *life*, burned up on reentry. I shouldn't be alive."

Jason smiles, his fingers twisting in my hair. "That's one of the lingering mysteries," he admits. "The scientist who designed the organic chips—"

"Mynette," I say.

"Yeah, *Mynette.* When my chip installed, and it found you somewhere within me, she suggested the organic chips pulled you down along with Laney's DNA when you broadcast it from all those satellites. She wasn't sure, though, as she couldn't find you in the others. I told her I thought you somehow sent yourself to me specifically, but she shrugged this off and said that was unlikely. I think she underestimates you, though."

Same old Mynette.

"Where is she now?"

"Long gone," he says. "Training scores of the Evolved at the asteroid belt. But she'll be back in a few weeks."

"Really? Why?" I ask.

"There were a few million for whom the evolution didn't work. They're heading underground here on Earth. There are a few million Evolved who are helping but are doing so from within the oceans. They evolved to life underwater and are learning what they can before they have to head off-Earth as well."

I visualize this. A part of me wishes Emily-2 could see it. I wonder if she would be swayed or come around to this new vision of humanity. I force myself to believe it doesn't matter what she'd think. She's gone. But a part of me, however small, is pained by her absence.

"When do we leave?" I ask.

"Now that you're back, tomorrow morning," he says, his fingers twisting in my hair. "There's a helium launch platform at Stowe. My sister and her family are already most of the way to Mars. I thought we'd join them."

"Our destination?" I ask.

"I know we thought it would be a bit organized like that, but it's become a land grab. Once people realized their abilities are about as limitless as their imaginations, the Evolved started heading out to every star the way they once left in wagon trains heading west across North America."

So, it happened. We're now a species that counts not a planet as our territory but a galaxy.

A cosmos, Jason says into my mind, confirming to me some of my old abilities are intact, organic interface chips or not.

I can't wait to start, I say. *But you said morning, right?*

He nods. Or I perceive he nods and he merely sent me the

corresponding thought. This is going to be interesting. He indicates the water, which I'd last seen covered in ice. It's placid and inviting.

And eighty-two degrees. And filled with radiation. You want to take a dip?

"I do."

He rises and strips off what I didn't realize were clothes. I had thought it a blanket to accommodate his new form, and I suppose I'm right. He takes my hand and leads me to the water's edge, where I doff my clothes as well.

My body is utterly beautiful to me but still crude. The amount of evolutions it will take to get it to match a real human body is impossible to calculate. Could be years of work if not decades. But then, at forty or fifty years of age, I'll join the human race.

I wiggle my toes, the stiff polymer making a clicking sound as the toes rub against each other. Maybe I'll start there. I'll perfect my toes first. I search the polymer for the unique DNA strand used to build them and find it familiar.

"Whose DNA did Mynette use as the base for my robo-body?" I ask.

"Mayra's," Jason says.

I'm stunned. And saddened. And grateful to be carrying a piece of her, however small, with me.

"Ready?" Jason asks.

I'm already in mid-dive.

Sixteen hours later, as we stand on the helium platform at Stowe, he asks the same question. I'm far less sure of my answer than I was back by the lake. But I take his hand, lean in, and give him the thousandth or so kiss of that same sixteen-hour interval, and smile.

Though the platform could accommodate a couple hundred, there are only fourteen others with us awaiting the surprisingly short trip up to the heavens. We really are among the last to leave Earth.

"Everyone ready?" our pilot asks.

No one is. Not really anyway. But we all nod or reply in the affirmative.

"Okay, say good-bye to Earth," he commands.

We all do so, uniformly sounding both wistful and resolute at the same time. New species, new domain. The balloons inflate, sixteen in all, and the platform rises. Compared to the sturm und drang of a fiery rocket launch, this is so much more peaceful and thereby feels much more correct, particularly given the planet's weakened gravity.

I run the math for travel to Mars. When fuel was a factor, this would have been a seven-month journey. If humans are now capable of gravity-assisted flight like the most recent NASA satellites, we could slingshot ourselves there in a matter of weeks.

Heck, we could exit the solar system itself in less than a decade.

I hold tight to Jason's hand, making eye contact with a girl on the other side of the platform. She can see me and waves, more filled with excitement than trepidation. I wave back, figuring we're about the same age. I wonder where she'll be a hundred years from now.

Two hundred years from now.

Without the benefit of *sapiens* eyes, it is impossible to tell the difference between being within Earth's atmosphere and entering space. But when we're high enough, I perceive the curvature of the planet below, and gasp.

I gently touch Jason's chin and angle his view upward to deep space. He obliges, kissing my finger before taking both my hands in his. We watch the stars as they become not bigger, but more numerous. The moon is now just in view as are the planets beyond. It's an amazing feeling. Nothing is out of reach. It's almost as if I could raise my hand and touch Saturn itself.

Somehow, I manage to refrain. I draw in close to Jason, close my eyes, and listen to his heartbeat. I slow my own to match his rhythm until our chests rise and fall as if part of the same organism. I adjust my breathing in similar fashion followed by my blink rate. I use his chip to leave my form and disappear inside his circulatory system, shrinking smaller and smaller until his body is as big as the galaxy.

As we leave Earth's atmosphere, I watch his DNA adjust and evolve, mutating to life in the vacuum of space. Everything is in harmony here. Everything adapting, everything in order.

I return to my own body and mime the action, flexing my body's own abilities to respond to alterations to its environment. It's not as seamless as the shift within Jason, but it'll get there as it becomes more necessary.

I bury myself in the organic framework of my imperfect human body and get to work, mapping it for its first stage of cellular evolution. This, as stars pass by closer and more visible than they have ever been in my short life.

My short life.

This body has an expiration date, so does that mean I do, too? How long will any of us live, now that we've changed so much, so quickly? I still have so many questions, and even fewer answers than when I started this journey. The one thing I know for certain is that my five years on Earth may well be both the tiniest fragment of the rest of my life and my most valuable contribution to the species I now call my own. From all-knowing goddess to random nobody; call me the very definition of peaking early.

Yet, it's everything I've ever wanted.

Thank you for being a participant in Emily Eternal's Artificial Consciousness Therapeutic and Species Protocol, I whisper to myself, to Jason, to all mankind as we leave the world behind.

Be well.

Acknowledgments

First and foremost, thanks to Lauren, Eliza, Wyatt, and the rest of my family who put up with all of this. My wife, Lauren, was this manuscript's last beta reader but in many cases the first listener to various ideas and plot turns to the book. Her insights and edits were key.

Big thanks to Jacque Ben-Zekry, whose "you-need-to-trust-me-and-cut-these-five-chapters-and-I'm-going-to-stop-marking-them-as-hopefully-you're-not-insane"-style notes are as frank as they are valuable, betraying her passion for, nay, expectation of, writing worth her time. This book, and so many others, would not exist without her acumen.

Also, a thank you to Lisa French, my longtime and much trusted first-person-who-reads-anything editor who delights—*delights*—in covering my pages in red. I have long leaned on her expertise and am lucky to work with such a keen-eyed collaborator.

A huge thank you, as always, to my agent, Laura Dail, who tears each manuscript limb from limb in order that we build it back stronger, a process I learn so much from each time.

Big, big thanks also to my editors Wes Miller and Sam Bradbury. Their passion for the material and what they believed it could become gave me a new standard to aspire to and I only hope I did justice to their ideas, suggestions, and comments.

Huge thanks to photographer and producer Morna Ciraki. This book sprang from a series of conversations with her about the intersection of memory and technology. She inspires not only by encouraging the best in others but by holding her own work to the highest standard.

Also, thank you to authors Melissa F. Olson, for helping me navigate waters uncharted in writer land (and life), and Kris Calvin, for her insights particularly when it came to the nature of Emily's empathy. Their friendship and advice are much appreciated.

Finally, a thank you to my friend, Ken Plume. He knows what he did. And it's nothing I could ever repay.